THE SONG BEFORE IT IS SUNG

BY THE SAME AUTHOR

*Interior*
*Look At It This Way*
*Masai Dreaming*
*In Every Face I Meet*
*Leading the Cheers*
*Half in Love*
*White Lightning*
*The Promise of Happiness*

# THE SONG
# BEFORE IT IS SUNG

## JUSTIN CARTWRIGHT

BLOOMSBURY

Copyright © by Justin Cartwright 2007

All rights reserved. No part of this book may be used or
reproduced in any manner whatsoever without written permission
from the publisher except in the case of brief quotations
embodied in critical articles or reviews. For information address
Bloomsbury USA, 175 Fifth Avenue, New York, NY 10010.

Excerpt from "Little Gidding" in *Four Quartets*, copyright © 1942
by T.S. Eliot and renewed 1970 by Esme Valerie Eliot,
reprinted by permission of Harcourt, Inc.

"Reason To Believe," Words and Music by Tim Hardin,
Copyright © 1966 (Renewed) Allen Stanton Productions and Alley Music Corp.
International Copyright Secured. All Rights Reserved.
Used by Permission.

Excerpt from *To the Lighthouse* from Virginia Woolf, copyright 1927
by Harcourt, Inc. and renewed 1954 by Leonard Woolf,
reprinted by permission of the publisher.

Published by Bloomsbury USA, New York
Distributed to the trade by Holtzbrinck Publishers

All papers used by Bloomsbury USA are natural, recyclable
products made from wood grown in well-managed forests.
The manufacturing processes conform to the environmental
regulations of the country of origin.

LIBRARY OF CONGRESS CATALOGING-IN-PUBLICATION DATA HAS BEEN APPLIED FOR.

ISBN-10 1-59691-268-5
ISBN-13 978-1-59691-268-7

First U.S. Edition 2007

1 3 5 7 9 10 8 6 4 2

Typeset by Hewer Text UK Ltd, Edinburgh
Printed in the United States of America by Quebecor World Fairfield

For Penny, Rufus and Serge

Where is the song before it is sung?
— Alexander Herzen

# PROLOGUE

As Conrad Senior flies towards Berlin, he is thinking about thoughts; so many thoughts piled up, such a quantity of half-remembered knowledge, so many emotions brought up from the well to spill out: the unrolling of history – a river into which you can't step twice, a collection of biographies end to end, a hilltop to survey the surrounding plains and so on – but also, more so, the anxieties prompted by the spooling of time and the awareness of its unstoppable nature; and random thoughts – Einstein buying a vanilla ice cream sprinkled with chocolate when he first landed in New York – the bank's accusations, sexual encounters, the relation between friendship and envy (La Rochefoucauld), the aromas of bread rising, randomness, the softness of a horse's muzzle (excepting the fishing-line hairs), the smell of books, the deep peace of libraries, the idea of patriotism, the scent of Greek hillsides, the significance of landscape, the strange deceptions of painting, the persistence of religious belief, the races of people, the love of animals, the power of music (*I can suck as much melancholy out of a song as a weasel sucks eggs*), the unknowability of another's mind, the idea of progress, the ever-presence of the poor, the truths of mathematics, the language of policemen, the hypocrisies of small talk, the obsession with self, the sickly miasma of money, the yearning for simplification, states of mind, regional accents, underwear, the nature of understanding, the isolation of dictators, personal hygiene, displays of food in shops, attachment to a lover's topography, cross-wiring

I

in the brain, celebrity, the truths of art, the roof of the world, cowardice . . .

And the garrotting of Axel von Gottberg.

This is one of the mysteries of consciousness, Conrad thinks, the difference between the thoughts you bid come to you and the ones that come anyway, sometimes as a blessing, also as a curse.

For nearly three years, Conrad has been thinking about Axel von Gottberg. Von Gottberg was garrotted on the orders of Hitler in August 1944. He was thirty-five years old, and looked, although not in profile, like him, with thinning hair and a longish, northern-European face. Northern-European hair is inclined to throw in the towel early. Thoughts of von Gottberg visit him at any hour of the day, without warning.

Actually, Conrad is aware that he is not thinking full-blown thoughts, but highlights, like the trailers at his local cinema complex; these thoughts are presenting themselves to him in a chaotic pageant. It is in the nature of air travel with its barely suppressed claustrophobia and its sexual speculation and dulled sense of movement that thoughts seem to be provoked to go on the exuberant march. (You can only think about thoughts, or consciousness, in metaphors.)

When he thinks of Axel von Gottberg, Conrad sees him as he was at his trial. There he is, standing in a capacious suit before the People's Court with his hands folded in front of him. This could be to prevent the trousers falling down, as the prisoners are not allowed belts and appear to have been given clothes from a second-hand store. The defendants are mostly aristocratic and the idea is to bring them down a peg or two, to make them accountable to the ordinary people, so that they can be hanged in clear conscience.

The film, which was commissioned by the State Film Superintendent, Hans Hinkel, to show what a fine National Socialist the judge Roland Freisler was, and what wretched traitors the accused were, is beautifully lit. It is as though the windows of the court are admitting a soft, warm light, a Dutch light, containing the texture of paint, to coat the defendant, the judge himself, and the upstanding members of the public, who, in contrast to the decadents on trial, are mostly uniformed. The unintended effect of this is to make von Gottberg look heroic. Von Gottberg speaks calmly about his career in the Foreign Service and politely deflects Freisler's criticism about his failure to join the Army and about his education at Oxford on a Rhodes Scholarship: 'An English scholarship,' says Freisler. 'But candidates chosen in Germany,' says von Gottberg.

Freisler's clinching remarks are that four years at Oxford and a lot of time hanging about in the Romanisches Café on the Kurfürstendamm are the ideal preparation for a traitor. As Freisler names this particular sink of decadence – the true voice of Nazism speaking against intellectuals – von Gottberg stands, balding head inclined. The scene doesn't make much linguistic sense because in the finished film each defendant in the trial of the 20 July 1944 plotters is edited in such a way as to give Freisler the last word, but still von Gottberg's calmness and composure are striking. He knows that he is facing certain death, because this is not a trial but a lynching: even before the court has sat, it has been announced that the defendants are traitors who will hang, in Hitler's own words, like cattle in the slaughterhouse. Hitler has said that this is an authentic German blood-revenge. He sets great store by the authentically Teutonic.

Freisler's only job is to discredit the defendants. Like his leader, he is prone to rages. He says the word *Schweinehund* at one stage which, until he heard it in Freisler's mouth, Conrad thought was an invention of British and American war-films. And it adds to the unreality that Freisler looks as though he has been pulled in by a desperate casting director. He models his hand gestures on the Führer's and contorts his face dramatically. Even some Nazis are embarrassed by his behaviour, but Hitler says that Freisler is their Vyshinsky.

Although the defendants' replies and interjections are edited, it is known that most of them were brave in the face of death. One, when asked why he joined the plot, said that he regarded Hitler as the instrument of all evil in the world. Another urged Freisler to get on with the hanging or he would be hanged by the Allies first. In fact Freisler is crushed by falling masonry a few months later when a bomb falls on the People's Court.

Von Gottberg, in this glimpse of him, remains polite, even resigned. He has done his best to demonstrate that there is such a thing as a good German. Perhaps he is too composed, too controlled: he is the only defendant not immediately strung up on a thin cord attached to meat-hooks in Berlin-Plötzensee Prison. He is kept for interrogation for another eleven days because he has high-level contacts with the outside world that some Nazis believe they can use to save themselves. When Hitler hears of the plan to keep him alive, he falls into a screaming rage, which in German is called a *Tobsuchtsanfall*, and orders his immediate death. Von Gottberg is hanged and his children, a boy of three, a girl of two and a girl of nine months, are taken away from their mother to an orphanage where the boy dies of diphtheria. Von Gottberg's wife is imprisoned. Hitler calls this *Sippenhaft*, another ancient German custom, of revenging yourself on the relatives of the person who has done you wrong.

Conrad finds it difficult to imagine how someone who has walked the same streets as he has, who has known the soft wet light of an Oxford winter, who has drunk at the Eagle and Child with E.A. Mendel – where he drank with Mendel fifty years later – could have ended up in front of Freisler, in a trial so unreal and so mad and so vicious that it points to something unimaginable about human nature. Certainly unimaginable in the low-roofed, hop-steeped Eagle and Child, which has been known to generations as the Bird and Baby. He is aware that his interest in von Gottberg, what Francine calls his morbid interest, owes a lot to the fact that von Gottberg was an Oxford man, a Rhodes Scholar, as he was. Rhodes Scholarships, despite the questionable character of their founder, confer a sense of destiny. Did von Gottberg believe in his destiny? Did he get the scholarship because he had a sense of destiny, or did getting the scholarship cause him to think he had a destiny?

Conrad knows that his own destiny has not yet been made manifest. It may never be. It may anyway be no more than to be assailed by thoughts. He has a friend, Osric, who thinks about sports all day: his thoughts range over the selection of teams, the policy of coaches, the role of luck and of mental toughness. It is this friend's duty to have an opinion on sports. He doesn't, of course, cover all sports, but the ones he loves need his constant attention. He has a particular interest in Russian women's tennis, but this, Conrad thinks, is not entirely high-minded: Osric imagines himself having sex with these coltish women. In fact when they bend over to receive serve, and arrange their thighs nervously, it is difficult not to imagine such a thing. But generally as regards sport his friend is high-minded: no less than a philosopher grappling with ethical problems and problems of perception, he feels obliged to add his opinion to all the others that nobody listens to. In this respect at least he is more like a philosopher than he realises.

I am troubled by the accumulation of thoughts, particularly by the half-dead aspect of them, like leaves in autumn, still there in outline but lacking life, Conrad thinks. In my thirty-sixth year they seem already to be piling up and I see no way of disposing of them.

The stewardess brings drinks on a trolley. Stewardesses – it is believed – are sexually avid. This woman is excessively friendly, chirping in a high girlish voice, *Bloody Mary, with Worcester sauce, yes, spicy? Nice one.*

Her features move about in pursuance of a little personal drama as she prepares his Bloody Mary: it looks as though her cheeks and eyes and lips are all directly attached by wires, like puppets, to the emotional centres of her brain. Maybe this trip to Berlin, which he can't afford, will clear away the dead material. *Nice and spicy you said yes? Here we go sir.* How many meaningless conversations have we had? How many pointless exchanges?

He drinks the Bloody Mary deeply; he feels the vodka, and its advertised spiciness, warming him. He doesn't usually drink in the morning, but he has a sense of well-being, because he will be fulfilling some of the promise E.A. Mendel saw in him fifteen years ago. He will be paying back a debt, the nagging debt of being cherished by Mendel. When Mendel left him his papers and letters three years ago, he wanted Conrad to understand that for nearly sixty years he had felt guilty about his repudiation of von Gottberg, his friend, when he went back to Germany:

*Dear Conrad, I leave you my papers and my letters relating to Axel von Gottberg. You may be surprised; you may even wonder what to do with them. It is true that you were not my most brilliant student, but I think, my dear boy, that you are the most human. You know that I took a position against Axel, and you know the reasons why, but perhaps you don't know that many people blamed me in some way for his death. It has been a terrible burden to live with this.*

*In these papers you will find every letter he wrote to me, and copies of my replies and letters to him, as well as many other papers and cuttings and so on. You will also find letters his friends wrote to me and various other references to him.*

*The truth is, Axel was a man of courage and action while I was a man who loved libraries and enjoyed gossip.*

*It may be that if I hadn't warned my friends in America and here about Axel's notion of himself as a world-historical figure – he believed to the end that he had some sort of dialogue with Churchill – the Allies would have given more support to the July plotters. And it may be that Axel would have been spared his appalling death. Did you know that a film was made not only of the trial – there's a copy of it in the Imperial War Museum – but also of the hangings? This film was made expressly for Hitler's benefit. It is believed to be lost.*

While he was alive Mendel had never once suggested that he

wanted Conrad to have these papers. He knew that Conrad's years since leaving Oxford had not gone smoothly – so perhaps he was offering him a way of establishing himself, a post-mortem gift. But he had made no suggestions about how Conrad should apply his advanced human qualities to the question. Three years ago, when he first read the papers, Conrad saw an opportunity. This, he thought, is the sort of thing television will go for. And then he imagined a play, the final meeting of von Gottberg and Mendel in All Souls in 1939, just before war was declared: von Gottberg tries to justify himself to his friend and also he tries to explain how important it is to save Germany and Europe from the Nazis and the communists. Mendel is sceptical, but affectionate. Mendel's own account of this last meeting is in the form of three letters to friends. In each letter he gives a slightly different telling, but essentially he regards von Gottberg as a dangerous fantasist, with a taste for high-level intrigue, who sees himself as a man with a destiny, the agent of history. The idea that history has agents is deeply repugnant to Mendel. It runs contrary to everything he believes about personal responsibility. It lies at the heart of fascism and all other forms of totalitarianism.

Conrad had a modest book contract but he has long ago spent the advance. Neither the play nor the documentary has been taken up despite many lunches, most of which he has had to pay for himself. And his editor at the paper – he's only freelance, not staff – thinks that he is wasting his time. Actually she thinks he is losing his grip, and becoming obsessed. And it is true that he thinks von Gottberg, at thirty-five, looks just like him. This trip to Berlin to meet an unreliable informant who claims to know the whereabouts of some film may be one indulgence too many for his editor. He has to produce an article on Berlin's boutique hotels and chic restaurants to justify it; she has given him a modest allowance in cash. And now he thinks of women in positions of power, and the strange coolness they cultivate as an antidote to the more womanly qualities, which he has always appreciated, unlike so many of his friends. The publisher's editor

7

who gave him the advance to edit and collate Mendel's von Gottberg papers always asked him how he saw the marketing pitch. She had enormous success, so far unrepeated, with a book on dating for the over-thirties. She was terrified of being dragged down by this book into a donnish, male, old-world morass. She feared that she would be tainted by nose-hair and cluttered rooms and obsolete male scents. Women in positions of power lack the confidence to follow their own instincts, he thinks.

He has often pondered the nature of the complicity between men and women, particularly in the sexual realm. It may be that you can't have sex with a woman boss because, in the traditional sexual grammar, women are the object. He has never had any employees, except for a Polish cleaner who lasted three weeks: she was like a pupa, strangely pale and unformed and unalive, with many sick relatives in Gdansk. Perhaps they were bleeding her dry.

And he thinks about the Oxford streets and quads where he has walked, the cobbles of Magpie Lane – cobbles are enormously evocative, like the scent of forgotten objects and remembered melodies – and the crumbling Headington stone of the old colleges and the deeply worn steps of the Bodleian Library and the chequered floor of St Mary's and the flags of Balliol (not so old but weathering down nicely) and the grand stairs up to the hall, and the gate on to Christ Church Meadow (giving admission to a sacred landscape), and the glimpses of secret gardens of *Magnolia grandiflora* and aristocratic old climbing roses and, underneath his feet, miles of books, stoically waiting, and the sound of bells and the filtered voices of choirs, and strained piano notes flying from the Holywell Music Rooms.

Von Gottberg went back to Germany taking the imprint of Oxford with him. And for sixty years, E.A. Mendel walked around this little rat-maze of stone and stained glass and richly fired brick, guilty about von Gottberg.

Von Gottberg's ninety-three-year-old wife, Liselotte, and one of his children, Caroline, have received him at their country house, which is now given over to a religious foundation in his memory. This is the house to which they fled when the Russians approached. The old lady said Axel loved Oxford. The daughter, Caroline, now sixty-three, had slightly staring, apparently sightless eyes, the result, he guessed, of a kind of mysticism: she could see beyond the merely corporeal. As they sat in the garden to talk, he saw that they were both sanctified and burdened by being good Germans. When he asked about von Gottberg's feelings towards his Oxford friends, whether he felt he had been let down by Mendel, Lionel Wray and others, Caroline looked to her mother for an answer. When there was none, she spoke – Conrad remembers dandelion heads floating behind her, past the latticed brick of the old house – saying that there may have been this problem: my father was a German patriot, he wanted to save Germany from Hitler. I think that some of his Oxford friends believed he wanted glory for himself. That is my understanding. He wrote to us the night before he died, and we did not receive this letter although my mother was told in 1946 by a chaplain that what he had written was that he regretted most that he was unable to use his experience and his insights to help the country he loved. And when Conrad asked her, Do you think that means he believed his friends had let him down, she said, You should ask my mother. The old lady, who was smiling at very low wattage, said, Yes, I think he was disappointed. Yes.

Conrad mentioned the letter to the *Manchester Guardian* that had so upset Mendel: Some of your husband's friends were worried about that letter. Liselotte said, When I met him in 1975, Mr Mendel said that he now believed that Axel wrote that letter because he wanted to deceive the Nazis. And literally what Axel wrote was true: where he was working as a prosecutor, he saw no discrimination against Jews in 1934. But, as you know, he tried to withdraw the letter the day after he sent it. Mr Mendel said that as a Jew he had felt that it was impossible for Axel to have written that letter without compromising himself. But he wrote to Axel in 1939, saying that he would always regard him with the warmest affection. Everyone always loved Axel, she said. And Caroline said, I think the Oxford friends thought that Oxford was, how you say, the centre of the universe. My father loved Oxford, yes, but Germany came the first.

Conrad was invited to supper in the vaulted dining room. Liselotte had gone to bed. He ate with Caroline and some solemn Christians; it seemed they were subdued, still stunned by the murder of Christ, the Nazis, the beastliness of the human race, their closeness to an authentic martyr. He slept that night under a stag's head in the local inn, the Schwarzer Bock.

But he knew that families cannot be fully trusted: they manufacture their own myths. He didn't tell them that the film of von Gottberg being hanged, naked, might still exist.

PART ONE

# 1

*WHO ASKED YOU?*

Difficult question. Nobody and everybody. What Francine
meant was why did he think he had some obligation or right to
rummage about collecting – not a very systematic collection –
ideas? She said he was like a shoplifter in a supermarket. What
she meant too was that he lived in a chaotic state, constantly
picking up ideas rightfully belonging to other people – and other
contexts – and trying to take them home. There was a certain
portion of truth in her charges. She also implied – in fact she
actually said it that night – that he had no ideas of his own.

'That's nonsense, of course,' he said, foolishly imagining he
was being asked to contribute to an entertaining theoretical
discussion. 'To understand ideas, to be interested in ideas, you
have to have ideas.'

'Here's an idea: why don't you get a job?'

'I'm working on Mendel's papers.'

'Are you?'

'Yes, I am.'

'And what does that work consist of?'

'Research, reading.'

'Oh, I see. And who is paying for this research?'

'You know the answer. But remember, we very nearly had a
TV deal. And there are still people interested.'

'Your life so far has been a series of nearlies. I've got some hot
news for you: no one is interested in E.A. Mendel. He had an

13

idea in 1953 but nobody can remember what it was. That's why the publishers aren't giving you any more money and that's why the TV deal got nowhere and why nobody wants your film version of his story. Of course I am not in the creative world, but even I know what goes on at the cinema: morons eat popcorn while watching cars exploding and aliens turning into spinach. They don't want some bollocks about the history of ideas.'

When Francine was angry she developed a kind of torrential force that could not be stopped. He watched her with admiration as she gathered herself. He had the feeling that he had written the script for her, but he had no hand in the delivery. Sometimes she started quietly, inviting him to say something provocative. At other times she wanted to deliver a peroration without contradiction, as though she had already run through the early charges and was now simply summing up for the benefit of the jury. A not very intelligent jury. He knew that she had a desire for certainty, for the incorrigible proposition. And this made it very hard for her to live with someone as unformed as he was. For a while she had called him the questing vole, but that was while she still found him amusing. Now she thought his curiosity was an excuse, a form of evasion.

Her face, with its seeping medical tiredness, had a high, feverish colour now, siphoned from the depths by resentment. Her eyes were cloudy, the way they used to be during sex, as if her anger had produced a flash of blindness, like looking at the sun, and her throat was becoming pink and russet, and slightly mottled – mushroom colours and textures. The violence of her feelings towards him was causing this discoloration. Mushrooms have a strange and mysterious life cycle, much of it underground. And on the surface Francine appeared calm, although the fungal colour was becoming more intense.

'Conrad, I go out every morning at seven, I return home at seven – if I'm lucky – I've been peering at samples and slides, I have even seen a few patients, I have grabbed ten minutes to eat a piece of microwaved pizza in the canteen, and you have

been reading the letters and ramblings of a long-forgotten –
rightly in my opinion – Oxford don, who knew just how to
flatter you by talking of your human qualities. And, guess what,
the marmalade is exactly where you left it at breakfast.'

The charges were true. But his alleged human qualities seemed
to Conrad to be important, if still unclear.

Francine continued: 'I have decided to leave you. I can't live
like this. I need some support.'

At the time she surprised him with her resolve. A few months
later she said that she had been seeing another man, the consultant
who was her boss, a man very highly regarded in obstetrics. He
had recruited her to his team. He was fifty-one years old, sixteen
years older than her. That word 'seeing' troubled him. He found
it hard to believe that it meant fucking. It was too brutal. He had
hung around outside the hospital for a few days and once had seen
them leaving together. (He had plenty of time to observe the disor-
dered comings and goings of the patients while he was waiting.)
What had surprised him was that he was not present in their lives.
Somehow he had imagined that Francine and John would be crippled by the knowledge of him, that his spectral form would be
visible between them, that they would be slipping away nervously,
alarmed by the foolishness of their actions; but no, they walked
happily down the front steps of the hospital in Whitechapel and
linked hands as they turned down a side street. What hurt him
most was that she appeared happy, carefree, girlish. Even her hair
seemed to have acquired new vivacity.

In another context, John might have looked to him like any
other decent, utterly unremarkable English professional man, but
here, leaving the hospital with Conrad's wife, he had princely
qualities. Here, he was a man known and admired for his
pioneering work on the incontinence in women caused by child-
birth. Francine was a suitable tribute for his achievements.

She tried to dress up her defection as a gift from her to Conrad:
'I have a career, my career path is more or less fixed now, but
you, you still have some growing up to do. I realised you didn't

want to be tied in this way. I am sure you will see it for the best in time.'

She always needed to tidy things up mentally, as if by naming them they were settled. It was – he thought – a scientific habit: taxonomy applied to the emotional life.

'With my human qualities still unexplored.'

'What?'

'What you said about me and Mendel.'

'Yes,' she said impatiently. 'You and your human qualities.'

It was clear that she had come to this meeting determined to be brief and final. Her neck coloured again anxiously at the delay.

'In medicine, we don't have enough time to investigate human qualities. We are too busy with human beings, in person.'

'And is John leaving his wife?'

'That's our business.'

'Is he too old to have more children?'

'Jesus, you can be offensive.'

'We were going to have a child, remember?'

'We were. But I had to delay, remember, when I got the research job and you found – what a surprise – that you weren't earning as much as you expected when you went freelance.'

'Well, you're fine now as long as wifey doesn't take all his money.'

'I'm glad you said that, because you've reminded me that underneath all that airy-fairy charm you are just a vicious little prick. People like you who sneer at honest endeavour and science and actually doing something for people, while reading the fucking *Guardian* and having an opinion on everything, from politics to football, to, I don't know, immigration and the Iraq War, without really having any in-depth knowledge of any sort, are the real worry for this country. Anyway, now you can go and explore your human qualities in depth and at leisure.'

Francine asked him to leave as soon as the flat was sold – as she said, a free spirit can operate anywhere.

\* \* \*

Mendel and von Gottberg had gone to Palestine for three weeks in the winter of 1933; he decided to follow in their footsteps. He took a loan on his credit card. He was encouraged by the fact that the surrealists advocated *dépaysement*, the policy of uprooting yourself from your home country, to increase your sensitivity and understanding, qualities he was clearly in need of. Although he could only afford a week of *dépaysement*, it seemed to him a good moment to go. The seventeen boxes of papers, which he had arranged and re-arranged and tried to catalogue, reproached him with his lack of progress. The problem was that he was looking at the letters for a kind of meaning, some hints from Mendel to him, perhaps some clues to his own destiny.

Actually he found that it wasn't that easy to go to Israel without friends or letters of introduction. The Israeli agents at the airport questioned him closely about his motives and his intentions. He explained that he was going on holiday but that made them suspicious. He stood for half an hour with his baggage, which earlier an excitable dog had okayed, while they made phone calls. With reluctance they allowed him to proceed. At Tel Aviv the plane landed to some rousing folk music; there they questioned him again and asked him to list the people he was seeing. There was only one, a film-location manager whose name he had been given. The agents particularly wanted to know if he had friends on the West Bank. They wore sunglasses on the tops of their closely shaved heads, giving the impression that office work bored them, that they would prefer to be vigorously employed outside. And this, he thought, is what has happened out here in the Levant, as Mendel described it: Jews have become outdoorsy people.

The Mediterranean, lapping the town, was unexpectedly glamorous, but Tel Aviv had a rackety, half-planted feel and he remembered what Mendel had written:

*I have realised — it was a true revelation — that I have a kinship with these strange Levantines, who are like relatives one hasn't seen for twenty years. They make me uneasy, even afraid. German Jews,*

*who are arriving by the thousand, are going mad at the disorder,*
*seeking bus timetables. They cannot believe that the buses do not depart*
*on time, if they arrive at all. Axel finds the food oily. It is oily, but*
*I have convinced myself that it is my ancestral cuisine. I eat on bravely.*

Conrad took a shared taxi to Jerusalem and he found himself
looking closely at the other passengers, remembering Mendel's
description of the people as odd and fascinating. Some were backpackers from New York's suburbs, he guessed, the girls wearing
little squares of cloth on their heads to indicate a willingness to
muck in with the harvest and an eagerness to embrace the spiritual
challenges ahead. There were English Hasids, the men strangely
abstracted as though this earth, this taxi bus, these numerous
children, these wives with the chestnut wigs and full fecundity,
were in a way not fully present, unavoidably inhabiting the same
space, but ephemeral, shadows cast by their husbands' radiance.

By the time the taxi van had reached a mountain pass, he
wondered how the soft pale people from North London and the
eager backpackers saw the landscape outside, now turning from
the coastal plain to a tumultuous upland littered with the painted
shells of armoured cars, left – he discovered – as a reminder of
the war of 1948. What did they see in these tortured, pumice
rocks and grudging trees and steep, parched valleys? Did they
see a land of milk and honey, a landscape that had been deep in
the race memory all through the diaspora, or did they see, as
Mendel did, an unfamiliar and unnerving otherness?

Conrad himself knows that you can hold at the same time
different landscapes in your head – or in your fibres – for instance,
the broad openness of Africa and the distilled beauty of Oxford.
He also finds himself seeing John and Francine conversing about
bladders and urine samples in the lab and then, back in the little
flat John has taken, he sees the warm strawberry rash rising up
her throat as John, with the scientific and practical qualities, so
different from his own which are essentially meaningless, removes
his scrubs and reveals his highly meaningful self to his research

student, who has now forgotten for ever that she is married to Conrad. He feels a sharp pain, as though he has in some way been erased, his very existence questioned. And he wonders how the lovers can reconcile the madness of sex with the scientific life. The answer – the Orthodox children with their insane side-locks seem to have been put here to illustrate his train of thought – is that we are not wholly rational, and never will be.

To prepare himself for this trip and to think about something other than Francine and John in Whitechapel, he has read Amos Oz's autobiography. Oz's mother was never able to adapt to the landscape; goose-girls and deep resinous forests were more real to her than Arab shepherds and olive trees. In Jerusalem with the blinding white rocks and the thin soil, she felt lost: eventually she killed herself, leaving the eleven-year-old Amos. And maybe this is what Mendel meant when he described the country as strange and his kinship with the people who had been Levantised as unsettling, even frightening.

And Conrad sees Mendel, small and plump, with the tall, thin von Gottberg, approaching Jerusalem and he wonders exactly what thoughts assaulted them, because Jerusalem is a city like no other, a city that attracts the irrational and the mystic and the fanatic, as if there are certain loci on this earth that exhale some of the vapours of human longing that have been breathed on them over the millennia. Once Conrad heard wild bees in a cleft in a rock in Africa, and the fanning of the wings and the diligent murmuring suggested some message, like the intimations of music, which came from beyond the rational. Jerusalem is the world capital of the irrational, with longing and loss and despairing hope to boot.

And into this place – they arrive on donkeys from Transjordan – come Elya Mendel and Axel von Gottberg. Even on a donkey it is clear that von Gottberg is born to ride. Whereas Mendel has only once ridden – coincidentally on a donkey – on the beach in Bournemouth. In the photograph of the event, the donkey wears a straw hat and the infant Mendel is holding an ice cream.

He wears a sailor top and small black spectacles, so that he looks like a bee, a Jewish bee. Mendel tells friends gleefully that on the outskirts of Jerusalem they were stoned by Orthodox Jews. Von Gottberg's feet, in calfskin boots, are almost trailing in the powdery dust.

Outside the King David Hotel where they are staying, a photographer captures them. Mendel is smiling, a smile that Conrad recognises across sixty years. It's as though a smile is ageless, or perhaps eternal, independent of the decay and collapse of the surrounding features. Von Gottberg has his arm around Mendel's shoulder: some way behind them is the stone façade of the hotel, and behind that a glimpse of the Old City. In this photograph they look as though they have been posed for Nazi propaganda, the tall, athletic, aristocratic Count Axel von Gottberg, of Pleskow, and the smaller, softer Elya Mendel, of Hampstead, who could be thought by the ill-disposed, from his complicit smile, to have cabalistic knowledge. Conrad knows that look, intensely curious, half-amused, expecting something enter-taining to happen, as happy to hear gossip as a new idea. Conrad is staying in the old Petra Hotel, not far away, but he ventures into the King David to get the fabled view of the Old City from the terrace.

The Old City glows in the late-afternoon light. It is not obvi-ously a Jewish city: he can see churches and the Dome of the Rock and beyond that the cemeteries rising above the Garden of Gethsemane and up the Mount of Olives. The walls are mainly Ottoman with some Crusader sections, but the stones were quar-ried near by and re-used after every conquest, so that this city – viewed from above the swimming pool from which the voices of children are rising – is as no other city he has ever seen, sema-phoring significance. And this is the pattern: ideas and creeds are now represented by unheeding stones as the ends of human longing. For two thousand years – longer if you count the Mesopotamian diaspora – the Jews have held this landscape in their minds. But over there, pulsing, is the golden Dome of the

Rock, where the Prophet Mohammed ascended on a horse for his Night Ride to Mecca, and beyond that on a hill is the spot where Jesus ascended into heaven, and then beyond that the hills of the Judaean Desert, which seem to have a separate illumination, so that they are pale and bleached, with the dark shapes of clouds – the clouds themselves are not visible – moving swiftly like airships over the landscape.

And Conrad thinks that here in the Holy Land Mendel and von Gottberg may already have been aware of some sort of historical juncture in the relationship between Germans and Jews. On the one hand the aggrieved and resentful Germans were being offered a Faustian deal by Hitler and on the other the rawly human but vulnerable Jews were arriving here in their confused thousands, on the move again. But they could not have had more than an inkling of the nightmare that was to come.

Von Gottberg's letters show that he was always keen for Mendel's approval: Mendel was the same age as von Gottberg, but seems to have arrived, like an egg, fully formed into the world and, strangely for a young man, to have come equipped with a serenity and wisdom. Conrad wonders if von Gottberg resented, at a deep Germanic level, Mendel's urbanity and his protean – Jewish – qualities. Von Gottberg's family had lived in the same pile for six hundred years, while Mendel's had arrived in England via Riga and St Petersburg only nineteen years earlier.

As Conrad walks down to the Jaffa Gate and into the Old City, he finds himself under siege. He is entering a city out of an orientalist's sketchbook, with spice stalls and pushcarts and shops selling nuts and feral vegetables and parched herbs and chunks of meat; Bedouin women sit gloomily with isolated tomatoes spread on cloths, and then a group of Orthodox priests passes, plump from the devotion of crones, and young boys rush about with beaten-copper trays of tea and Palestinians are sitting at a table attached to a hookah, and now some Jews in fedoras with threads of the tallith underneath their overcoats come sightlessly by, and Arab children are buying candyfloss in colours that do

not exist in nature, and then Conrad enters a long tunnel of tiny
cave-shops selling jewellery and souvenirs and he stops for a mint
tea in a courtyard that leads off the teeming street. He sees
Mendel and von Gottberg here, Mendel eagerly listening out for
traces of Aramaic and Russian and von Gottberg trying to estimate
what point in history this overwhelmingly aromatic and exotic
place has reached and Mendel fascinated by the sense he has —
or is acquiring — that human objectives can easily be in conflict.
As if to prove the point, German Jews are sniffing vegetables
fastidiously, resisting Levantisation from inside their Bavarian
jackets and loden coats. Conrad sips his mint tea — a large bunch
of mint thrust into the pot — and wonders what it was like to
be here without the knowledge of what was to come. The knowledge that has made us.

Mendel and von Gottberg stop at the Lutheran Erloserkirche.
Although von Gottberg has given up active Christianity, he is
a believer in Christian values. Mendel, although a non-believer,
is a Zionist and believes in the preservation of Jewish cultural
values. It's strange, Conrad thinks sitting here, near the church,
now accepting some pistachios and some more tea, that belief in
the existence or non-existence of God is no impediment to friendship and understanding.

The young Palestinians wear cheap trainers; their hair is
geometrically cut. He wonders if they ever have distinctly secular
thoughts. And he wonders if on this trip the two friends talked
about Jews in Europe, because already in Germany Jews are under
notice. On a personal level, as he knows, human beings — for
example, he and Francine — can have irreconcilable differences.
He thinks about having Francine back, if she asks, but he knows
it would be impossible because he cannot imagine forgiving her,
not so much for kicking him out, but for allowing her body to
be a receptacle for someone else's semen. How can he explain
that in rational terms? He can't. And he can't even explain to
himself, as an atheist, why this idea of the transfer of human
substance, this sacrament, should be so painful to him.

He feels cold now as the sun goes down. The Old City seems to be closing down too: as the shopkeepers pack up, the bare electric light bulbs strung out along walls are beginning to shine bright. The sky above the courtyard is the colour of dark crustaceans, a pigment with a mineral content, elemental specks of colour not fully ground in. Tomorrow he will follow von Gottberg and Mendel along the Via Dolorosa to Golgotha to see where Christ died and the madness began.

The Arab owner of the café tells him that his brother lives in London. These days everyone in the whole world has a brother living in London. And Conrad has had this kind of conversation many times. It always leads to misapprehensions and pointless exchanges of information, which become increasingly stilted.

'You know Hackney?'

'Yes.'

'My brother say is very bad.'

'It is a poor part.'

'Many Jews.'

The protocols of Zion will be next, or the theory that Mossad bombed the Twin Towers.

'Thank you for the tea.'

'Wilcome to Jerusalem. I born here.'

'Thank you. I was born in Cape Town.'

'Israelis take my home.'

'I am very sorry.'

'You wilcome. No pay.'

In his hurry, he turns the wrong way and is lost. Where, a few alleys away, all was movement and bustle, he is now in almost empty lanes stalked by cats. An Arab child stares at him. From a dim doorway a woman calls the child; he hopes this is not a response to seeing him. He wonders how he appears in his khakis and T-shirt. Perhaps he looks sinister. These jumbled alleys and turnings and stairways have no obvious plan. He passes a small café, half of it below street-level, where a group of young men is watching a football game on television. The field is so green he thinks the football must be taking place in Germany or Scandinavia. The verdure in this chalky, bone-coloured place looks lurid and unreal. A goose-girl would happily lead her gaggle of geese across it. He comes out of an alley into a square, and there ahead of him is an Armenian church. From the church he hears someone chanting, perhaps a priest. He puts his head inside the heavily brocaded doorway, into the scented and lamplit vestibule. A man, perhaps a verger, directs him towards the Jaffa Gate. God bless you, he says, as Conrad walks out past the church under an arch, the stone strung with electric wires which also drape doorways and blind balconies.

Can we know anybody else? Other minds? Can I know von Gottberg and Mendel, or even Francine? Does John already know her better than I do? Or maybe we find what we want in other people, and so we never know them.

*Who asked you?* she said. He could have quoted Eliot:

> *We shall not cease from exploration*
> *And the end of all our exploring*
> *Will be to arrive where we started*
> *And know the place for the first time.*

Although he has a talent for quotation, he didn't quote Eliot in reply because he doesn't believe its implied meaning, which Eliot probably picked up from Buddhism, that life has patterns according to which we must try to harmonise ourselves. Life has no purpose: that is its stark beauty. That's one lesson he learned from Mendel. Here, as he walks, he hears all sorts of prayers and imprecations rising, those who are dispatching them evidently unaware that nobody is listening.

Sitting high in the Ottoman crenellations above the Jaffa Gate he sees the casual outline of two Israeli soldiers against the crustacean sky. If life has no meaning then this city, with its tumultuous longing and bitterness, is a monument to the power of delusion. And this delusion also has a kind of beauty; and he remembers what George Grosz wrote, that the commanders in the field paint in blood.

The imams are calling as he walks back, and from a mezzanine room, somehow awkwardly stranded by ancient architectural upheavals – these old buildings and stones are jumbled and re-ordered after thousands of years of recycling – he hears wild, muscular-Jewish music, and then he sees the shadows on the wall of men dancing. The shadows at least are hurling themselves about in a madcap way, as though the harvest had been good or they were moonstruck or – more likely – expecting the Messiah at any minute.

His room is small and sparsely furnished, with a view of a courtyard. Actually it's less of a view than a meniscus, a little sliver of wall and some stone paving down below, glazed by the passage of feet. He likes strange, unknown rooms. They give him a low charge of excitement.

Mendel wrote to a friend that von Gottberg was a great dancer. He had known the inside of every nightclub on Kurfürstendamm: *I am, as you know, a very poor dancer. Axel was dancing with the wives of the British officials. What a flutter in the dovecotes.* And it was this flutter in the dovecotes that was to change both of their lives for ever. Unlike Conrad, Mendel and von Gottberg had come with introductions; they had met with everyone from Zion-ists to Orthodox prelates and British officers. Mendel writes that he would have been glad to meet the Grand Mufti, if he were prepared to speak to Jews.

Conrad cannot sleep. He lies pleasurably in the mean bed and thinks, tries to think, more measured thoughts about Francine. He understands her contempt for him. His grandmother's house in Cape Town had flypaper in the kitchen; many of the little shops in the Old City have it, hanging down over the strange cuts of meat or the sticky pastries. He remembers as a child waiting to see a fly landing on the paper: and this is how Francine sees him, waiting idly for some minor sensation, while she goes out on the world's business. And it is true that helping women deliver their babies as she does, sometimes having to slice them open just above the pubis, is activity of an entirely different order. Once upon a time they had discussed films and books and ideas; she had been charmed by his inchoate eagerness. What charmed her then now seems infantile to her. The scientific life has got to her, as though all those chemicals and miserable people and – let's face it – death, have somehow driven her into the arms of the superior class who deal with the real world, who have the power of life and death and who know folly and self-indulgence when they see it. Francine cannot bear to see people chomping their way to the grave, slurping sweet drinks or puffing on cigarettes or dipping into buckets of popcorn: in her estimation he is really just a high-minded version of these slobs who exculpate themselves from the consequences of their own folly in torrents of banality. And this is one of the reasons he loved Mendel, because Mendel never ceased from exploration. And Conrad sees now, in this cell just outside the resonant walls of the Old City of Jerusalem, that what happened to von Gottberg and Mendel must be explored even though he cannot justify it to Francine – God knows he has tried – and it may be that the only reason is that he owes a debt of love to Mendel, who recognised his human qualities, and gave him a surprising legacy.

He sees more clearly now. In the morning I will begin to put this story in order, as Mendel wanted. He sees Mendel's creased smile, and he sees von Gottberg standing before Freisler, his hands crossed in front of him, ready to be sacrificed.

And von Gottberg was almost exactly the age I am now.

# 2

MENDEL AND VON Gottberg are standing outside the boundary of the Dome of the Rock, which they know as the Mosque of Omar. The dome is gleaming. It is too bright for this climate, a great gold cupola high above Jerusalem winking and conducting heat and radiating it out over the Old City, like the RKO Radio Pictures trademark.

The faithful are gathering for prayer and the muezzin are calling. It's a sound that stitches together the Muslim world, a defiant, plaintive, poetic call. They stand under the shade of a cypress as the worshippers arrive and wash themselves at the tiled basins into which water gushes from giant bronze spigots. Water and paradise are closely associated. The faithful drift into the mosque, its magnificence and space and colour the simulacrum of paradise. Down below, in an alleyway, Jews are praying in front of the Western Wall; their heads nod and dip and nod again. They are not worshipping the giant blocks of stone in front of them as it appears, but they are inspired to piety by the remains of Herod's temple. It is their direct line to their real and imagined past.

'Down below,' says Mendel, 'they are plotting how to get up here into the pound seats. You believe in destiny, Axel, don't you? That is their destiny.'

They often discuss the purposes of history. To Mendel's amusement, von Gottberg sees patterns in history.

As they leave the haram, von Gottberg stops and holds Mendel's arm.

'Elya, I am going back to Germany.'

'Don't leave us.'

'I have to go.'

'Why?'

'My country is sick.'

'Can I ask why you, especially, have to go?'

'It's my country. Somebody has to take care of it.'

Mendel thinks that his friend sets too much store by his own destiny.

They walk out of the Old City down towards the Kidron Valley. Mendel walks surprisingly quickly, efficiently but not gracefully. He and von Gottberg have often talked on Addison's Walk in the spring, deep in fritillaries, scilla and windflowers, and in the autumn brushing through leaves and the spiralling, helicoptering seed pods from the limes. Perhaps it reminds von Gottberg of Unter den Linden.

Von Gottberg has cherished his talks with Mendel, more than anything at Oxford. They have argued about the nature of ideas; Mendel has begun to tire of philosophy, but loves the history of ideas. He doesn't see – he is wilfully blind – the forces behind history and philosophy. Sometimes in Oxford von Gottberg has detected a certain loneliness in his friend. He loves the company of women, but he is a virgin. Von Gottberg knows that Mendel observes his easy successes with women and so he plays them down and sometimes he withholds information from him.

As they walk down the dusty track into the Kidron Valley, they are, in their Oxford fashion, discussing philosophy. Under their feet are flints and stones the colour of bones; some of them may be bones. There are tombs here cut into the rock. The biggest, Absalom's tomb, has a hole high up on its face, as though a mortar shell has gone right through the rock.

Mendel says that Jerusalem is a place of irrationality. Von Gottberg thinks that Jerusalem is just a stage in man's journey to self-consciousness.

'Ah, the *Geist*. Hegel always pops up when you are at a loss to explain.'

'You should remember what Hegel said: "The actual is rational." '

'Meaningless. Absolutely meaningless. Sonorous nonsense.'

They love high-minded walking.

At Absalom's tomb, in fact the tomb of a member of one of the Hasmonean priestly families at the time of Christ, they buy some bread from a Bedouin, who heats it on a brazier (it is very cold, although there is some sun on the high ground) and the Bedouin gives them a twist of paper with coarse salt in it. The bread is sprinkled with a dried herb, perhaps oregano. Mendel says that this bread has been baked since the time of David, and the herbs come from the mountainsides. He takes pleasure in this continuity.

'Count von Gottberg and Mr Mendel.'

Two young women are coming down a track towards them. One is Elizabeth Partridge, the wife of a second secretary at the High Commission. It seems to Mendel that she is not here by chance. She introduces the second woman who is wearing a silk scarf wound around her neck and over her head.

'This is my cousin, Rosamund Bower, Mr Mendel.'

'Elya, please. This is the land of the muscular Jew. In fact a wholly new breed of informal Jew, who likes outdoor activity. Absolutely delighted to see you in daylight.'

'You were deep in discussion,' says Elizabeth. 'Interesting, I hope?'

'Yes, Axel was trying to tell me that I misunderstand the nature of human ends.'

'And do you?'

'Not always.'

'Does he, Axel?'

'It's hard to say, because nobody can agree on human ends.'

'Too clever for me, I'm afraid. I'm rather simple,' she says, laughing girlishly in the direction of von Gottberg.

Mendel notices her small, childish teeth, which are strangely lascivious. He has never before thought of teeth as part of the sexual weaponry. The second woman who he has at first decided is the less attractive, the alibi type, he sees now has a dark, rather serious look, which suggests a rich inner life. Her lips appear to be naturally outlined in some mineral substance. She leads Mendel towards some caves.

'I think it is amazing that these tombs are carved out of solid rock.'

'Yes,' she says, 'the tomb with the hole in the top, Absalom's tomb, has that hole because it was completely buried over the centuries and grave robbers got in from the top.'

'I wonder how long it took to carve out. But of course time, and any idea of its short supply, probably hadn't occurred to the Hasmoneans.'

'Do you always talk so profoundly?'

'Believe me, I'm far more superficial than I appear. It's just a habit you cultivate in my line of work. What's yours?'

'I was at Oxford for a year, in fact I used to see you always surrounded by acolytes. Now I am trying to write a novel.'

'What sort of novel are you writing?'

'I'm a great admirer of Virginia Woolf.'

'Marvellous writer. I've met her.'

'Did you like her?'

'She frightened me. She sent me a postcard afterwards, saying any time I was in London I should knock on her little grey front door and she would let me enter.'

'Rather risqué.'

'Yes, I thought so.'

'And did you knock on her front door?'

'No, I was too nervous. Far too nervous. We met last night briefly, but I didn't catch your name a few minutes ago, I'm afraid. Rosalind?'

'Rosamund.'

'Why were you following us?'

'Well, we're not actually following you. It's just that your friend Axel arranged last night to meet Elizabeth here and she thought I should come to protect her. Is he very voracious?'

'I think he is. Surrounded by servants all his life and milkmaids, of course.'

'Is he a Nazi?'

'Good God, I hope not. No, he's far too intelligent for that.'

'Oh look, they're wandering off.'

They follow the other two at a distance in the direction of the small village that stands above the valley. All around are graves, slabs of stone, some neglected, one or two with small piles of rocks on them.

'What are you doing here?' he asks.

'Oh, Elizabeth and I are cousins, as she said. She is a little bored here, I think, so she invited me to stay. She and Roddy have an old Turkish house, very solid. I was in Italy trying to write my novel, so I came by steamer to Haifa. Do you know I heard about you all the time in Oxford, but we never met.'

'More's the pity.'

'You're supposed to be brilliant. Dazzle me.'

'Am I supposed to be brilliant? To tell you the truth I talk far too much, but only the credulous are taken in. Will you tell me about your novel?'

'Are you interested or being polite?'

'I'm deeply interested.'

And she sees that he is. He smiles but it is not patronising or cynical. His eyes, behind his glasses, are very dark, the irises abnormally large. As they walk up through the olive trees where goats are foraging in their irrepressible, intelligent way, she tells him that it is the story of one young woman watching as her lover is taken from her by a friend.

'Has this happened to you, or is that too direct a question?'

'They always say write what you know.'

She is no older than him, but he has seen that life can quickly produce wariness; the blitheness of extreme youth has gone, but

31

still she has a kind of directness he finds attractive. At Oxford he soon discovered that he was drawn to these intelligent, upper-class girls. She stares down the dry wadi, in the direction of the Dead Sea.

'I am over it now, I think. The book is my therapy.'

'I met Dr Freud once, a very strange man.'

'Gosh, you have met everybody. Why is he strange?'

'Sorry, I tend to blurt things out when I am excited. After five minutes he proclaimed, "I see you are not a snob." '

'Why?'

'I don't know. Perhaps he has psychic powers. Please tell me more about your book.'

'I'm finding it very hard to write because I am not sure if the life that interests me will interest other people.'

'May I read it? Do you have it here?'

'I've only got a few chapters typed. In my bag. I carry them everywhere. It comforts me.'

'Will you let me read them?'

'I would be honoured, actually, if you would.'

The village, Silwan, is very simple. These Arab villages appear to be slowly falling down, roughly at the same speed as other parts of them are being built. A mosque, with a pencil-slim minaret, stands in the middle of the dusty, crumbling houses with cool dark interiors. They have tea and coffee in a courtyard served under a cypress tree out of the cold wind. Elizabeth is wearing a straw hat, tied around the crown with a huge floppy pink bow: the brim spreads extravagantly on one side and hangs over her eyes, so that when she talks to von Gottberg she has to raise her face slightly, which, Mendel sees, is done in a consciously provocative way. Both the women have shining waved hair, and their eyes are made up to look wide and expectant.

'Shall we leave them?' Mendel asks.

'All right. Elizabeth, let's meet up again at the King David for a cocktail. We'll meet you at six or so. Elya is going to teach me how to speak everyday Hasmonean.'

'Toodle-oo,' Elizabeth says, and turns back to von Gottberg. They hear his extraordinary laugh suddenly breaking to the surface.

'In Russia there is a saying that you sometimes feel like the fifth wheel on the wagon,' says Mendel when they are at a distance.

'Yes, I am afraid my cousin is not happy with Roddy. He is rather earnest and works all the time.'

'And Axel is providing a little diversion?'

'Yes. She hopes so anyway. Where shall we go?'

'Let's walk up through the Jewish cemetery. And then to the Garden of Gethsemane,' he adds.

'No need to be ecumenical. I'm half Jewish, although I was never brought up with any Jewish faith. Or indeed any faith. When you are here, do you long to see where Jesus walked or where Solomon's temple stood, or to climb King David's tower?'

'Nothing to do with King David, of course.'

'Do you see a Jewish homeland?'

'Yes, I think Jews must have a homeland. We Jews.'

She rests her hand on his forearm.

'Elya, can we go back to the hotel now? I have the manuscript and I want you to read it. I won't be able to rest until I hear your opinion.'

In the bar of the hotel she orders a Tom Collins.

'Would you like one?'

'I've never had one.'

'You don't know what you are missing.'

She removes her small hat, which is clinging to the side of her head, and shakes her dark, waved hair, as if expecting clouds of dust to emerge, as from a beaten carpet. Her hair is centre-parted, the waves tumbling in an orderly fashion to just above her collar. Mendel feels quite drunk after his first deep draught.

'Can you read the manuscript in your room?' she asks.

'Of course.'

He feels suddenly bereft, and stands up.

'Shall I meet you down here?' he asks.

'Don't be silly. I'm coming too.'

The lift, one of the earliest in Jerusalem, is piloted by a robed servant, perhaps a Sudanese. A Nubian. Rosamund and he stand some way apart; lifts sometimes produce this awkwardness about proximity. His room is on the sixth floor. The operator uses a brass handle to bring the lift to rest.

'It's a little cluttered, I'm afraid.'

In the short time he has been here he has collected pamphlets and maps and books and a Roman head and a small carpet, rolled up. After clearing a space they sit in the two padded and studded chairs, which have fanciful Ottoman legs, splayed outwards. She pulls the manuscript from her bag.

'Here we are.'

She stands and goes to the window.

Outside, the Old City is glowing. The light in Jerusalem has a desert quality, adamantine in the day, but softening and golden in the evening.

'God it's a marvellous sight. I'll order from the bar. What would you like? I'm going to have another Tom Collins.'

'So am I,' says Mendel, giggling. 'When in Rome . . .'

Once he has started to read, he looks up only to smile until a waiter in a white uniform with a red sash over his shoulder appears.

'Wonderful,' says Mendel, but she doesn't know if he is talking about his second Tom Collins, which he drains excitedly, or her novel.

'Do you mind if I have a shower? I'm dusty.'

'No please, go right ahead. This is very, very good, moving, this opening scene of the break-up. You are a marvellous writer.'

He can hear the shower – the showerhead is enormous, as big as a French sunflower drooping at sunset. The sound of the water on the marble, by way of her body, distracts him. She is in his bathroom, just through there, naked.

She comes out in a bathrobe with a white towel around her head.

'Elya, I wonder, are you the sort of man who needs a woman

34

to ask him a direct question? I think you are, so let me ask it: would you like to make love to me?'

At twenty-four, he is finally naked with a woman. Their love-making is not awkward, as he had feared his first sexual experience would be. She anticipates his uncertainties.

'Oh Elya, you are so beautiful.'

He knows he is not beautiful, but he finds her tone and the way she speaks to him intoxicatingly strange, as though she is from another place, one where he has never been, one which has its own language. He finds as they make love that he has passed through into a world that was always there, but behind a screen, indicated to him only by rodent scratching or the calls of small, unseen nocturnal animals.

When he comes, far too quickly of course, he weeps with joy as she breathes Tom Collins into his ear.

'You probably thought I was providing cover for Elizabeth.'

And the idea that she has set out to seduce him makes him feel doubly esteemed. They lie in bed and eat green-and-mother-of-pearl pistachios as the softening sun leaves the ancient walls in shadow, but lingeringly embraces the Dome of the Rock, the Mosque of Omar, like a favourite child before sleep.

He wonders if she feels the same sense of being blessed as he has next to her. She can't, but still he feels that he has never been happier and that this moment has somehow resolved – perhaps as Axel's thesis and antithesis is resolved – many of the contradictions in his life.

'Now read on, Elya.'

He reads aloud now and she is thrilled by his understanding and his extraordinary, liquid, exotic cadences, which make her book seem more human, richer, than she could have hoped. He reads, thrilled by the feel of her thigh against his. He worries that he is too plump or too hairy, but he soon loses himself in the book. She has an extraordinary, comic grasp of social relations and tensions, as well as a sardonic wit. The heroine, Claudia, has a bold approach to life: *It's not only our fate, but our duty to lose our innocence.*

35

'Do you believe that?' Mendel asks her.

'I don't think I'm talking about sexual innocence. More that we should not be under any illusions.'

'As Joseph Butler said, things are what they are. Why should we wish to be deceived?'

'Exactly. Whoever Joseph Butler is, or was.'

He knows that they will make love again soon and he feels that he is living in a moment that can never return. He reads:

> 'Do you have feelings Claudia?' Esmond asked.
> 'Of course I have feelings. Do you?'
> 'Yes I do. Of course I do, but they are not important to me. I try to be more decent, more civil than I feel. That is how I get by.'

'Do you have feelings, Elya?'

'I do.'

'Do you have feelings for me?'

'That's a strange question under the circumstances.'

'You wept, but perhaps you wept because you had lost your innocence. We hanker after innocence.'

He puts the book down and turns to look at her. He is still wearing his glasses, which he fears loom rather large now that he is naked.

'I have the most extraordinary feelings for you. Quite astonishing, even frightening. I feel blessed.'

He can't get over the fact that he is lying next to this young woman, that her breasts are now touching his chest, that he met her only yesterday, that she says he is beautiful.

'Were you very hurt?' he asks.

'I was terribly hurt. Rationally I knew he was highly unsuitable, but that didn't stop me loving him. Do you think women sometimes embrace hurt?'

'I don't know enough about women, to tell the truth. So far I've always been considered rather safe in a taxi.'

'No longer, Elya. Those days are behind you.'

She slides on top of him: it is almost unbearably sensual to feel her body on his. She sits up, astride him. She utters tiny shrieks and her eyes seem to cloud over. He feels exalted although he has a nagging sense that his life and his emotions have been too quickly and easily subverted.

Down in the bar they meet Elizabeth and Axel, both a little tight.

'Elya was reading my book. Sorry we're late.'

Axel is leaning back on his seat, in a lordly way, at his ease.

'They are cousins, you know,' he says.

Elya wonders if he imagines that this is drawing them closer. He sees that Elizabeth and Axel and Rosamund are complicit. Perhaps they think it is amusing that he should be drawn into this ménage. All the things he had never experienced, until an hour ago – Rosamund wiping herself with a hotel towel, dressing again with such insouciance, dabbing scent behind her ears and hooking up her brassiere deftly and re-attaching her stockings – these things to them are routine. He feels hurt, as if he is being patronised, but as he has never been able to strike an attitude for long he soon gives in to this warm, physical well-being, while still going over the precious details, both the magical and the practical, of their love-making. At the end of the lounge an Egyptian band starts to play 'Happy Feet', and Rosamund immediately jumps up and leads Axel on to the dance floor.

'Are your feet happy?' Elizabeth asks him. She looks at him in that over-the-shoulder fashion; her lips are deep red and shiny.

'Cheering up.'

'Shall we give it a whirl?'

'I don't really dance, I must warn you.'

'Just hop about enthusiastically. That's the secret.'

The band gives the song a certain Middle Eastern plangency; he doesn't care how foolish he looks as he tries to follow Elizabeth. She holds him quite firmly; of course he has danced before, but now he too is in on the secret: dancing is a sort of surrender to the sensual, to the clear message that music is life, and life is love and sex and longing, strangely and incomprehensibly distilled. And he sees that there are various forms of understanding that are not susceptible to strict logic, but which still have very real effects.

Rosamund and Axel appear next to them suddenly, and she blows him a kiss. Axel leans over to him, affecting a heavy German accent. '*Zeitgeist*. Good, *nein?*'

An army officer cuts in and he finds himself dancing with the officer's wife. She is bright and cheerful, like the small birds in cages attached to the walls in the Old City, incessantly flitting and chirping dutifully.

'Lovely girl, Elizabeth. And what do you do?'

'I teach at Oxford.'

'Oh gosh, you must be jolly clever.'

'Not really. I am like a monkey, I learn tricks easily. Are you enjoying living here?'

'Nobody likes us, not the Arabs and certainly not the Jews, which makes life a little trying.'

'Yes, I have relatives here who seem to think it's all my fault.'

'Jolly argumentative, aren't they, don't you find? They argue like billy-oh about almost anything.'

'It's an old Jewish tradition. It's the *Midrash*: life must be constantly examined.'

'Gosh, jolly interesting. Actually, I try to keep out of politics. Richard says it's best.'

'I'm sure he's right.'

'I know that Hitler is being beastly to the Jews, but Richard thinks that Hitler is right about the communists. They're the real problem, he says.'

Later the four of them leave the hotel and go off to a house in the Old City and smoke hashish. It's almost dawn when Elizabeth and Rosamund leave to go home. Roddy will be waiting. Axel hugs Mendel briefly and says, 'Lovely, lovely girls.'

When Elya lies on his bed again, he can smell Rosamund's

perfume faintly and, he imagines, the more mysterious scents of her body. He thinks of his mother at home in Hampstead sewing intently as his father reads the newspaper.

*Dear Mama. Tonight I lost my virginity and smoked hashish for the first time.*

She would be happy: she thinks her own life is too ordered.

And he thinks about what Axel said to him as they inhaled the hashish: *I must go back, Elya, dear friend. Please understand.*

# 3

WHEN CONRAD GOT back from Jerusalem, he found that
the struggle for the ownership of the Holy Places had a parallel
in his own life. In six years of marriage, he and Francine had
accumulated quite a lot of stuff. Now he was being asked to go
through an inventory to decide who had what. In Jerusalem the
contest between the religions was a bitter struggle for the possession of places, many of them of doubtful historicity. What he
wanted to discuss – or contend – with Francine was the human
issue. How, for example, was she able to accommodate herself
physically and emotionally to someone so different from him?
What was it like to live with someone else, to breathe their air
and experience their little night noises and foibles? Was it easy
to feel a different skin against yours after nine years? And, if it
was easy, what was it that he lacked that this other person had?
It was a mystery, an existential mystery, and he would have liked
to get to the bottom of it. But when he tried to get on to these
topics, Francine saw not some interesting ontological issues but
jealousy. Jealousy, *tout court*.

'Don't give me the philosophical stuff. I know it's painful for
you, but I love John. You have to accept that. You and I are not
suited. You think running off to Jerusalem – how did you put
it? – to get closer to Mendel and his German pal is somehow
important. It is so damned airy-fairy. For nearly ten years you
have been telling me your ideas. None of them, not one single
one, has come to anything.'

'That is not totally accurate.'

But before she could develop the aggrieved lobster-thermidor colouring, he added, 'At least from where I am standing – admittedly the non-scientific vantage point – I would have to say that there has been some bad luck and some near misses. But yes, in material terms you are right, although you seem to conveniently ignore the fact that ideas have value in their own right. And – no, wait a second – also I accept that you believe you love John. Love is, after all, even for the people who understand the ins and outs of biology – no innuendo intended – an irrational, even subjective matter.'

'Conrad, in case you have forgotten, we are here to discuss which of our possessions you are going to have and which I am going to have. I have made a list and I have checked the things that are unmistakably yours or unmistakably mine. After that I propose that we have a choice each, one after the other until we get to the end of the list.'

When he looked at the list, there were items on her side that seemed far from indisputably hers. For example, any wedding presents that originated on her side of the family were treated as hers alone.

'I don't remember your mother saying that the Boda Glass was yours. The tag read, as far as I can remember, "For Franny and Conrad, from Mummy". I remember distinctly feeling a little queasy about the "Mummy"!'

'Look, she gave them to me. She is my mother and she never liked you. You've had six years of use and broken about one in three of them anyway.'

'Now I would like to break the rest of them at my leisure.'

'Oh Jesus. I'm on call tonight. I can't spend the whole afternoon discussing every item.'

From the bakery below, the smell of yeast fermenting was strong and pleasant. The bakery smells, the hints of artisanal life, are what he likes most about the flat.

'I tell you what, I'll have the bed. Presumably you have one that works well for you?'

'Oh my. I see the way this is going. You can have the bed. I'll have the desk my father gave us.'

Her choices had a basis in economics or utility; his were provocative or whimsical. For instance, his fourth choice (how demeaning he found the system, in fact how demeaning he found all forms of practical organisation), was a small Roman head he had bought in Bristol. It was probably worthless, maybe even a fake, but he had grown fond of this modest bust of some late-Roman Bristolian in his best toga – three diagonal folds were visible under his chin – with the sightless seer's eyes suggesting some desirable and ancient ease of mind. What Ovid called *otium*.

'Are you interested in what I did in Jerusalem?'

'Not especially. I find your aimless journeys and impulses depressing. Also I know that you have no money.'

'Not exactly aimless. But still, OK, let's keep within the world of objects. Things. As you so rightly say, we are not here to divide up our ideas, our loyalties or our finer feelings. Just the fucking bits and pieces. And talking of money, when are we selling the flat?'

'Which I mostly paid for.'

'I think you will find it is in our joint names. Anyway, you and John between you already have enough for a little hidey-hole in Whitechapel, it seems.'

'You are such a bastard. I don't want to talk about John. I don't want to cause unnecessary distress.'

'Only necessary distress. You know what I found in Jerusalem? I found that you were never meant to allow possessions to take the place of ideals.'

'Luckily for you, that's never likely to be your problem.'

'You looked beautiful on our wedding day.'

'Why did you say that? Why now?'

'I said it because you had serenity then. Now all you think about is your work and – what you said, your words – your career path. Before we go back to looking at the crockery and debating ownership of the Dyson, what is a career path? To me it seems like planning your own funeral fifty years in advance. All the way to the grave. No thanks, I don't want a career path, I want to follow, in my aimless and depressing way, the life that interests me. How do I know what will interest me in ten years' time? In ten years' time I might want to farm coconuts in Mozambique or learn Sanskrit, or fuck pigs, I don't know. But I just don't want a career path.'

She wasn't listening. She was opening up a flat box that contained a collections of schnapps glasses, unused, unseen, for six years. He could have gone on to tell her about the benefits of *dépaysement*, the opening of your mind to wonder, but he knew that she was in no mood for this kind of thing.

Is he trying to get close to Mendel? Did he really say that? One of Mendel's favourite themes was the impossibility of knowing another mind. Take Francine's mind. He finds it astonishing that for all these years he believed he knew her mind quite well. He thought he understood her tastes, her determination to understand how things worked, her anxieties about disorder, and still he thought that deep down she loved him, but somehow it seems her face, with its almost-too-strong nose and her widely spaced eyes and distinctly ribbed lips – the top lip protrudes slightly – has fooled him all this time. It suggested a kind of softness; he could never have guessed that she would dispose of him so decisively. He imagined that they had exchanged enough of their human essences to become in some way one person. He had often lain in bed – the bed he had just been granted – and thought about the minute sloughing-off of skin, the exchange of air as they lay close. He had adapted himself happily to her night habits. (She sometimes appears to be awake, with her eyes wide open and her teeth grinding lightly.) And not to forget in this round-up the semen rushing eagerly on its short, Darwinian sprint, the bed-sheets made not grubby by the spillage, but intimate, even numinous; how she would eat breakfast standing up, unaware that he saw her absolute belief that she was going to be late as endearingly irrational. And

44

all this she has ignored, because John's claims to intimacy are stronger than his.

If he doesn't know her mind, how can he know Mendel's? We see through a glass darkly, von Gottberg's wife, Liselotte, had written to Conrad of her experiences. But this idea of darkness, he thinks, is romantic, a mistake, because it suggests that we are moving towards light, that we must look closely for the truth, that there is some end in view – religious or personal or historical or philosophical. He remembers so well that the last time he saw Mendel, breathing air and oxygen through a plastic tube, he said with his faintly ironic smile, 'Life has no meaning. I rejoice in that. Things are what they are. There is no more.'

Mendel had written that to him the history of ideas was often more interesting than the ideas themselves: what he meant – Conrad believes – is that the search for meaning is more revealing than the nostrums, the prescriptions, the ideologies, concocted in the name of this search. But still he is far from clear about what Mendel had in mind for him. Maybe all he had in mind – surely plenty – was an extended tutorial in how to live your life. Francine intended something similar, if a little more practical.

'Conrad,' she said, 'I know you don't really care, but can we get this sorted? Once and for all? And fairly? You have a talent for putting off very simple matters. In fact you find them almost intolerable.'

'I do.'

'It's a kind of resistance to reality.'

'Oh thanks for that. And I thought I was just lazy. That's the scientific mind for you.'

'I was being polite.'

'I was thinking about how you could possibly have sex with John.'

'Shall we stick to the programme?'

'That's another thing I find difficult.'

For no good reason he debated her every choice, the wedding photographs, the used chequebooks, the Dualit toaster, the curtains he had never liked. He made a stand over the books and his demands were mostly met, because he had, somehow, a moral lien over them, although not of course over the medical textbooks. In idle moments – plenty of those in the last nine years – he has looked through them. It is amazing to him what these doctors know. She thinks it is a matter of pride with him to decline all opportunities of practical knowledge, but the truth is that when he looks at these textbooks he sees mountains of facts – even protein molecules require pages of explanations and tricky little diagrams – mountains that he could never have scaled.

Before his rapid decline, his father had often talked about Everest. Mountaineering represented not man's ability to conquer some turbulent geology, but his ability to make life in his image. Later when he discovered that even the best intentioned can be disappointed, his father lost his faith in the human enterprise. But back in the fifties it was a young man's task to subdue chaos wherever it was found; in personal relations or in the garden or in the colonies, the imperative was much the same. And Conrad sees that ideas have their time: von Gottberg, with his spirit and destiny, belonged to a different time. Mendel, back then, was already interested in the effect of ideas, often deleterious. He hated particularly the lie at the heart of Marxism, that ordinary people are suffering from false consciousness. And when, soon after his trip to Jerusalem with Mendel, von Gottberg went back to Germany and wrote his infamous letter to the *Manchester Guardian*, things were never the same between them. Von Gottberg wrote that the *Guardian* was wrong to say that there was discrimination against Jews in the courts in Hamburg. He had never seen it, and he was working there as a prosecutor. He had even spoken to some active storm troopers who, though they supported their leader's race policies, said they would never have countenanced violence against Jews.

And now, in this wrangle, Conrad saw what he already knew, that there was no hope of recovering what he and Francine had lost.

46

'Fran, take whatever you want. And we'll sell the flat whenever you are ready. Or you can buy me out. You decide how much it's worth. I don't care.'

This insouciance upset her more than the wrangling. Maybe she thought it was a ploy. Her throat was colouring and her tired, tired eyes, flecked with late-night blood spots, looked at him for the first time today.

'What's the matter with you? Why are you doing this to me? You know we were going nowhere.'

'Going nowhere. It's a common but untrue belief that life is a journey.'

'Please, Conrad. Please, please, spare me, spare us, this hell.'

'You take whatever you want. And pay me out when you can. I mean it.'

She started to cry, but resisted his attempt to put an arm around her.

'No, Conrad. I've made up my mind. Conrad, you are an extra-ordinary person, wonderful really and I loved you. But you have, I don't know, a kind of contempt for me and the world I live in which has hurt me terribly.'

'I don't have a contempt for you. Not at all, I admire you. It's almost unbelievable to me what you do and what you know.'

'Yes, unbelievable is the word. But you are engaged, in your estimation anyway, in the higher pursuits.'

'That's just not true. But you know, you are what you are. You once said to me, "Who asked you?" and the answer is nobody. Nobody asked me. But it's in my nature. And, by the way, the contempt is largely from your side, from the practical side of life, towards the airy-fairy, represented by me. I never wanted to hurt you. Never.'

'You see where we've got to? It's hopeless.'

'Do you love John?'

'Yes. I love John.'

'Do you know what Axel von Gottberg's brother called him on the day he was hanged by Hitler? He called him an outcast dog.'

47

'Am I supposed to see a connection?'

'No. But to me it suggests that desperate people will do or say anything. Are you desperate?'

*Zur selben Stunde starb Axel in Berlin-Plötzensee.* That was what von Gottberg's wife wrote in her memoir: one brother called the other an outcast dog in the same hour as Axel died in Berlin-Plötzensee. This is where all his talk with Mendel led von Gottberg, to a blank wall in a prison, a wall decorated with meat-hooks to which thin cords were attached to form nooses. How could you call your own brother an outcast dog? What is it about us, we presumptuous human creatures, that makes us on the one hand desperate for order and certainty, and on the other craven, vicious murderers? I don't know and, for all her knowledge, Francine doesn't either.

When he looked at Francine she was ticking the list frantically and he saw with an upwelling of sympathy that rose like a tidal bore from within him, starting somewhere at the bottom of his torso, that her face was blotched now: the colour had escaped from the neck. All her composure was in that moment gone. She was a frightened woman, young but not very young, and she was exhausted by her work, by his intransigence, by her childlessness, by the realisation that life is full of disappointments. He put his arm around her now, brushing away her muted protest. He kissed her and she was trembling and he was shaking too, because there was something exciting about taking back, even for a short time, his sexual property, that another man had used.

Afterwards they lay together silently, their skins damp. For both of them what had happened was shocking, although of course they had made love thousands of times before. How strange then, he thought, how perverse, that this love-making should seem illicit.

His father loved a singer called Tim Hardin. He had a vinyl recording of his songs which he played endlessly and would sing in the bath. Now the words come to Conrad unbidden, and he sings:

*If I listened long enough to you, I would find a way to believe*
*It's all true, knowing that you lied straight-faced while*
*I cried. Still I'd find a reason to believe.*

'Tim Hardin?'
　'Tim Hardin.'
　'Conrad, I'm glad we did this. But it'll never happen again.'

*If I listened long enough to you, I would find a way to believe*
*It's all true, knowing that you lied straight-faced while*
*I cried. If I gave you time to change my mind,*
*I'd find a way to leave the past behind.*

'Do you still love me, Conrad?'

The bakery smells that rose up from below were strong now, coming in gusts. Their possessions, arranged as if in a charity shop, seemed to him utterly worthless, without purpose or substance. He could hear his father, singing quite tunefully in the bath. Two thirty-five-year-olds were lying semi-naked in the Camden afternoon, which intruded weakly through the dirty panes.

'Fran, even gannets mate for life.'

'Oh shit. I'll sort out all our things and make sure it's fair. I owe you that.'

She seemed to be eager to go. Perhaps John was waiting somewhere to hear how her encounter with the erratic one had gone. He watched her get dressed again. She usually goes into the hospital in jeans and changes into her blue scrubs there. In future John will be sharing this intimate knowledge of her, how she pulls on her jeans and leans slightly forward to do up the top button and how she passes both her hands through her hair, and then leans forward again to shake it for a moment, before raking it back. What do these little things mean? He couldn't believe this would never happen again.

His intimacy with Francine, whose buttocks, he noticed, were beginning, ever so slightly, to droop, would be relegated, like his father's singing, to a different and more treacherous intimacy, the realm of memory where almost anything goes.

When she had gone, he felt strangely exalted. He lay on the bed and then fell asleep for a while, and he heard his father singing *I would find a way to believe*. Sometimes in his memory his father shuffles, small steps, like a dutiful Japanese woman's, as he sings *It will never happen again*.

# 4

MENDEL WAS ELECTED a fellow of All Souls in the autumn after he returned from Jerusalem. In those days Englishness had a sort of radiance and Mendel's parents could not help basking in it, explaining to their relatives and friends that a fellowship of All Souls was the highest honour in the English academic world. Their son Elya's triumph had allowed them to feel that they were sitting in the box-seat, as the saying went. Actually their son was also an immigrant, six years old when his family arrived in Britain by steamer, but the children shake off the whiff of the old country very quickly even as it clings to the parents like some faintly noxious gas, for ever.

By the time Conrad met him, Mendel was that necessary figure, the publicly acknowledged wise man, known not just in Oxford but in the wider world. A few of these people spring up in every generation. So, reading the letters, Conrad was surprised and touched by Mendel's pride in his election to All Souls. We tend to think that well-known people were always celebrated.

Conrad visited Mendel once in All Souls, for lunch. It was 1991. He remembers the elderly college servant – a dying breed, said Mendel, and this one was clearly moribund – serving the oxtail soup with his thumb dangerously close to the brown Plimsoll line.

'Often he doesn't notice when his thumb goes in,' said Mendel. 'That's probably why the soup is served cool, for health-and-safety reasons.'

They sat in a small panelled room, the Common Room, which the Fellows used when there were not many of them dining. Mendel told him that dessert was always served here after dining in hall, a custom whose origins had been forgotten. The eggheads of all shapes and sizes, boyish, awkward – some, he fondly imagined, *idiots savants* – greeted Mendel before they moved to their tables. Mendel was like a saint in an obscure church, whose effigy or relics have to be touched or kissed or stroked when entering.

'They're always surprised, I hope pleasantly, to find I am still alive.'

These brainy folks seemed to be physically tortured by their intelligence, stooped, contorted, with out-of-control hair and clothes that ranged blithely between the resolutely tweedy and the hopelessly ill-assorted, as though great minds were unable to take in the merely cosmetic.

And now Conrad sees that those early days in All Souls, when Mendel was in love with Rosamund, had been wonderfully happy, the freedom to read and write and the encouragement to live the life of the mind unreservedly. In his own way, Conrad has been trying to do this for ten or more years, without much to show for it. And it is this aspect of the life of the mind, the snub to the free market and its bogus laws, which Francine resents most: where's the vaccine, where's the best-seller, where's the academic tenure? What's the product of this free-range thinking?

Yes, it must have been bliss, with Rosamund coming up from London for the weekends, and Mendel going often to London to see her and reading her new chapters with that wonderful enthusiasm and humour, and the love-making which was still new and utterly entrancing to Mendel; love and sex dissolved the protective deposits of cynicism and selfishness. And, Conrad guesses, caused Mendel to understand that there are many human actions that are animal or irrational in essence. Conrad himself knows this all too well. Dumped by Francine he feels jealousy and rejection, but still more strongly, the loss of innocence. He wants to believe in love and its redemptive power; in fact he loves the idea of love perhaps more than he loves Francine, although he remembers *The Leopard*: *Love. Flames for one year, ashes for thirty*. It's the nature of love that you enter the lists knowing you will both lose.

Rosamund and her cousin Elizabeth, who had become even more bored in Jerusalem, were making a visit to Germany and were proposing to see von Gottberg. Rosamund wanted Mendel to patch up his relations with Axel.

'He's very hurt, Elizabeth says. Please write to him, Elya.'

'I will write him. But what he wrote to the *Guardian* was unforgivable, although it is possible he had his reasons.'

'Elizabeth says he is trying to avoid joining the Party.'

'The only way to avoid that is to emigrate.'

'You are a hard man. And I thought you were soft.'

'I have surprised myself. Perhaps I was reacting as a Jew. But Axel must have known exactly what laws were passed. When we were in Jerusalem we met German Jews arriving in their thousands. What were they fleeing? A few cartoons showing them heavily bearded? No, loss of property, loss of jobs, loss of life. What he wrote was that the only hardship the Jews were suffering was because of "aid" for German Jews from abroad. And he cited the storm troopers as witnesses of their excellent good treatment at the hands of the authorities. Do you know what angered me most? It was the idea that Jews should be grateful under the circumstances. Only the wilfully blind cannot see. Anyway, now you and Elizabeth can see for yourselves. But in my mind Axel has passed from the grey world to the black-and-white. Books have been burned. Jewish shops have been expropriated. Axel knows these things. His idiotic letter is not in keeping with his beliefs and character, or if it is, he has deceived me and all of us.'

There is reference to a letter from von Gottberg, trying to explain himself, but Mendel dismisses it: 'He always takes refuge in generalities: "Europe must see that the true spirit of the German people is being subverted." Et cetera, et cetera.'

'Still, Elya, write to him. He loves you.'

'I will write to him, for your sake.'

He writes a conciliatory letter to von Gottberg, saying that he hopes and believes that they will always be friends, and that he was probably unaware of all the circumstances surrounding the writing of the letter to the *Guardian*. *But, Axel, you must know that what you wrote was foolish and – if not strictly interpreted – untrue, dangerous. It was not worthy of you. Please come and visit me in All Souls whenever you can.*

Conrad wonders if it is possible to read this letter as von Gottberg read it. They could both see that Europe's dark prejudices were surfacing in Germany, but neither of them could have any idea of the horrors to come, because, given the stock of available human experience, they were unimaginable.

When Elizabeth and Rosamund return from Germany, Rosamund writes to Mendel to break off their relationship. Mendel is heartbroken, but grateful, so he tells friends, for the happiness she has given him. He is, of course, primarily grateful for the sexual experience, previously a mystery to him. He cherishes it and husbands it.

Conrad wonders what happened in Germany. There is no sign in Mendel's papers that Rosamund met anybody else and her novel, when it was published early the following year, was apparently a minor success, thought by *The Times* to display 'an amusing, if rather shallow understanding of the surface aspect of our times'. Mendel kept the cutting alongside her letters. He wrote: *Nothing has changed. In my present mood I am happy with this situation. I see ahead of me a long, enclosed tunnel of work.*

Later there is a letter from Elizabeth saying that Rosamund has decided to return to Germany to oppose the rise of Nazism. She will be sending reports back to the newspapers; her uncle is a proprietor. But there is no mention of Rosamund's feelings for Mendel. He writes that he consoles himself with the knowledge that he was made for the contemplative life.

Conrad is sitting in the flat, now on the market. Without Francine's presence, he has noticed, it is deteriorating. He is unable to control the remains of meals and dirty plates and crumpled bedclothes. He seems to cause seismic upheavals with simple acts like opening a jar of coffee or looking for a book. Mendel's papers, which he is trying to put in some order, are resisting, faithful to their progenitor's spirit; he was famously disorganised. The collected letters of E.A. Mendel are far from collected. In fact they may be more dispersed than when he took delivery of them two and a half years ago. Many times he has been warned – Francine has warned him – that they should be kept in safe storage. For the moment they are still in hundreds of books and loose files of papers and seventeen cardboard boxes in what used to be his study but which has now become an all-purpose room containing items of clothing, plates, books, newspapers and socks. He hadn't realised until Francine moved out just how much stuff came through the letterbox every day. With her fear of chaos, she must have been up at dawn clearing up. Or clearing up when she came in from a hard day in the hospital. He feels retrospective guilt. New pizza-delivery services are multiplying, and working drivers with their own vans offer to move his possessions. Sometimes he looks at these flyers and marvels at the grammar and spelling. Utility companies and phone suppliers and holiday companies are offering deals. Often they come with mission statements. He understands that they are for mom and apple pie of course, but why are they issuing these quasi-philosophical statements which can't possibly mean anything? If it is true that language corresponds to some fundamental order in the brain, these folk are in serious trouble. A company that is offering to deliver salt for his water-softener (he doesn't have one, as far as he knows) describes itself as 'caring'. Caring salt. Or perhaps the proprietors are generally caring people and they want it to be known. He spends far too much time reading these bits of paper.

Am I heartbroken, like Mendel, he asks himself?

He hasn't spoken to Francine for ten days or so. She last rang to say that the agent was a little concerned about the state of the flat. It wasn't presenting well. Could he tidy up? He promised to give it a bash, but so far the moment has not presented itself. Although he is not actually discouraging interest in the flat, he likes the status quo. The bakery smells soothe him and he is able to apply himself to Mendel's papers, trying to understand what happened all those years ago.

Sometimes he goes out to meet friends. They appear to feel sorry for him, as though he has lost something. Nobody takes account of what Francine may have lost. He sees clearly his diminished status through his friends' eyes. The truth is, he is not heartbroken. He is beginning to feel liberated, freed of the awareness of Francine's disapproval. Although he must get someone to clean up, so that she won't have fresh grievances: in this way he is not yet entirely liberated. He remembers his friend Osric saying at first that his divorce was wonderful: he was able to eat scrambled egg in bed at three in the morning while watching women's tennis if he wanted to. Later he admitted to being lonely.

He imagines Mendel in his rooms at All Souls, properly heartbroken, first love turned to ashes, and, jumping forward, he sees von Gottberg in front of Roland Freisler at the People's Court, as though, somehow, there is a connection. This scene of von Gottberg being accused by Freisler of the perfect preparation for a traitor, loitering in cafés in the Kurfürstendamm after going to Oxford, an English university, on an English scholarship, haunts him. He thinks about it every day. He replays it, as if the film is inside his brain, right in his being. If Freisler had known his history a little better he would have realised that Cecil Rhodes's tendencies were closer to Nietzsche's than anything currently popular at Oxford. Rhodes truly believed in the Übermensch and the world spirit. But Oxford, to some people, is even now a provocation.

It occurs to him, in this flat above Baiocchi's Bakery, The True Taste of Italy, that he is living more fully in Mendel's life – All

Souls and Oxford are very real to him – and more fully in von Gottberg's life – sometimes when he wakes in the night he believes that he was present at the People's Court – than in his own. It is a strange but comforting feeling that the outside world is becoming less substantial to him. Perhaps I am beginning to understand what it is to live someone else's life. And possibly, he thinks, this is what Mendel had in mind for me, that I should apply this understanding to his life and give it its final shape. And this is perhaps what novelists do. The reality they create is just as valid as any other. Or more so. This is the sort of talk – although of course he is talking only to himself – that drives Francine mad. If she were here he would not have been able to resist trying it out on her. His mind is moving very lightly so that he thinks that appearance and reality and false consciousness and dualism are just fancy terms for the idea that the world is imaginatively constructed.

And now Conrad decides to clean the place up. He has the idea that if he cleans up he will possibly be better able to order Mendel's papers and so to determine their meaning, which needs panning out. When this meaning is discovered, he thinks, it will be nothing more than a few gleaming specks. His mind, moving a little too fast, like a man running down a mountain, skips to the Klondike and men in shabby clothes standing in icy streams staring hopefully at sieves.

He has no plastic bags, but the bakers below give him some used flour bags and offer him the use of their dumpster. He buys a freshly baked ciabatta, lightly dusted with flour, and takes it upstairs with the bags. As he cleans he leaves a light talc everywhere. He wonders how he could have used so many toilet rolls in so short a time. He carries the stuff downstairs; Tony Baiocchi and one of his sons, who wears a diamond ear stud, help him throw the flour bags into the dumpster.

'Where's your lovely missus the doctor, then? We ain't seen her for a little while.'

'We've split up, Tony.'

'That's a crying shame. She's a lovely gel. I thought you was perfect together.'

Upstairs he takes a look at himself in the bathroom mirror. He wonders if he is looking haggard and eccentric, but actually he quite likes the way he looks, a little dishevelled, but interesting; small pouches have formed under his eyes. He has not taken much note recently of the time; he feels no need to go to bed at any particular hour, or to get up if he doesn't feel like it. This irregularity has led to these eye-pouches. *Perfect together*. They were never perfect together. But he sees again the sense that other people have that Francine is something special, a lovely gel, who lent him some lustre. The world doesn't give much value to high-minded thinking.

Successfully completing manual tasks always leaves him invigorated and he sits down among the cardboard boxes with renewed purpose. Just then the phone rings and he hears a woman's voice, clear but delivered at elderly registers.

'I would like to speak to Mr Senior.'

'Yes, that's me.'

'You won't know who I am, but I am Elizabeth Partridge. The novelist, Rosamund Bower, was my cousin.'

'Good God. Sorry. Apologies.'

'You probably imagined I was dead.'

'No, no, not at all, I just had no idea what had happened to you. Although of course I knew that Miss Bower died in 1984. And I have some of your letters.'

'Yes, I know that Elya Mendel gave you many of his papers. I have some of his letters as well as some letters from Axel von Gottberg, and I wondered if you would like to have them. Elya suggested it before he died.'

'Jesus Christ. Sorry again. Yes, please, I would love to see them.'

'I'm in Ireland, but I will be in London next week for an operation.'

She speaks, as clearly and as harshly as a bell, with the authority of someone who has been around servants and dogs and horses all her life.

'Did Mr Mendel write to you often?'

'Oh yes. He certainly did. We were terribly close, particularly after Rosamund chucked him. Axel wrote to me often. I also have some of Rosamund's letters from Axel. Are you married?'

'I am, but it's not going well. She's gone.'

'It's a mistake to think of marriage as the final solution. Your voice is slightly odd. I hear that's how the young speak today. Is that what's called Estuary English?'

'Probably. I hope your operation is not serious.'

'At my age everything is serious. But this is just plumbing. Do you know, I never took it seriously when people said growing old is awful. But the truth is that it is awful. Things conk out.'

'I've got a lot of questions for you.'

'I'll do my best. Fortunately, my brain seems to be holding up surprisingly well.'

'How many letters do you have?'

'At least a hundred.'

'Good God.'

'You seem to have a rather limited vocabulary. In those days one wrote. Goodbye.'

'When are we going to meet?'

'I will telephone you when I arrive at Basil Street.'

He thinks when she has gone that she probably slept with von Gottberg. He finds it quite shocking, even thrilling, that someone who knew them both so well is still alive. From her letters, he has come to know her, but it never occurred to him that she would still be alive. She must be ninety-two or -three at least. He tears at the ciabatta with his hands and eats it excitedly. The room is pleasantly farinaceous. He has spoken to someone who slept with von Gottberg. He is stuffing the bread into his mouth. He is easily excited. His mother used to say that he was highly strung. Von Gottberg was highly strung; his hands would grasp and furl and unfurl when he was excited by ideas. In the face of enormous danger, mortal danger, he would become calm and detached. At his trial, after being tortured for days by the Gestapo in Albrechtstrasse, with only the sure prospect of death, he was calm. A few months later, when Helmuth James von Moltke was sentenced to death, he welcomed Freisler's remark that the Church and the Nazis demanded the same thing, the whole man. He would be hanged – von Moltke rejoiced – for his thoughts.

And this is something Mendel must have understood, that a deep belief, however irrational its origin, can be the source of strength and unimaginable courage. Perhaps the only source of strength.

# 5

WHEN ELIZABETH PARTRIDGE calls him a few days
later she asks him to come at tea-time, which he takes to mean
four o'clock. He emerges from the underground at Knightsbridge
and walks down Basil Street to her club. It is a place that accom-
modates members, mostly women, up from the country, women
who don't want to be startled in any way by the new realities of
London. So he imagines; he always, constantly, unstoppably,
makes these judgements. The brass doorplate has been polished
for so many years that the inscription, 'London and Counties
Club', is as indistinct as the epitaph on an ancient tomb. He
rings the bell and a porter in a faded dark-maroon uniform –
the colour of an old apple variety – trimmed at the cuffs and
lapels with gold thread that has lost its lustre, opens the door
and, limping, leads him to the reception desk where he presses
his hand down on the burnished brass bell which produces one
exhausted ping.

'She won't be long,' says the porter, who opens a small panelled
door and passes through it. He appears, when the door shuts, to
have vanished behind a large vase of delphiniums.

Everything in the place is faded. Even the delphiniums are of
a washed-out blue. It's an effect decorators often strive for, the
gentle deterioration of fabric and carpet and paint, the suggestion
that here at least there will be no absurd – vulgar – newness.
Even the lift with its concertina doors and brass buttons and
mahogany interior is perfect. Conrad likes it. He likes strange

things: there is no pattern to his tastes, another aspect of his life that upsets Francine, who finds whimsy self-indulgent. But what he likes is the confidence demonstrated by the committee, or whoever the presiding genius of the place is, that in this corner of Knightsbridge at least there is only one possible style appropriate for its members. It's akin to the belief that God took time out to endorse the Anglican church – its rituals, its tasteful hymns, its worn-out kneelers, its flowers, its surplices, its holy innocence – with his special approval. We are all God's children of course, but Anglicans are his favourites, because of their demeanour.

He is inspecting a thickly varnished oil painting of a horse in a landscape, when he is called.

'Are you here to meet someone, sir?'

He turns to see a cheerful young woman in a heavily threaded violet suit. The threads are on the outside, in a fine arachnid web, as if hovering above the material itself.

'Yes, I am here to see Elizabeth Partridge.'

'Ah, Lady Dungannon. She is expecting you. Please go through to the lounge and I will tell her ladyship that you have arrived. Would you like tea?'

'Oh, yes, please.'

'Ordinary tea, or herbal?'

'No, no, not herbal. Ordinary tea. Builders' tea, please.'

He imagines that 'builders' tea' is the sort of phrase that plays well here. He waits in the lounge, where the brass clock on the wall ticks loudly. The lounge looks on to a small courtyard. Elizabeth Partridge, he has discovered, was married to an Irish peer who died nearly thirty years ago. He tries in the loud silence to imagine what it is like to be as old as she is, to have witnessed so much, the parade of ideas, absurd fashions, hopeful politicians, corrupt regimes, dictators, murderers, sexual encounters, musical styles, marriages, bereavement and above all the restless, insatiable appetite for happiness, for explanations, for fulfilment and also for art and beauty and music. Every generation uses and transforms what has gone before. As Eliot said – approximately – every generation takes what it needs from art. If you live for ninety years, you must lose faith in human judgement, so fickle, so self-regarding, so dangerous.

He hears the lift lurching and coughing upwards. The doors open somewhere above and close clumsily and noisily. There is a moment of indecisive whirring as if it is gathering its elderly senses, and then it jolts into action again. The doors open and he can hear the porter making polite encouraging noises to someone. The young woman's voice now joins in.

Into the lounge comes Elizabeth Partridge in a wheelchair, pushed by the porter. She sits in the chair with dignity, although age has cramped her so that she is curled, rolled, almost into a cochlear posture. The porter wheels her into place and helps her into a florally abundant armchair. Her face, heavily made up, has a mummified look, the porcelain appearance of time stopped, a broken clock, so that she can never get older and, with her carefully arranged woman-aviator's hair, will go to her grave in exactly this state. He thinks of her in the Kidron Valley, when she and von Gottberg were certainly having an affair, and he tries to imagine her tilting her head to look at him over her shoulder from under a large hat, her hair in shiny waves partly obscuring the view.

'Ah, hello,' she says. 'You must be young Master Senior. Pass me the bag, Miss Trentham. Is the tea coming?'

'Tea is on its way, Lady Dungannon.'

'Sit down, my boy. Sit down. It's not a cocktail party, more's the pity.'

She laughs and her laugh is so high and girlish that he is instantly charmed. As a small boy he liked older people, although his Aunt Dorothy with the bristly moles on her cheek repelled him when she kissed him.

'Why, Conrad, did Elya choose you to be his biographer?'

'He doesn't actually say biographer anywhere. I think he just wanted me to have his papers and look after them.'

'Thank you,' she says to the young woman. 'We will be talking for a while. Did you say tea is on its way?'

'Yes, it is, Lady Dungannon.'

'Jolly good. In this folder I have all the letters from Elya and from Axel, as well as some other bits and pieces. But before I give them to you, I want to ask you to do one thing. I feel I can ask at my age.'

She reaches across and places her hand on his wrist. It rests there with an avian lightness for a moment.

'Yes.'

'I want you to remember that Elya trusted you. He told me just before he died that you have some sensitivity.'

Conrad feels that dangerous surge of childish gratification rising up in him.

'To be honest, I don't know why he said that.'

'He was an excellent judge of character.'

The porter brings the tea. There is a long pause, some sighs, some clattering of bone china as he unloads his tray. Here, it is still a mark of civilisation to cut sandwiches very thin and to stack them in neat triangles. In the outside world people fill sandwiches and baguettes and bagels to bursting, but that is not the way here: watercress, cucumber and Cheddar are strictly confined. The tea comes in a pot with a matching jug of hot water and a strainer.

'Would you pour, Conrad? My hands are a little shaky.'

The ritual – perhaps it's the point of all rituals – draws them into a complicity. On her forehead he sees the thin indelible pencil mark of a blue vein, threatening to emerge from under her pale skin, which is only lightly coated on to the bones of her face.

'Yes, so you mustn't use his papers or the letters I am going to give you to make a fast buck.'

'No, no, of course not.'

Actually he is stunned both by the – justified – suspicion and by the phrase.

'No. You must not. The point about Elya is that his life's work was the understanding of human aims. As a matter of fact I think human longings is a better phrase. He believed that we make the best of the life we are given. All those years ago in Jerusalem, I asked him what he did – I had no idea he was an Oxford don – and he said he believed that human beings spent a lot of time deceiving themselves. He was thinking about why this should be the case, d'you follow me? What he couldn't decide then was whether this is a necessary human characteristic. Axel, of course, believed in Hegel, who Elya thought wrote absolute balls.'

'You were very close to Axel, weren't you?'

'I was. I loved him. But so did my cousin, Rosamund. She left Elya and followed him to Germany, but it didn't work. No, she slept with Elya because she wanted to prove to Axel that she would do anything for him. It was his idea that she help Elya lose his virginity. She never really loved Elya, unfortunately. However much you admire someone, you can't force the body to fall in love, don't you agree? Rosamund loved Axel, and she took up with a friend of his, just to stay in Germany. You're probably shocked. People of your age think sex was invented in 1963, as Larkin said. It wasn't, believe me.'

She laughs again quite suddenly, improbably loudly considering the diminished sounding box from which the laughter emerges.

'Did he know about Rosamund and Axel?'

'Elya? Yes. You must read the letters.'

'And Axel von Gottberg? Elya Mendel always writes about his charm, but deep down he never trusted him after his letter to the *Manchester Guardian*.'

'No, that is true. Elya never trusted him after that letter, but also he never trusted him after Rosamund. What's odd, of course, is that people like us – Axel, Rosamund, Elya and me – were just young people in strange times. I'm not saying we were ordinary, far from it, but the times were extraordinary. And knowing Axel changed us all in different ways. The only advantage of growing old is that you see things from differing perspectives. Young people think they have made the world.'

Axel von Gottberg has reached out from the grave to change Conrad's life too, although he is not yet sure exactly how.

'Let's have a cocktail now. Will you order? I would ring the bell, but life is too short to wait for Alf.'

'I'll go and order. What would you like?'

'I'll have a Tom Collins. I gave Alf Lionel's recipe years ago. Lionel Wray, Elya's friend, notorious sodomite. Or so he pretended.'

He finds the young woman and gives her the order for two Tom Collins.

When he comes back Elizabeth is powdering her nose, looking into a small compact and moistening her lips.

'He was very good-looking, you know.'

'Who?'

'Axel. He had enormous charm and sex appeal. Elya had charm, but it didn't really have a sexual content. Women liked him and confided in him but he was often treated, I think it's fair to say, as what people these days call a walker. Although some of his students fell for him utterly. One young woman, he brought her to stay when we came back to England, to Sussex, was desperate to marry him. He asked me in the kitchen what I thought. She was talking to my husband, my first husband Roddy, who was killed in 1942, and I said, "Don't touch her with a bargepole." "Bit late for that," he said. "I mean don't marry her, she's away with the fairies, daft as a brush." "Yes, but she's very good in bed," he said. "Honestly, Elya, what kind of talk is that from a fellow of All Souls?" And he laughed. He had a wonderful liquid laugh, like a big warbling bird. But you know how he laughed, I am sure. Actually we all laughed like hyenas. I think it was a fashion.'

Conrad has an image of those dogs, Boston terriers, that barked at the circus to produce music. He remembers Mendel's laugh: it rose, it bubbled from a cleft in the rocks, from the Kidron Valley, distilled in Jewish time, from a biblical age of innocence.

The porter is cast specifically to lend verisimilitude to this scene. He appears with two tall cocktail glasses, each topped with a maraschino cherry and a slice of orange. He places the glasses beside them on little round paper mats and then attempts a sort of respectful, unobtrusive exit, which stops the conversation.

'Don't mind me, your ladyship, I shall be returning shortly with some mixed nuts.'

Nobody has spoken like this since 1953.

'Jolly good, Alf,' says Elizabeth.

Conrad wonders if it is possible to order your life so that you are surrounded and attended only by people called Alf who have been sealed from the world as it is. If you have money, it may be possible. He wonders, too, if there comes a time when you wish for stasis and are unwilling to take on board any new information. That seemed to have happened to his father; he wasn't prepared to take on a new world, because he believed it would be just as deluded as the one it was replacing.

'Chin, chin,' Elizabeth says, raising her glass. 'Do you know, Axel, as a good Prussian, always bowed his head slightly when he said cheers or *prosit*. Elya noticed it. He said it was a sort of submission to higher powers. You couldn't say *prosit* without, as Elya put it, an acknowledgement of higher meaning if you were Prussian. Higher meaning was exactly what Elya spent his life trying to debunk.'

'How long did Rosamund stay in Germany?'

'After Axel called off their engagement, she went back to Germany and lived with a German for a year, and even wore the *Herrenhut mit Schmuckband*, that funny little trilby hat with a ribbon, for a while, but she came back here just before the war started. Her man joined the Party – he was called Strelitz – and remained a true believer to the end. He was killed in 1945. What she really wanted was Axel. Axel visited her, and me, on his trips to London to try to stop the war. That was in April and May 1939. A year later Ros married an Englishman. Five years later Axel was dead, hanged. It was too awful. We were so young.'

'I've seen the film of the trial.'

'Is it terrible?'

'He is oddly serene. Ready to die.'

'He was horribly tortured. Fingernails torn out, and God knows what else.'

'Did Elya ever talk about that?'

'No. He couldn't bear to hear about torture or pain. He was a coward himself, by his own admission.'

'Did he ever say he felt guilty about undermining Axel's reputation with the authorities, here and in America?'

'He was accused of it. But he said any criticism he had of Axel was of his fondness for putting himself in the middle of any intrigue that was going. And of course his patriotism. Patriotism was a very dirty word in Oxford. What's the phrase, the last refuge of the scoundrel? He felt that Axel's attitude was *my country, right or wrong*. What Elya realised very early on was that Hitler was not like anybody who had gone before. He had read *Mein Kampf*. But no, I don't think he ever believed that he had been responsible for Axel's death in any way. Axel put himself in danger from the beginning, by joining the German Foreign Office and playing a double game. He went all over the place telling people about the resistance. It was surprising he wasn't arrested long before July 1944.'

Conrad sees that Elizabeth is becoming tired and agitated.

'I must go now and rest,' she says.

'Can I see you again?'

'If I live through tomorrow's op, I would love to see you. Come and stay with us in Ireland.'

'I would love to.'

'How old are you, Conrad?'

'I'm thirty-five.'

'Just the age Axel was when he died. My son is sixty-one. Astonishing. Now take the letters and remember what I said about your obligation to Elya.'

*   *   *

As he walks along Basil Street towards the underground with his precious parcel in his tennis bag, he marvels that out here on the street life is so different, as though he has stepped through the scenery, like the evanescent porter. And this too, he thinks, is English life, a series of cameos or farces played out in separate rooms. Elizabeth conducts herself as someone who is on a stage, surrounded by bit-part players like the porter, the Dogberry of this scene. That self-assurance of the English upper-classes, the belief, as Cecil Rhodes put it, that if you asked any man what nationality he would prefer to be, ninety-nine out of a hundred would tell you they would prefer to be born an Englishman – that assurance lives on long beyond any possible verification. And it was this confidence that the benefits of an exposure to English-ness – an inoculation of Englishness, as a Master of Balliol once described it – would benefit everybody, that led Rhodes to include Germans among his candidates. And it is by this strange philo-sophical route that Axel von Gottberg came to Oxford.

When he gets home Conrad delays opening the folder and spends some time examining the cover on which Elizabeth has written in bold, lost, copperplate: *My correspondence with Elya Mendel and Count Axel von Gottberg and my cousin, Rosamund Bower, and other papers. Dungannon House, Ireland.*

When he eventually opens the folder after making coffee, and checking his emails twice, the sight of the letters, the paper alone, with the intimate and confessional quality of handwriting, has a powerful effect on Conrad. As he starts to read the letters, he discovers that they are full of promises and new starts and partings. As he knows, the pain of parting can itself be a pleasure. It should be no surprise that sixty years ago people had the same feelings as he does, but it is. The effect is unexpected: Elizabeth Partridge has brought him closer to them all, as though he has been introduced to friends of a close friend. And in a way he has been. But still he finds himself unsettled: Elizabeth is ninety-three, but her lover – who was also her cousin's lover – is for ever thirty-five. There are pictures of people at a certain age that freeze them in time – he thinks of movie stars and sportsmen and revolutionaries – and this has happened to von Gottberg: he remains for ever young. Early death also confers certain mythological qualities, and he wonders whether Mendel resented this as the years went by.

All three of the others are very aware of Mendel, as if his example, his deep-mined wisdom, reproaches them explicitly. It is a burden to them, it seems, trying to live up to the standards of their friend. Von Gottberg suggests that it will be difficult to write frankly after he returns to Germany. Conrad has seen this clear suggestion in other letters; Mendel has perhaps underestimated his friend's difficulties in Nazi Germany, because he sees basic principles so starkly. One of von Gottberg's letters asks if he has friends left in England and in almost every letter he tries to envisage a new European understanding; he is alarmed by the gulf that he thinks is opening up between Germany and England. He is longing to see Rosamund again, as though he has great faith in his ability to explain to her how it can all be fixed. He arranges to meet her at Tempelhof, from where they will drive to the family home. His mother is dying to meet her. Absurdly, Conrad feels nervous about her reception.

# 6

*Darling Lizzie*

*He looks different in Germany. Of course he is at home. At first we found it difficult to speak. I don't know why. Six months have gone by and in that time so much has changed, not just for us, but for our countries. An awkwardness had sprung up. I can see that what Axel fears most is that we will all be separated. He believes, however, that Hitler and his awful supporters are the product of history. What he means is that we created the problem at Versailles, and Hitler has simply used the situation. The German people – according to Axel – don't want Hitler or war. I must say to the visitor like me they seem to be longing for war and they appear to adore Hitler. But I am getting ahead of my story, dear cousin.*

*We stayed the first night in Charlottenburg, which is enchanting. Axel is well known in every café and bar, suspiciously so in my opinion; his favourite is the Romanisches Café, where the avant-garde meet. Anyway, by the time we had a few cocktails and fried calf's liver – essential Berlin food, said Axel – we were quite relaxed. In the morning we visited the Schloss, of course, the usual over-egged gilt and rococo. From Berlin we drove north to the countryside. This is Axel's* Heimat. *His father was one of the Kaiser's trusted ministers and the family have lived here for six hundred years. Axel feels very deeply for his* Land, *and I can see now why he felt he could not*

71

*abandon his home and his family for a life in Oxford, although Elya thinks if he hadn't got a second he would have stayed on. We stopped a few times in small villages, sleepy villages. Some of the names of towns and villages sound Polish to me, and in fact we were not far from East Prussia. Axel is very good-looking, as we know, but at home he has something princely about him. The peasants who served us (emancipated 1807) seemed thrilled by his voice and his looks. It helps that he's a least a foot taller than anyone else, of course. You know how intensely Axel can engage you with those hazel eyes? We novelists often prattle about eyes, probably because it's so easy, but Axel's eyes have more depth than anyone's I have ever met. We stopped by a cornfield streaked and splashed with blue cornflowers and red poppies and he kissed me there, as though it had special meaning. He said he loved me and that not a day has gone by without his thinking about me. What's a girl to do? Strange, considering it was he who encouraged me with Elya. Dear Elya. I hope he has forgiven me.*

*Soon we were approaching the family pile, via the Gottbergerwald, a huge forest which has been in the family since the fourteenth century, or thereabouts. The house emerges as you approach and then disappears again. Axel was so pleased to be showing me his demesne. It's a Palladian house, built in about 1850 in reality, on the site of the original manor house. We approached it down an avenue lined with oaks and enormous medieval barns. He stopped the car on the last hill so that we could gaze down the avenue at the house and the lake behind. The servants were lined up to greet us and I wished I had more luggage to occupy them. Inside, Axel's mother, the Gräfin, sat in a drawing room overlooking the lake. She speaks almost perfect English, as good as Axel's, and she welcomed me warmly. She's a very grand lady. Axel's father is unwell and he has been recuperating somewhere, I think in their other house over the Elbe, so I did not meet him. Axel admires him very much, although he thinks he belongs not to the previous generation but to the one before that. Later Axel's older sister arrived; the coachman had gone to get her at another house – I am not sure if it is one of theirs – where she had been painting. She was married and lived in London for a while. She is a wonderful painter and wears elaborately printed dresses in a bohemian style that only a very few can carry off. She was wearing a hat with ostrich feathers. That night we ate in the grand dining room and Axel and his sister were delightful. Her name is Adelheid, although they call her Adi, and she is about to marry the richest man in the whole of Mecklenburg. It will be possible to walk from the Baltic to Berlin without leaving their joint* Heimat. *(I may be exaggerating just a little.) In the morning we went riding in the forest where Axel and his sisters had run half-wild most summers. He took me to a lake hidden deep in the trees, which he said was their secret place as children. When we came back his mother was very grave: she said that the Brownshirts had destroyed thousands of Jewish businesses and synagogues in the night. The police and the army did not intervene. The realisation that a gang of thugs is in charge of the country is terrifying. Axel, in his usual way, spoke soothingly of historical forces and the coming of the new order of labour, which is disguised by these upheavals. I wonder. But anyway, he has not joined the Party, a fact which is making life very difficult for him, his sister told me, although he denies it.*

*That night we argued as we used to, but now there was something desperate about it: Jews have been murdered, scores settled as if the days of the Teutonic Order are coming back. And yet here we were in the grand house, with Axel saying that the English are suffering for their dried-up rationalism, which fails entirely to understand that we are on earth in a context. As Elya says, Hegel is never far from his thoughts. Not, of course, that I have read Hegel, but the general idea seems to be that everything has a purpose and that all conflicts lead inevitably to a resolution. Axel says that Hitler must be given some rope so that he can hang himself. He says, when his mother is not present, that there are plans in the High Command to stop him if he invades Czechoslovakia. As we sat and talked it all seemed very remote, yet Berlin is only a few hours' drive away. You know in your bones that terrible dark days lie ahead, but Axel retreats into metaphor: Germany will find her rightful place in the new Europe that is emerging; these upheavals are a sign of the emergence of new forces, benign forces. (I'm repeating myself, but then so does he.) I have the impression that Axel has had affairs with many women in Germany as well as the ones we know about in England. It's as though he feels he needs to help women in the only way he can. You know when I wrote in* Shadows at Dusk, *'He can't get on with women, so he gets off with them' – well, there is something of Axel in that. The next day we went back to Berlin. He is keen to introduce me to all his friends, even the women who I just know he has been to bed with. He seeks out Jews too, and seems fascinated by the fact that Mummy is Jewish. He said to me at the home of one of his friends, 'I am not a womaniser.' What he meant, I think, is that he has some sort of higher capacity for understanding: in life, as in women. I love him, although I can see that this cannot end well. Already we have to talk in code in public. In Berlin he is worried about his landlady and about neighbours. One night at three in the morning he sent me away to a hotel. I was shocked, but he said that it had to be done, no more explanations. We drove out to visit one of his clients in a Jewish area and the house was daubed with a huge five-pointed star and* Juden heraus. *It was so shocking, so nearly unbelievable, that I couldn't see how Axel could stay one more day. I waited for him in the car, but again he told me it was a phase, an historical phase. I'm shocked, I am as much shocked by the fact as by his blindness. But he is very sensitive to feelings and the next day we drove to an old inn deep in the countryside, a lovely place which is adorned by a huge gilded bunch of grapes over the ancient doors, and we dined by candlelight on Sauerbraten and a plum tart. I think he was keen to show me a more tranquil Germany.*

*Oh, Elizabeth, I can't tell you how torn I feel. I love him, I am obsessed by him, yet I have a horrible, uneasy feeling. Particularly in relation to what's going on in Germany. Somehow he wants to put it right himself, or die trying. It's madness – he is only a newly qualified lawyer doing rather routine work, but he has this burning sense of duty to Germany, not this Germany, of course, but to a higher Germany, a Platonic Germany. He talked to me seriously of the 'valuations' of feudal Germany. I completely lost my temper, and he said, 'How beautiful you are when you are cross,' and I told him, weeping,*

*that he is the most beautiful man I have ever known. Oh, Lizzie, he
is unfaithful, he's mesmerising and he's also a little mad, but I love
him. He's asked me to marry him. I'm sorry, darling, I am rambling.
Let's meet in Cornwall, in the physical world, when I get back from
here. A dunking in cold seawater will set me to rights. I'm crying
as I write. I must stop.*

   *R x*

Conrad looks for the signs of tears on the paper, the watermarks
of misery, but he can't see them.

He reads on, letter after letter. It's dark outside but he has no
idea of the time. The letters are unbearable in their accumulation
of hope and ideals and of love and disillusionment. He sees in a
speeded-up version a sort of historical conveyor belt that never
stops producing this craziness from a deep unplumbable human
well. But it's when he thinks of von Gottberg standing in front
of Roland Freisler, dignified, resigned, his eyes molten from the
sight of evil, that Conrad finds himself weeping softly, because
this is the end of all these false hopes and ideals. It's as if it is
a medieval morality play that mocks the naïve traveller. He knows
that he is moved on his own account, because he is just as much
an item in this parade of human folly, he and Francine with their
false hopes, the child they failed to produce, the success he never
achieved, the warm urgent longing to live a higher life – details
unspecified, of course – that they once shared, the expectation
that somehow they were due fulfilment – equally unspecified –
and then the loss of love, the tiredness in her skin, the bitterness
in her heart. He quoted Malraux to her when she was still
listening: *Art is an attempt to give man a consciousness of his own
hidden greatness.* But she has come to regard his ability to remember
quotes as a monkey trick.

While Rosamund was suffering her agonies of doubt, over in
Oxford Elya Mendel was discussing with other Oxford philosophers the meaning of theory: What do we mean when we make
a theory? Are all philosophical questions purely linguistic? Is

philosophy grammar? Do ethics have any rational content? No, they don't.

Rosamund retreated to England and she and Elizabeth and some other friends, including the poet Emily Brittain, went down to Cornwall to the family house overlooking Padstow Bay, near Trevose. Back in England Rosamund felt, as she put it prosaically, that a weight had been lifted from her shoulders. They walked on the cliffs and swam where the water was deepest and most turbulent; they knew secret channels between the rocks. And Conrad sees them in those one-piece suits, sleek young women, on whom disillusion is falling like rain. Von Gottberg writes to her: the dangers to her in Germany would be great. She must know that he can never leave Germany.

'He believes in his destiny, Lizzie. He thinks that is going to be increasingly difficult for his English friends to understand.'

The beach under foot is pebbly. This roughness of the shingle, the eroded honeycombed rocks, the cold impersonal sea, the light-house at Trevose, the headlands that crouch down against the wind, the narrow paths between the stone walls are Rosamund's *Heimat*, she decides. And Conrad sees the myth of Englishness, which believes itself practical and down-to-earth and unshowy, can even be seen in landscape: *This part of the country with its small woods and simple houses and pounding sea is more part of me than any philosophy in the world,* she writes to von Gottberg.

Mendel tells Elizabeth that von Gottberg has written to him saying that he is in love with Rosamund and that he is going to marry her and that he hopes that he, Elya, will forgive him: *I wrote to him telling him that I have long since got over Rosamund but I think it is only natural to say that it makes me uneasy. Of course you must not mention this to Axel or to Rosamund. I do hope, however, that she is not going to try to make a life in Germany. This is no time for anyone, let alone someone Jewish, to be going there. As usual Axel has his head in some very thick cloud.*

Conrad wonders if Mendel was gradually, as people do, building up an intellectual case against von Gottberg, which was really a cover for sexual jealousy. It is easy to imagine the highly voluble, relentlessly cheerful and intellectual Mendel feeling that von Gottberg was a charlatan, attractive to young women – for instance, Rosamund – with his phoney-baloney spiritual and mythological tendencies, and his deep-forested Teutonic destiny. And of course his five thousand hectares, *mit Schloss*. Perhaps unconsciously in his gossip and in his letters, he was forming von Gottberg to his prejudices. Many people do this. Francine, for example, has made Conrad's lack of money into a moral principle: she thinks he has selfishly avoided the pursuit of money because (a) she, Francine, has a proper job and (b) because he wants to avoid responsibility. It suits her thesis to emphasise those aspects of their relationship, forgetting conveniently that he supported her – emotionally anyway – all through medical school and the hell of finding hospital jobs in the Health Service. He coached her too:

Why do you want to work at St Thomas's Hospital, Dr Swinburne? I hope I don't sound too pretentious when I say that St Thomas's represents to me something about medicine that my late father, Professor Swinburne, was always very keen on, the idea that hospital medicine is both the latest technology and a passing-on of wisdom down the generations. I love the fact that Tommy's contains both expertise and a long and inspiring tradition. And most particularly I really want to get the best possible training. Obviously I have limited practical experience, but I do believe that St Thomas's offers this, as well as a wonderful team spirit.

She was reluctant to learn his little speech, but he explained to her, although he was himself already out of the loop, that interviewers are not interviewing a candidate to discover her worth, but rather to see if the candidate can bring allure to their own lives and careers. What they are looking for, Francine, he proclaimed, is a stooge, a true believer. He doesn't proclaim any longer.

\*    \*    \*

Sitting in that interview, ten years ago, was his wife's lover, then a newly appointed consultant of Obstetrics and Gynaecology. If Francine's ghost-written spiel hadn't been so appealing, she might not have got the job. But he can't expect any retrospective gratitude now.

Mendel's way of tackling the growing tensions in Europe was to look more closely at ideas and their effects. Idealists, he wrote, have produced some of the most terrible cruelties in history. Although he saw that the philosophers around him were undoubtedly right to believe that ethics had no rational basis in logic, he came to see that we must act ethically according to common sense. He also saw, as he once told Conrad, that Oxford philosophers were going down a blind alley if they believed that there was some incorrigible proposition waiting to be discovered. In the thirties, he told Conrad, academics were in the grip of this fallacy. Most philosophers in Oxford, he said, believed in a version of determinism, although of course none of them had ever met a determinist. His reading of the history of ideas offered an entirely different perspective, namely that ideas and beliefs are often in conflict, so the important question, it seemed to him, was not the truth of the ideas themselves, so much as the resolution of them, and that could only be realised by understanding human longings. Conrad remembers not only the conversation in Mendel's rooms, but also the rooms themselves, with the mullioned windows looking out towards Christopher Wren's clock, and the panelling that the years had infiltrated so richly, and the Roman head on the mantelpiece, acquired in Jerusalem, and the books and papers stacked and scattered so profligately. In his journalistic fashion, Conrad's father had loved books, but in Mendel's world books were not objects of self-congratulation – upmarket interior decoration – but living things, as alive as the souls that produced them. In books you could find the whole history of mankind (he didn't exclude novels and poetry) a history that includes folly and heroism and idealism and cruelty; he said more than once, quoting an American poet, that books are the bees that carry the quickening pollen from one mind to another. And Conrad in his own fashion has always felt happiest surrounded by these living dead.

Francine demanded a regular cull of books as though there was a limit to the number of books you needed at any one time. Anything over that limit, for example, books you were never likely to read again, was an indulgence. But Conrad kept them, all except for best-selling novels. Now he's sitting in his own All Souls, in a crowded room above Baiocchi's Bakery, The True Taste of Italy, in Camden Town, surrounded, his feet actually lapped by, the souls of the departed in book form, reading the letters of Elya Mendel and his friends. Each time he sees von Gottberg's beautiful handwriting he feels a jolt. Von Gottberg may have proposed marriage to her cousin, but he continues to write deeply romantic letters to Elizabeth, remembering their walks in London and Oxford, visits to her mother's house in Kent and dancing at the Café Royal; they both loved dancing. She was married at twenty-one, her husband was a friend of von Gottberg's, but he was now in Athens on a posting. It seem certain to Conrad they had been lovers once and that this continued after her marriage. He was one of those people who insisted on maintaining his friendships with lovers.

He finds a letter from von Gottberg, mailed in Switzerland just after *Kristallnacht*:

*My darling Elizabeth*

*I understand that you were hurt that I proposed marriage to Rosamund. But let us be practical. You are married already. Please don't think I have lost my reason in the general madness of my country, but if I can persuade Ros to come and live with me, I feel we will all three be close. On your way to Athens, please come and visit me in Berlin and I will show you Pleskow. It's so beautiful in the winter. I am going to be there for three weeks. It's becoming increasingly difficult for me to speak clearly. You know what has happened now,*

*as Elya understood it would, and I didn't. In reality I did understand, but I was not prepared to accept it. I feel very foolish, and even humiliated. I have written to Elya from here – it is easier from here – to say how sorry I am about that letter. I still believe, perhaps I am deluded, that I can help Europe to find its true nature. (As I write this, I hear Elya laughing that amiable but deadly laugh!) Don't mention this letter to Rosamund; I know how close you are, my darling, but please respect my wish that what we have should remain intact, and sacred.*
*Love A*

The visit to Pleskow was not a success. Whatever happened angered Elizabeth, who kept copies of her letters:

*Darling A*
    *As you had told me, Pleskow was utterly beautiful in the winter and your sister could not have been more friendly, although I found myself wondering if she was comparing me to anyone.*
    *But I can't accept your views at all, darling! You have the attitude that you are for God and Ros and I must be for God in you. Of course I shall not discuss this with R, but you seem to me to be living a double life or worse. What I said, I stand by. Obviously I understand in the broader sense that you are deeply involved, as we discussed that night in the little house by the lake. You know my feelings about that, but, darling, it's not possible for you to share this life with anyone. I assure you, I do believe our love and friendship will survive whatever happens next.*
    *Athens is noisy and mindless. Roddy is gloomy. I wish I were at home, in my own little house. The glory has passed from the earth.*
    *Love E*

Dawn comes. It takes Conrad some time to locate himself. It's as if he finds himself in an unfamiliar room in a foreign country, without knowing how he got there, although he has been awake all night. Beneath him the bakery is coming to life: the ovens hum and whirr and the smell of the yeast as the proven bread is taken for baking is comforting. It tells him, more clearly than the murky view from the smeared windows, where he is.

# 7

VON GOTTBERG STILL does not believe that war is inevitable. He is working in Hamburg as a prosecutor, the only job he can find as a non-member of the Party. Still he is resisting joining. He wants, nevertheless, to play a part in his country's life and has applied for a post at the Auswärtiges Amt, the Foreign Office. He believes that the Nazi Party will leave the stage of history soon enough; it is just a symptom of the changes to come. Why join? One day the president of the lawyer's association calls him and explains to him that he wants to talk to him in person.

Two days later he presents himself. The president knows his father. They walk the length of the garden of the president's office, and out along the inner ring of the Alster. Von Gottberg knows that this is not because the president wants some fresh air, as he tells his secretary, although there is plenty of that blowing in up the Elbe from the North Sea.

'My boy, I can't endorse you for the Foreign Office, despite your father's good name. Your request was sent to me by Berlin for a reference, but my hands are tied. You are not a member of this association and that would be seen as a rejection of National Socialism.'

'I don't reject National Socialism if that's what it is. In fact I am all in favour of both socialism and nationalism. But I can't join the Party. It's not possible for me. I have friends in other countries who would misunderstand. My aim in joining the Foreign Office is to work for our country. I don't want a war, but if I join the Party I will appear to be in the war party. I would have no credibility at all.'

'Just join the association. Not the Party. Then I can write you a glowing reference.'

'Mr President, you are a member of the Party, I assume?'

'I am.'

'Do you want a war?'

'Of course I don't want a war. Nobody in Hamburg wants a war. But the problem we all have in every professional association, as you know, is that we have been required to swear an oath. Germany is going in one direction and you either jump on the train or you are an outcast. Can I tell you in confidence that none of us is happy? We tell ourselves we can work from the inside, we can make things better. Now, let me speak quite frankly, if you don't join the Party or our association, you will end up in a concentration camp or in exile.'

'I will give you my answer tomorrow. And I thank you.'

That night von Gottberg is dining with a friend from Göttingen, Dietlof Goetz. Goetz is very strong, darkly good-looking, and he loves all sports. Von Gottberg finds him wonderfully uncomplicated and honest. As they leave the restaurant – they have been eating green-eel soup – they see a commotion on the Lombardsbrücke. A man is running, pursued by three Brownshirts. Dietlof steps forward without hesitation and punches one of the Brownshirts in the face, and they block the way of the other two, who turn away reluctantly and morosely with their companion, whose nose is bleeding freely. The man who was being pursued, a Jew obviously, comes back. He removes his hat. He is a man of about fifty. He says nothing beyond *thank you* to Axel, but grasps his hand in his two hands briefly, and then Dietlof's, before hurrying away. He is wheezing.

Dietlof is exhilarated as they stop at a bar for a beer.

'We can't beat up every Brownshirt in Germany,' says Axel.

'We must try. It is our sacred duty.'

'What have we become, Dietlof?'

'I am leaving. I am going to America. There is no future here.'

'Look. Let's walk a little, I want to talk to you.'

'One more beer. It's thirsty work beating up these animals.'

They leave the bar. Dietlof is unconcerned that the Brownshirts might be looking for them. But Axel is nervous until they break free of the close alleyways and walk along the lake where the rigging of moored yachts is slapping and chiming against masts and spars. Goetz is in his uncle's shipping business in Hamburg, but his family home is also in Mecklenburg.

'Dietlof, can I speak honestly to you? I know I can trust you. I have been talking to my friends in England and there is a chance we can stop the war. If everybody like you leaves, there will be no future – as you say – for our country. Another war will be a complete disaster, again. The Nazis apparently are unable to see that the whole world will eventually be against us, including America.'

Von Gottberg explains that there is resistance to Hitler in the Army Council and that General Beck, the supreme commander, is absolutely against any foreign adventures. There is a plan to deal with Hitler when the time is right. His friends in England are absolutely against a war too. It only requires all sides to hold their nerve.

'Dietlof, it is our destiny, our duty, to stay in Germany and fight for the country we love. My dear friend, when I saw you punch that bastard, I felt strangely exalted. It doesn't need many of us to stand up for Germany, for what you and I would call the true Germany. But first, and this is what my work is, we must persuade our friends in England and America to allow Germany some return of pride and dignity. It they don't do that, Hitler will flourish on the people's resentment. Believe me, Dietlof, we need you. You must stay.'

Dietlof Goetz was to say years later that Axel von Gottberg's passion, his eyes brimming, his voice quivering with emotion, made him ashamed of his plan to join his brother in New Jersey. Von Gottberg convinced him by the Alster that it was only by demonstrating to the world that there was another Germany, not seized by madness, that they could live honourably. The life of exile, he said, is a half-life.

Later that month von Gottberg writes to Elizabeth Partridge saying that he has met a girl from Mecklenburg, who is the sister of his old university friend Dietlof Goetz, and that he is planning to marry her. He has written to Rosamund too, explaining that he hoped they would always be friends, and wishing her well. *But, Elizabeth, you know that I will always love you. If you hadn't been married I believe ours would have been a match made in the heavens.*


Down below the bakery is making its first deliveries of the day. The bread is stacked on wooden trays to be loaded into the vans. Conrad sees the tortoise shapes, the brown carapaces, from above and he is reassured. Human life depends on small rituals and the daily bread is surely one of the most basic. No wonder the Church appropriated it. He sits among these papers, anxious that they should not miscegenate with the earlier papers that lie in disarray around the flat. I am losing my hold on order, he thinks. I am more engaged with Mendel and von Gottberg than I am here, in my own home. I must see my friends. Although they have become strangely silent. Perhaps Francine has been briefing against me. I must re-enter the physical world, as Rosamund put it.

What happened at Pleskow, he wonders? Letters are only the outcroppings of an underwater reef. Elizabeth Partridge will tell him what Axel von Gottberg said to her that evening in the little house by the lake. But he knows already that von Gottberg joined the lawyers' association and soon after that, the Party, because he was appointed a counsellor in the Foreign Office, Information Department. With the new job he moved back to Berlin, and into a small apartment. Every morning he walked to the Information Department in Kurfürstendamm. Sometimes he was summoned to the ministry at Wilhelmstrasse. And at the same time he began to attend meetings of the Kreisau Circle, a quasi-religious opposition group which met on Helmuth James von Moltke's estate, Kreisau.

How much of this double life did Mendel understand? Mendel, tucked up in All Souls, was fearful of what might happen to him if Hitler invaded, and was considering an escape to America. He saw clearly what Hitler was, and it frightened him. Oxford became unbearable to him: quoting Hugo von Hofmannsthal, he wrote: *I feel like someone locked in a garden surrounded by eyeless statues.*

# 8

A NURSE FROM a private hospital in Marylebone summons Conrad: Elizabeth Partridge, Lady Dungannon, wants to see him. He takes some time finding suitable clothes. He has neglected his wardrobe and he is conscious that his shaving has become irregular, so that he never quite completes the job. He shaves carefully although the blade is blunt – it is one of the razors in cheerful pink plastic – all women's things must be cheerful – that Francine has left behind. And he brushes his hair, trying to spread it around. Like Axel von Gottberg's, his hair is thinning alarmingly. John, his wife's lover, has thick, wiry school-prefect's hair, even though he is sixteen years older. Perhaps his wife prefers this kind of growth. What else has she been keeping from him?

He has the impression as he hurries to the underground that Elizabeth must be dying. The nurse, to be fair, gave no indication of imminent death. He is supposed to be showing a potential buyer – WITH READY CASH – around, but he has left a note on the door saying that the key is with Tony, the baker. He asked Tony to be as quiet as he could – the machinery they use to wash the bakery is noisy – while the prospective buyer is upstairs.

'You don't really want to sell, I'll turn 'em up full blast. I'll bang all the trays together. It'll sound like a fucking mad house.'

'That's the idea, Tony. Good man.'

Tony is always dusted with flour at this time of day, so that he has a ghostly appearance, not necessarily the ideal person to let in a cash buyer. Francine has implored him to tidy up, but it hasn't been possible at such short notice, although he has managed to organise the papers into drifts and has hidden the dirty dishes under the sink.

What he wants to ask Elizabeth is exactly what happened on her visit to Germany. What had Axel said that upset her? And also, he wanted to know when she saw him last. After years of reflection, old people reorder their lives. We all do it in our way. We construct our self-image as if we are hoping for some retrospective distinction, a vision of the person we believe we are supposed to be; without being able to see a template, we carry on relentlessly, like bees obeying an order they don't understand, until death makes it all irrelevant. Why is it important to practise wilful amnesia and invent myths? Francine's mother, the professor's widow, describes their life together in implausible terms, an improbable idyll of happiness and contentment and domestic bliss. In truth he was a philanderer and caused her much pain. These old women – Liselotte, Gräfin von Gottberg, and Elizabeth Partridge – are living with the memory of the man who meant most to them or gave their lives retrospective significance. And this is what Francine is accusing him of, of trying to give himself some phoney significance by attaching himself to Elya Mendel. Except, as he has told Francine – more than once – he was chosen by Mendel.

'So you are the chosen one?'

'I didn't say that. I simply said he chose me to edit his papers.'

'To do what with exactly? So far, all I can see is a neurotic muddle. You're like a dog running for a stick. You have no plan.'

'No career path. You're big on career paths, aren't you?'

He could have said to her, Look, Francine, these papers contain some deep significance, some big issues, the man of ideas versus the man of action, the contemplative life against the active life, false ideologies, the curse of the twentieth century, or you could see them as just one thing, one human thing, a plea from an old man to me to recount fairly what happened between him and von Gottberg. Who cares, she would have said.

For scientists what happened in the past is filed away. They don't see ideas in the same fashion. Instead they see them as building blocks, pointers to how things work. They, unlike us, live in a world of certainty, or at least in the conviction that certainty can be achieved. Although she told him once that sixty per cent of all theories posited in science magazines prove to be absolutely untrue in time.

Now, a little floury himself – he can feel the flour when he rubs his eyes – he is on the train with the people who aren't really rushing anywhere at this time of day. Some of them seem to have only a tenuous grip on life. Every time he emerges from the flat he finds himself marvelling at people: every one with his or her own mind, own worries, own ambitions. What's the point? Why did evolution find that it was more effective to have an individual mind? Perhaps we would have been better off like tadpoles, all obeying simple rules. Perhaps we are, as the Austrian poet Hugo von Hofmannsthal once wrote, on the same plane of reality as tadpoles or even plants and minerals: *In these moments an insignificant creature – a dog, a rat, a beetle, a crippled apple tree, a lane winding over a hill, a moss-covered stone – mean more to me than the most beautiful, abandoned mistress of the night.*

Although, Conrad thinks, a beautiful mistress of the night could be just what he needs. He often looks at women on the underground and wonders what they would be like in bed. Would they be eager or timid or loud or quiet? Would they be concerned with their own pleasure or with their partner's? This is an important divide, he has found, and not easily judged on appearance. Elizabeth Partridge suggested to him she has had a full sex life. It's as though your life, on some measures, is validated by the amount of fucking and heartbreaking you have been involved in and also by the number of breasts and clitorises and cocks and inner thighs and mouths you have travelled intimately. The body is a terra incognita which must be explored in order for you to achieve the desired self-esteem, to complete the dots, pointillist style, of your self-image. Sex has become a sort of religious career. These old ladies, he sees – his mind always tends to speed up with the humming, rushing, whining, rattling trains – set a great deal of store by their memories, because memories are a form of immortality.

Elizabeth Partridge has chosen her hospital on the same basis as her hotel, as a reminder of the old order. The nurses wear tasteful blue uniforms and little coronets, like napkins elaborately folded in seaside hotels. What these details signify is that the secret England is still there, unaffected by the coarsening of life outside. The receptionist is wearing a tailcoat, apparently without embarrassment.

In her room, overhung by flowers of exquisite breeding in tall cut-glass vases, Elizabeth appears very small and mortal: the jungle is advancing to reclaim her. Her face under the cheekbones is a pale lilac, something like the colour of a budgerigar's breast. He places his half a dozen tulips apologetically beside the bed.

'Ah Conrad. Lovely flowers, thank you. Sit down, my boy.'

'How are you?'

'As you can see, I am alive. Or at least I think I am.'

Her voice, however, is weaker, as though the body's decline draws on the essential substances impartially, even on something so precious as the means of speaking. Conrad's treacherous eyes fill as he remembers his father in mute agony, twisting and turning and his mouth opening and closing convulsively, as though he had something important to say before he went, but could not. He hung on for eight days in this appalling state.

'You look wonderful,' he says.

'My boy, the important thing to know about Axel is that he was a patriot. Germany was everything to him. When I visited Pleskow he asked me to marry him. Can you believe it? He was engaged to Fräulein Goetz, he had rejected Rosamund, and now he was asking me to marry him. I reminded him that I was married. I reminded him that he had broken Ros's heart: I told him that she was devastated by his letter, but he said that he and Ros had an enduring relationship. You must never abandon someone you once loved, he said. I was shocked, because he seemed to me to be so troubled. I didn't think his behaviour was rational. I told him it was impossible for us to marry. He would have liked me to say that I loved him.'

'Did you love him?'

'I did. But I couldn't throw up everything for him. I couldn't wound my cousin, and I certainly couldn't live in Germany.'

'Were you lovers?'

'You're a very direct young man.'

'I'm sorry, but I feel that I have to know what happened.'

'We were lovers. In Pleskow, even there, after what had happened. So I was a louse too. People often are in these cases, don't you find?'

She reaches slowly for some water. Her arms are fragile, and speckled like the hen's eggs in children's books. He helps her. She drinks, a small, birdlike sip.

'Where was I?'

'You were saying that you loved Axel von Gottberg.'

'He said something to me which, in fairness to Elya, I think I should tell you. He said that as soon as he wrote the infamous letter to the *Manchester Guardian*, he knew that he had lost Elya for good. Since then, he said he had been working to prove that he was worthy of Elya. I found it immensely touching. That night in the little house by the lake he told me at least some of what he was engaged in. It was highly dangerous. The concentration camps were filling up already. He also said to me that all he could offer me as a wife was German-ness. Strange word. But what he meant was that this was a German problem, to be solved by Germans. The Jews were not the main point, at that time. Hitler must be removed by Germans. He was sure of that. He wanted me to tell Elya, and to tell him also that he was engaged in secret opposition. We didn't know the extent of it until later, but of course Elya just thought it was his usual self-dramatisation

93

when I told him. I think it was difficult from Oxford to understand – in fact it was hard to understand from wherever you were – what the atmosphere was like in Germany. It was terrifying. Kafkaesque. But Axel chose the heroic life, whatever his friends believed.'

She lies still for a moment, her lips possibly forming some more words, but in the end no words emerge for a while.

'You said you saw him again?'

'Just before the war started, he came to England. He wanted to explain to people how to deal with Hitler: the German mentality, Versailles and all that. We met in Kent. He had seen Elya in Oxford and the Rhodes people had fixed him up with various meetings and private talks. But also his friends, the Astors and so on, had influence. He met Halifax and Chamberlain at their house in St James's Square.'

'Why did his Oxford friends distrust him?'

'They thought, to put it bluntly, that he was working for the Nazis. He seemed to be able to go anywhere and do whatever he liked. They found this suspicious. They also thought that he said different things to different people.'

'Did he?'

'I think he did. He was naïve in some ways. It's clear that when it comes to us gels, he said all sorts of things. The problem, as I said, is that he wasn't able to speak freely by this stage. He had to be careful, because he was in the resistance and working for the Foreign Office at the same time. When he saw me at my little house in Kent he was distraught because he felt nobody at Oxford was taking him seriously and that none of them trusted him. It was humiliating for him. Deeply, deeply humiliating. Oxford meant so much to him. And yet they thought he was a Nazi or, at best, deluded.'

She appears to fall asleep. For a moment he thinks she may have died, but the rose patterns on her satin dressing gown are rising and falling gently.

'He took me to Sachsenhausen, you know. We stopped outside

in his little car. The guards came out to see what we were doing, we sat for so long.'

The room is richly scented. The heat – hospitals are always overheated – is causing these flowers to signal to summer insects. Life, even at the plant level, is a slave to attraction. The women in this story – the gels – were drawn to Axel von Gottberg, but others were deeply affected by him too. Even Roland Freisler, the prosecutor, seems drawn to him as he stands there, his hands clasped – Conrad suddenly remembers that the hands were not shackled in court – Freisler shouting at him, but at the same time impressed by his dignity, perhaps aware for a moment that his grotesque screaming and acting are shameful, coarse, so that he speaks more quietly, even conspiratorially. Axel, doomed, has a certain resignation, perhaps even a serenity, that Freisler acknowledges. And the attraction is in the fact that von Gottberg looks like a German hero. Freisler does not. Hitler does not. And this may be one of the reasons that Hitler and his friends, having killed millions without a qualm, are unhinged by these aristocrats who, if there were anything in race-science, *Rassenkunde*, would be on his side. Hitler is reported as saying that the aristocrats had betrayed him and he should have acted against them from the beginning. Others who knew him said Hitler was never the same again.

'You look like him.'

She is smiling, slightly crumpled after her absence.

'Like Axel?'

'Yes. You are thirty-five?'

'Yes.'

'Axel was thirty-five when they hanged him.'

'I know.'

'He was an astonishing person. Women saw it immediately. He was fervent. Are you fervent?'

'I don't think so. Sadly.'

'Are you successful with women? I imagine you are.'

'I am not successful with my wife.'

'Yes, now I remember. You said you were separated.'

'Yes.'

'Is it because of this, the papers Elya left you, and so on?'

'Not really. We are very different. She's a doctor.'

'And you?'

'That's the problem. I can't honestly say.'

'I may not be the person to give advice, but keep at this task. In their own way, both Elya and Axel were great men. Elya was a wonderful judge of people. The fact that he asked you to do this is an enormous compliment.'

'Thank you.'

'I am so glad we have met. Elya asked me before he died to speak to you. He wanted you to have my side of the story. He spoke about you.'

'What did he say?'

'I told you that he thought you had special qualities.'

'Do you remember what they were?'

'I can't. Not exactly. I don't think he said.'

'Did he say what he wanted me to do?'

'Nothing specific. He thought you would know.'

He doesn't know. They are interrupted by a nurse in blue, who comes to take Elizabeth's temperature and blood pressure.

'Lady Dungannon, you have some other visitors in the waiting room. Shall I tell them to wait a little longer?'

'I had better go,' says Conrad. 'Goodbye, Elizabeth.'

He kisses her lightly, his lips just brushing her budgie cheek – he feels anything more vigorous might injure her – and tears start in his eyes. I am becoming unhinged, he thinks.

'Goodbye, my boy. Come again tomorrow. There's more for us to discuss.'

As he goes out he sees Elizabeth's visitors, a man in a loden overcoat and two women in country clothes, one in a green padded coat and the other in a tweed skirt, holding her Barbour over her arm. They have a weathered look as though they spend a lot of time outdoors.

'I'm sorry if I kept you,' he says.

'Not at all. I hope we didn't rush you.'

'No of course not. She's just having her blood pressure done.'

'I'm Nancy Cutforth, this is my sister Bunty Miller, and this is Esmond O'Driscoll.'

'I'm Conrad Senior.'

They shake hands and he feels their fragility relayed down their arms like telegraph messages.

'Too damned hot in here,' says the man.

'You could take your coat orf, Esmond.'

'Jolly good idea.'

'We're all gaga, as you can see.'

They laugh, and he remembers what Elizabeth had said about laughter.

'I'm on my way.'


He walks up from Marylebone and into Regent's Park. She is going to die tonight. He feels sure of it, although he doesn't believe in any kind of presentiments. He wonders who the three elderly visitors are. They have a kind of patina, like old paintings, which people of his generation will never have. Their world may have contracted, but their values are immune from further change, although they are beleaguered. The shrinking of their circle as the years pass must be frightening. His father had no friends by the time the dementia set in; everyone had abandoned him. His father ended by the sea, raging, a sort of provincial Lear.

He crosses the bridge into that part of the park he likes best where there are a few buildings, a college, a park-keeper's neat house, and then he goes out again through the circular rose garden. Across the football prairie he see the zoo's mountains. Once he heard a lion roaring in broad daylight, hoarse, reverberating, a challenge thrown down into nothingness. No response came back of course. It's late afternoon now. A few people are playing football. There's an all-Asian game over there: he can see small figures, perhaps Filipino or Malay. There are dogs, going about their optimistic lives, accompanied by their owners, who look less optimistic, some of them even depressed. One of Rosamund Bower's books has a scene set here in wartime, by the boating lake.

When he gets home he finds messages from Francine. She is angry: the agent said that the flat was a mess. The client – the cash buyer – spent exactly one minute looking at the place. The chaos appalled her. And the noise from below was terrible. She's sending in industrial cleaners in the morning, and whatever they find lying about will be thrown out.

He feels at a great distance from Francine. Her complaints don't touch him at all. After nine years, he's free. Is he attractive to women, as Elizabeth Partridge put it? He hopes he is. Francine is on duty. He leaves a message apologising, explaining the urgency, and starts to pack his papers as neatly as he can. His loyalties are now directed entirely towards Mendel and von Gottberg. He has no more duties here. He is completely free to explore his human potential, to tell this story.

In the night Elizabeth Partridge dies and the circle closes.

What Elya Mendel wanted, he sees, was that he should collect all these conversations and letters and memories, and turn them into something coherent, a narrative.

# 9

OXFORD THE ENCHANTED: Axel, Count von Gottberg walks down the cobbles of Magpie Lane. He walks around the familiar and beloved place as though he is trying to feel its topography under his shoes. He passes through the gate on to Christ Church Meadow. Small boys in bright scarlet from Magdalen College School are playing rugby, tiny figures on the vast green sea. As he gets closer he sees how white their legs are, and how fragile, barely able to carry them into a run. They have curious blue patterns on them, as though their pale white skin is showing the veins beneath. A whistle blows and they stop and gather around the master in charge, who is wearing a cricket sweater and baggy trousers. Across the meadow, where dun cows are grazing or lying down, he can see the river and on it, between the burgeoning trees, boats passing, some in a leisurely Ratty-and-Mole way, others with sculls flashing in the weak sunlight. The English have a special relationship with water. He walks right down to the river and then along past the pouter-pigeon college barges. Looking back to the colleges he sees a Renaissance city – spirit and history in local stone. This stone is a pale russet, the colour of the old apple varieties his grandfather had collected at Pleskow, Gravenstein and Cox's Pippin and Egremont. He feels a kind of ache, which in reality is for his youth, and the girls he has known and the carefree years, but also a heaviness about what is to come. Even now he could choose to stay here and pick up the easy friendships. He could leave his homeland for the life of an émigré, to be treated with politeness and condescension.

He loves the landscape because he was happy here. There are places he has been, Hamburg is one of them, which he knows to be beautiful, but which have no pull on his heart. Other places quicken the spirit because of what they evoke: they for ever speak of blitheness, a state of happiness he can't hope to feel again. Elizabeth said Pleskow is the only place in Germany where the madness has not yet struck. And Pleskow is the landscape to which his heart is given, and Pleskow is in Germany. His family has lived there for six hundred years, which is longer than most of these colleges have been standing. His English friends don't understand this deep allegiance. It's spiritual and they reject the notion of spirit, but spirit is after all only the word that describes what is inalienably human.

He walks in a large arc towards the Botanical Gardens and Magdalen. The punts are drawn up beside the bank, forming a wooden platform extending right into the current, like a Roman military bridge. He strides along Addison's Walk. The fritillaries are not yet out and the water behind is like ale. He and Elya walked here. Their differences were all in the pleasurable inconsequential world of philosophy then. And now? He remembers Elya in Jerusalem, so happy after his first sexual experience with Rosamund. Transfigured. Elya on the one hand ancient in his understanding, on the other a plump eager boy in love. A Jewish boy. Unmistakably. Now we Germans have created a cordon sanitaire around the word *Jew*. As if Jew is something like bacillus. Just as he, Axel, cannot use the word Jew any longer without shame, Elya cannot speak of Germany or Germans without contempt. But there is a secret Germany. One lunatic cannot destroy that in a few years. This Germany that Hölderlin and George describe as *Geheimes Deutschland* is a Germany of the mind.

*The fable of blood and desire, a fable of fire and radiance:*
*The pageantry of our emperors, the roaring of our warriors.*

It is the longing for something nobler, which nobody here can understand. He swings back down through the Parks where the narcissi and daffodils are taking over from the crocuses. When he first came to Oxford eight years ago, he remembers his astonishment that spring at the thousands of bright, undaunted flowers breaking out of the damp, cold soil. Gardening is perhaps the art in which the English have most excelled. It suits their temperament, something to be quietly proud of, and something very private. Every college has a garden. Even now as he passes Rhodes House he sees the border, piled with compost, the rhubarb-coloured stalks of peonies already shining between the pale-yellow and white narcissi. On the other side of the road through the gates that will never open until there is a Stuart on the throne again – one of those much-loved Oxford whimsies, like the fact that the time at Christ Church is always set five minutes later than Greenwich Mean Time – he sees one of the most beautiful borders in Oxford, which extends a hundred yards or so to a bust of Cardinal Newman. He walks past Blackwell's to Balliol. The porter, Jimmy Tibbs, greets him as if he has never been away: 'Good morning Mr von Gottberg. Keeping well, sir?' He leaves a note for the Master, confirming that he has arrived safely and has arranged for his bags to be picked up at the station.

He wonders if Tibbs sees him as an enemy yet. He walks back – it is nearly time – past the Easter Island Roman heads, through the courtyard of the Bodleian Library out to Radcliffe Square beyond. The Square, grouped around the Radcliffe Camera, the most extravagant building in Oxford, and contained by St Mary's Church and Brasenose College to the west and south and the Library and All Souls on the other two sides, seems to him to be the heart and the soul of Oxford. As cyclists come by in the thickening light, he hears snatches of laughter and conversation. He looks for girls who might be the girls he knew, as if by wishing it he could cause them to appear as they were. Yes, we are for ever tied to the place where we were young and happy.

He enters the lodge and asks for Mr Mendel. 'You're expected. Mr Mendel's rooms are in the great quad, staircase four, sir.'

He emerges facing Wren's sundial on the Codrington Library. He finds the staircase. It is one floor up; his feet ring on the stone. He knocks. 'Come in.' There is Elya, standing by the fireplace in which a coal fire is burning. He has a book in one hand.

'Axel. Welcome to my little house in the woods.'

Elya is wearing a grey three-piece suit, which is bulging in the middle slightly. His face, however, has lost something of its boyish roundness. Axel seizes him by the shoulders and kisses him twice. Three years have passed since they were together in the same room.

'Lovely rooms, Elya. God, I envy you.'

The main room is panelled, a sitting room full of books and broken-backed armchairs and a table covered in periodicals and papers and on the mantelpiece, among other mementos, is the Roman head Elya bought in Jerusalem. Through a door he sees a bedroom with a candlewick bedcover and lopsided wooden light stands.

'Axel, it's marvellous to see you. A miracle. Oxford has been a mausoleum without you. I've got a bottle up from the cellar. Would you like a glass? It's the college's special reserve. Claret.'

Even as he says *claret*, he gives it a little ironic emphasis, to suggest that Jews don't really drink claret.

They sink into the swayed armchairs, their feet upturned towards the fire. They lie back. Elya is less elegant, being shorter and plumper, but right at home, ready to talk. He's always ready to talk. He tells Axel what has happened in Oxford: who has been elected to the post of Professor of History, what has happened in the parliamentary elections, who put up as a Mosleyite and the strange mood in Oxford, knowing that war is coming.

'Is it coming, Axel?'

'I hope not. I'm trying to stop it.'

'All by yourself?'

He asks the question without malice, but with a certain amusement.

'No, obviously not all by myself. Can I clear up one thing with you first? It's been on my mind. Are you still angry with me about Ros?'

'Axel, I am deeply grateful that I knew Ros, but that was years ago now. And as I wrote to you after you took my advice, I am very pleased that you are not going to marry her. I didn't think it would have been fair. Can we leave it at that, my dear friend?'

'Thank you, Elya. Elizabeth accused me of being a womaniser, but I hate to see it in that way. Ros will always be dear to me and to you, I am sure. And your letter was fair and true: I should never have asked her to marry me. As you said, it was selfish and dangerous. How's my English, by the way? It's been worrying me that I haven't been speaking it much. As you can imagine.'

'Your accent has always been better than that of almost anybody we know. Mine is ridiculous, a sort of émigré Wurlitzer. I sometimes think, Axel, that speaking such *echt* English has caused people to misunderstand you. They can't believe that you are really, deep down, where it matters, German. But you are.'

'For better or for worse. When we were in Jerusalem you told me that deep down – *au fond* – you were Jewish. Although an atheist. I think it's the same thing. When you say I am obsessed with spirit and such other woolly notions, what is one's identity? What's the difference? You have in your cultural memory, from your family, from your religion, an instinctive Jewishness. I have an instinctive German-ness.'

They are off.

'Axel, one thing has changed. The German instinct is now to obliterate those they see as lesser people. Do you know what one of my colleagues said to one of your chaps who was advocating more colonies for Germany at a meeting the other night? "We Jews and the other coloured people beg to differ." *Wir Juden und die anderen Farbigen denken anders*. You must be careful Axel, how you make your case. The mood has changed. People here are saying the Nazis are bastards and we want to crush them to dust, and that is how they think now. Don't rely on the old college scarf. Your people have changed everything. They are trying to take over the world in the name of Geman-ness as you call it. German-ness has some prior claim to life.'

'There's another Germany, Elya.'

'This isn't the *Geheimes Deutschland*, I hope?'

'It is in part. Yes, but, Elya, there are people of influence even in the Army Council who plan to get rid of Hitler.'

He is conscious of whispering now. Mendel pours the claret. The bottle is dusty.

'Elya, I want to tell you something: I will not be able to talk to you freely again. Even in the meetings I am having in London, it will be difficult. I am not sure if people here realise the sheer madness of life in Germany. But, Elya, I can only go on if you tell me that whatever happens you trust me, however it looks. If you can, I particularly want you to put in a word for me with Michael Hamburger. I'm going to New York in two weeks' time to address a conference, and I want to go down to Washington to tell Michael the details of the opposition in Germany, and to ask him to give us some help. Can you do that?'

'I will write to Michael and ask him to see you, of course.'

'Thank you.'

'But you must understand, Axel, that things have changed. It's no longer about some high-minded chaps getting together to sort things out. You in Berlin, you the opposition, chatting about how awful Hitler is while thousands of Jews must emigrate and others are imprisoned and Germany grabs the lost lands, how does that look? It's not easy for us to understand, dear friend. What you see is the task of saving Germany. What I see is somewhat different. I see the end of mankind. There is no halfway with this creature.'

'Elya, the only way to stop him is to allow the German people their dignity. He's offering them that, but his way will lead to destruction, utter destruction.'

'What are we supposed to offer? A few more Jews, a few Slavs, a few small countries? There may be some people in Whitehall who still want to deal, but these are the people who haven't read *Mein Kampf*. You don't seem to understand: the Sudetenland was the end. You will risk your reputation by talking to these people.'

'Germans are not a flock of sheep. Everything has a cause. Germany felt trapped, humiliated until this lunatic offered them a way out. But there is another Germany, Elya, which only needs encouragement. You are going to sneer, but there is a decent, a noble Germany.'

Outside clocks strike all over Oxford. Axel jumps up and runs to the window.

'I wanted to marry Rosamund, but you were right: it was not possible to bring her to Germany. I am getting married in September and I would love you to come to the wedding. It will be in the parish church at Pleskow. Her name is Liselotte Goetz.'

'I don't think I will be able to come. I'm congenitally timid. But please, let me offer you my warmest congratulations.'

Axel stares out of the window where the gas lights are soft, blurred by the damp mist that has come in.

'I will never see Oxford again.'

'Stay the night. You can sleep on the sofa.'

'I've left my stuff at Balliol, but I'll bring my pyjamas. We can continue to talk, I hope.'

'Of course. You look tired, tired to the marrow, Axel. Are you in danger?'

'We all are.'

He wonders if Elya really understands what is at stake. Dear Elya, who, for all his intelligence, loves gossip and friendship and comfort. Now, above all, he wants Elya to trust him.

'When I come back from my Balliol dinner will you tell me, absolutely frankly, where we stand?'

'What do you mean, Axel?'

'I mean can our friendship survive? Do I have reserves of trust to draw on, whatever happens?'

'When you come back from dinner we shall talk. Axel, I'm concerned. Why do you say you won't see Oxford again?'

'I have that feeling. In reality, it's more than a feeling, it's a certainty. As I walked here, round the Meadow and so further, I knew it. I don't think the world as we know it will survive what's coming unless we can stop it. Never mind Hitler for the moment, the East is gathering itself. A new barbarism is coming. If we can't persuade the German people that they can get what they need without Hitler, he will lead them into the jaws of the Russians. We have to keep peace in the West. But I must go. Nobody keeps the Master of Balliol waiting.'

'Not even God.'

Elya swings his plump leg over the side of his armchair, so that he is facing Axel.

'My dear friend, I beg you to bring your eyes down from the heavens to the ground. The most important job at the moment is to stop this madman with his racial policies and his desire to conquer the word. Forget about the Russians. I know the Russians. Whatever they are, they are not the main threat to the world. We can't offer Hitler concessions so that the Russians don't come and take your country. Hitler must be stopped, *tout court*. Next thing Hitler will be killing thousands of Jews, not just the ones he thinks are particularly dangerous, but just because they are Jews. *Kristallnacht* was just the supporting programme. Things are what they are, Axel, here and now. Don't try to pretend they are something else. You can't allow Hitler to murder Jews or to take Czechoslovakia so that the Russians don't come. And by the way, you are going to be late.'

Of course Elya doesn't understand. Western Europe is a bulwark against savagery, a repository of civilised values. Germany and England must never be set against each other and weakened.

'To be continued, dear Elya,' he shouts as he leaves the room and jumps two at a time down the stone stairs, across the quad and out of the porter's lodge. The duty porter is startled: perhaps he has never seen anyone running in All Souls before.

'Late, I'm late,' Axel shouts.

Alone in his rooms Mendel plays a gramophone record. A yellow Deutsche Gramophon record: Furtwängler conducts Beethoven's Ninth Symphony. Certainly if music is the touchstone Germany is the most civilised country on earth. In what sense, philosophers ask, can a piece of music be said to have meaning? Music evokes great emotion, but does it contain meaning? And how does it evoke emotion? This recording always causes him to feel deeply personal thoughts, linked to ideas about places and memories of Rosamund. Nietzsche believed that music revealed the pain and suffering at the root of human existence. And what Axel would say is that mystic experience, for example, the concept of a sacred Germany, which is a state of mind, are just as real in their effect as this Furtwängler recording on me. I am listening to this record and my emotions are stirred, and Furtwängler is, apparently, a Nazi. And Axel's man, Hegel, says that art contributes to the synthesis we require between the personal and the external worlds. But the Nazis see art as particularly subversive. Art has no morality, yet art can cause people to think about the abstract and the mystic.

The third movement is so beautiful; with the evening charged already, Elya feels himself and the world at a juncture. Beethoven was almost deaf but gloriously defiant when he wrote this; his pain and suffering are very evident. It's not simple: Axel is unable to distinguish this secret Germany from the actual Germany that is spinning into the abyss. And I, he thinks, cannot separate Axel the saviour of Germany from the Axel who has had sex – how many times? – and shared intimacy of thought and body with Rosamund, my first love. Rosamund is Jewish yet she is hopelessly in love with him still. Elizabeth, thank God, hasn't told her that Axel proposed to her at Pleskow. There is something deeply dishonest about Axel, for all his charm and his warmth and easy friendships. He claims to love women, but women to him are part of his domain, which is granted him of right. Perhaps it is just the basic aristocratic instinct, unknown to Jews from Riga.

He goes down to the Common Room to eat something. The food is usually very bad. He takes a collection of Turgenev's short stories. Reading at table is supposed to indicate that you don't want to talk, but everyone knows he is unable to stay silent. John Plamenatz, a Montenegrin, who was elected at the same time as him, comes over.

'I just have to sit with you, Elya, in case some Englishman wants to talk to me. Englishmen make me feel very alone.'

'I am an Englishman.'

'A sort of Englishman.'

'You think I am trying, like all Jews, to make a good impression? An amateur gentile?'

'No, you've done that long ago. You've become a necessary figure . . .'

'A licensed fool.'

'No, you are a public figure, but you haven't lost your insecurity. I hear Axel von Gottberg is in town?'

'Yes, he's on an important mission.'

'Do you believe him?'

'I believe he believes he is on an important mission. This is a wonderful time for the world-historical figures to emerge.'

'Is he a Nazi?'

'I don't think he thinks he is a Nazi.'

Axel returns at eleven. He is exhilarated. The Master of Balliol and the Warden of Rhodes House have been very helpful. The Prime Minister and the Foreign Secretary have both agreed to see him. He finds Elya in his rooms reading and listening to Beethoven. Elya lifts the spindle off the record and close the box.

'Saved the world?'

'I'm trying.'

'Did you have a good dinner?'

'Master's lodgings. Very good. The best wine, of course. And you?'

'Brown Windsor soup, a cool lamb cutlet and spotted dick. It's the price you pay for the honour of a fellowship, you eat absolute muck. Sometimes I take the train up to London just to eat my mother's pirogi.'

'Elya, after my meetings in London I am going to Washington.'

'So you said. Are you doing it for the Auswärtiges Amt or for your friends?'

'Please trust me. There are certain compromises I have been obliged to make. For the greater good.'

Elya looks at him through the round glasses. Axel knows that he is not so much thinking of what to say, as deciding what not to say.

'Is Wilhelm Furtwängler a Nazi by conviction or out of expediency?'

'That is a strange question. I think he is confused.'

'Are you confused?'

'No. I have had to make compromises, as I said, but I am not confused.'

'What were you going to ask me?'

'When you write to Michael, whatever your doubts, please remember what I asked, that you trust me. That's all I want. Nothing is as it seems to be.'

'Of course not. Lionel's coming over to see you. Do you mind?'

'No, not at all. I'm delighted. But don't tell him about Hamburger, please, or Balliol.'

'No. But cloak and dagger is not really our crowd, as Lionel calls it.'

'Our crowd. It's very strange how one short period in one place like this can have so much influence, don't you think? Our crowd. In three years here I felt we were at the centre of the world. More so than I do in Berlin. Berlin, the town, seems to be floating somewhere on the fringes of the world in a sea of unreality. Do you know the Nazis took over the department store where we have all shopped for more than a hundred years? They just told the Israel family to go. It brought home to my mother exactly how ruthless they are. You will say it's taken her a long time, but it's the crudeness of their thinking, their absolutely unnecessary cruelty, that has affected her so badly.'

Axel is still buoyed up after his dinner; they talk excitedly in front of the fire, which Elya prods vigorously from time to time, as though it is a reluctant farm animal. Elya ranges from the recent elections, to Munich, to the Jewish refugees flooding to Hampstead. His voice is as seductive as ever, as liquid as the calling of doves in Jerusalem, and then dissolves unexpectedly into giggles. He recites one of Lionel's scabrous poems, which concerns Penelope Betjeman's love of horses. He quotes Turgenev saying that, though he is fascinated by radicals, he is quite unable to be one himself.

'That's me, I'm afraid,' he says. 'I have no capacity for action. All I can do is talk.'

Axel knows that behind his back people say that Elya lacks courage and is too eager to please, but Axel sees that Elya is a product of his history: he has been uprooted and is only shallowly planted in this soil.

They hear Lionel's booming voice some time before he appears.

'I want to see my Junker friend,' he shouts. 'I want to see the duelling scars on his bottom. Let me in.'

Lionel comes crashing in. He is large and roughly carved. Axel, who is himself quite tight, can smell alcohol on him as they embrace.

'How is life in the Third Reich?' he asks, as Elya pours him a drink.

'It's difficult.'

'I hear you have a plan. Are we allowed to know what it is?'

Axel knows that any talk of the real Germany will get him nowhere.

'No plan. Just trying to help. Elya recited to me one of your latest poems.'

'Filthy, I trust.'

'Absolutely.'

Lionel slumps in a chair. These chairs have been so battered over the years that they can be sat in from any direction. Lionel places his large head on the worn carpet.

'Axel says, I believe, that the thing about Hitler is that he is playing on something real and that is the sense that most Germans have that they have been treated badly. The ordinary person remembers unemployment and chaos only too well. We – you and I – have to start from that position.'

'Elya, can you start from that position?'

'No, I've told Axel that it's not possible. I start from 1933.'

'But let's accept, Axel, as a theory, that the German people are keen to have their amour-propre restored. Then what must we do?'

Lionel is gazing at the roof as he speaks and now he raises his head to the horizontal in order to sip his drink.

'Western Europe must acknowledge Germany's right to regain the lost lands. Then they will see that Hitler is not the only way.'

Lionel stands up surprisingly nimbly and his drink falls to the floor.

'Goodbye, Axel. You were once my friend. Did you miss *Kristallnacht*? Were you out duelling? Yes, you were my friend. I even imagined I could spend my life with you. Now it is my greatest wish that I never see you again. You may not be aware of it, but you are a Nazi.'

He lurches towards the door and can be heard stumbling down the stairs. Elya and Axel are silent.

'He's drunk,' says Elya finally.

'But he meant it.'

'I'm afraid he did.'

They talk until about 3 a.m., when Axel, turning from the window, finds Elya asleep. At six, when Mendel wakes on the sofa, he sees that Axel has gone. At eight he returns, haggard, his skin pale, his eye sockets deep and dark.

'Where have you been?'

'I've been walking around Oxford.'

'Are you all right? Lionel was drunk. He's often drunk and outrageous these days.'

'I've tried to explain. But I see I have no reserves of trust left after all.'

'You do.'

'Goodbye, Elya. I am sure I will never see you again.'

Later that morning Mendel writes to Michael Hamburger in Washington:

*Dear Michael*

*Axel von Gottberg came to see me in Oxford. He is having meetings in London. He has asked me to put in a word for him. When he travels to America to address the Huntingford Institute he is hoping that you will be able to effect some high-level meetings for him. You can imagine particularly to whom I refer.*

*His friends at Oxford, and I am one, believe that he is at heart – I mean ideologically – a Nazi, although he is far too intelligent and complex a person to accept that as a simple fact. For a start it would be beneath him socially. He has been obliged to join the Party, as of course he could not be in the Foreign Office without membership. But he seems to be licensed to travel and talk to whomsoever he likes. At best he is a German patriot of the old school, a fact that makes him antipathetic to Hitler, if not to all of the ideas behind Hitler. You will no doubt receive him with all the cordiality our friendship indicates, but I feel I must warn you that both Lionel and I – and others – believe that, for all his undeniable charm, he should be treated with caution. He has a great taste for high-level intrigue.*

*Life in Oxford at the moment is nervous as if – as Somerset Maugham might say – a tropical storm can be felt in the air.*

*Yours affectionately*

*Elya*

Nine days later, Hitler invades Czechoslovakia and Elya Mendel's nagging guilt in writing to Michael Hamburger, the President's counsel and Supreme Court judge, warning against his friend Axel von Gottberg, is soon forgotten.

# 10

ELIZABETH PARTRIDGE'S FUNERAL is to take place at Booby Bay, Cornwall, in a little church on the edge of the water near the house that she and her cousin, Rosamund, loved. She will lie next to Rosamund and their grandparents. The train down is whipped by rain as it crosses into Cornwall. Conrad can't imagine living down here. The landscape is grudging and windswept. He takes a taxi from Bodmin Parkway and is driven by some rural bore who thinks London – *Lunnin* – is Gomorrah.

'I couldn't live in Lunnin with all them Pakistanis and such, what they call Muslims and mullahs. I don't know how you can do it. If they don't like it, they can always go back where they came from.'

'I like them,' says Conrad.

This is not strictly true. He only knows three, one who sells him his newspaper and two who run the local tandoori takeaway, a hatch in the wall, which he has used a lot recently.

This shuts the driver up for a while.

'Do you come down here often?'

'First time.'

'Boo-iful place, Cornwall.'

'Compared to what?'

'Well, you can just see.'

He can see very little from the back seat as they head down a deep tree-shrouded valley where the new leaves are being thrashed by the wind. He is wearing a dark suit borrowed from

Tony at the bakery, who goes to a lot of funerals. Tony says they are dropping like flies. Conrad is not sure who he means. Tony is sorry Conrad will be moving out. He sees Conrad as something of an exhibit, the man holed up with a thousand books and some fancy ideas, who doesn't know his arse from his elbow, despite all the books. The books are now mostly in storage, and the flat, newly sanitised, is comparatively austere.

Francine has written him a curious letter. Her style is usually more direct, a phone call or a terse email. Now she is demanding a face-to-face meeting. He wonders what she wants.

The other night he went out with his journalist friend Osric, who has just returned from Baghdad. Something has happened to him after three months there. Instead of coming back with his sympathies and human understanding deepened, he appears in the face of suffering to have decided that Western life has become over-analytical. Life, apparently, is a struggle for survival and we had better realise in the West that it always has been. We are in danger of disappearing up our own fundaments, he says. We think the soldiers, the grunts, the jarheads, the squaddies are morons, but actually they have seen life at the sharp end. He has left his girlfriend who also works for the *Herald*. 'You see what I mean? I come back from hell where nobody reads the fucking *Herald*, and I have been reporting on people so crazy, so fucked up, so deluded by religious manias of all sorts, that they want to kill all of us. I was at a protest with our boys one day and some kid there threw a bottle at the Land Rover. "Shoot the little cunt," I shouted. "Shoot him." You know what they said? They said, "Calm down, mate, you sound like the bloke we had in from the *Sun*." And they laughed. When I tell Sarah what happened, she is shocked and suggests I get counselling. She wants me to go to some therapist in Hammersmith. I have seen a man's legs blown fifty yards in different directions and I have seen a woman's head, still with the jihab on, lying in an ornamental fountain in the fucking lobby, and now I'm supposed to go and give face-time to some quack in a denim jacket, circa

1974, and listen to him talk about post-traumatic stress. This would be from a tosser whose knowledge of the world extends all the way to Barnes where on a bad day a duck can run out of the pond and give you a good nibble.'

Conrad laughed.

'It's not funny. I'm serious.'

'You're not really, Osric. You just need a little counselling.'

They were getting drunk in a bar in Shoreditch.

Francine seems to be hinting in her letter that things are not going all that well with John. It's difficult, she writes, both working on his team and seeing him after hours. Conrad has heard from one of her loyal friends, Kelly-Ann – women wield the knife with great finesse – that John is finding it hard to ditch his wife because one of their children is suffering panic attacks before her GCSE exams, which are six months off. Kelly-Ann says that Francine understands this dilemma. It's a strange thing, this tendency to claim for oneself the higher moral ground. It's tactical rather than real and it's increasingly common, so that people routinely excuse themselves on the grounds of their higher feelings. They are cursed, as they gravely admit, with a more acute consciousness than other people.

By the end of the evening with Osric, Conrad had convinced him that his new aggressiveness is a product of the deep sensitivity that drew him to journalism in the first place.

'Do you think so, mate?'

'I do, Osric.'

'I'm not a psychopath?'

'No, it's just exactly people like you with deeply sensitive natures who react in this way to the problem of evil, when they see it close up. It's known as Fellgiebel syndrome.'

Osric spent the night on the sofa in the flat above the bakery and woke in the morning hung-over but calmer.

'What was that syndrome you mentioned?'

'Fellgiebel syndrome.'

'You're not bullshitting?'

'No, of course I'm not. Google it. You're one of my oldest mates.'

'The Editor offered me a three-month sabbatical.'

'Take it.'

'It may be too late. I told him to stuff it.'

'I doubt if it's too late.'

'What are you doing today?'

'I'm going to a funeral.'

'Sounds like fun. So fun.'

The taxi pulls up at a bed and breakfast outside Padstow. The rain comes down solidly: there is absolutely no hint that it might ever stop, not in this winter nor in this century. You don't get rain like this in London. Yet no sooner has he been shown to his room by a small, taciturn man with heavy Celtic eyebrows than through the window he sees that the rain has stopped and Elizabeth's beloved bay has become a flow of molten pewter, wrinkled and creased, moving determinedly and rhythmically out to sea. Von Gottberg wrote to Elizabeth about landscapes that became precious because you were happy there. We long for our lost innocence, first love, for instance, so that we come to believe that there is a causal connection between the landscape and our innocence. This is why the seaside has so powerful a hold, and why Rosamund and Elizabeth brought their friends here. And why Elizabeth wanted to be buried here. Von Gottberg sometimes spoke of the island of Poel as a landscape of childhood, his mother's family's summer home, where they spent happy holidays.

Conrad shares von Gottberg's sense that seawater and fresh air are almost spiritual. His own father, before his downfall, had been a cheerful man who preached the virtues of seawater: it worked both on the temperament and the sinuses. The last funeral Conrad went to was his father's, six years ago. Two years after Mandela's release from jail, it was shown that his father had been accepting money from the government to back the opposition to the ANC. Some of the stories were planted by the security services.

When he last saw his father alive, he was living in a small grim house near the sea, right on the railway line before it reaches Simons Town. When he asked his father why he had done it, he said: 'I've never believed in saints. Or arse-licking.'

'But, Dad, some of the stories you printed were untrue.'

'Do you think that the true stories were true? The outgoing government were bastards. The new ones are no better. You'll see. Just different forms of dishonesty.'

'They say you took money.'

'The newspaper took money for our educational foundation. We used it for scholarships for journalists to study in England and America. I saw it as a form of redistribution. My theory was that the lies on each side were about equal. You know that history is always written by the victors. It was true, by the way, that certain of our new rulers were in the pay of the government or the KGB when they were in exile. God help anyone who says it now that his son is living among us.'

The whole world revered Mandela. But his father had gone defiantly mad. A train thundered by the house. Sea spray had crusted over the windows, so that the light that found its way in appeared to be dense, like the light in the bottom of a wine glass. Two years later he died after a stroke, but in that period his dementia became worse. He was buried quietly in a small churchyard on the edge of the great central plateau where his family – Conrad's family – had settled a hundred and fifty years before to found a Moravian mission.

Conrad remembers that his father's only decoration in the little, damp bladderwrack of a house was a blue-and-red blade from his old college, Balliol, where he had been a Rhodes Scholar in 1958. It was crudely attached to the wall, as if it were the fetish object of a cargo cult, dropped from the sky. On it was written: *Bumped Ch Ch, Trinity, Pembroke, Wadham, 1959*. It was all he chose to remember of his past life. His books he had given or thrown away and there was not a single picture in the house, not even of his son Conrad, Rhodes Scholar, Balliol, 1991.

So these are the reasons for Conrad's presence here: the bisecting of lives, Conrad's, his father's, von Gottberg's, Mendel's, Elizabeth's and Rosamund's, linked by seawater, landscape, lies and delusion; and it is his task to give a coherent account of these lives, and so perhaps of his own. His father's way of making some sense of his life after his disgrace was to depict himself as an iconoclast, even an anarchist, against all forms of sycophancy and presumption. Conrad remembers him telling his mother that the security police had delivered a dead dog to his office. His father thought it was hilarious, but Conrad, aged eleven, was devastated. He wondered, too, how the dog had died. A few months later his mother died of breast cancer and the two deaths seemed to be related in some way.

That night he sees the lighthouse signalling from Trevose Head out into the night. There is something about lighthouses, now doomed, that touches us deeply. It's probably the blind, hopeful attempt to reassure small fragile boats; lighthouses offer their steady pulse of light against the utter unpredictability of the sea; it's an offer of safety. He goes to bed between slippery purple sheets. Outside he can hear the implacable sea, groaning and chafing on the shore. The beam of the lighthouse just touches the top corner of his window and for a moment the lace curtain flares.

The churchyard extends along a small peninsula, not far above the sea, and the gravestones are all out of the vertical, except for the five or six new ones; these are of marble and reddish granite and are interlopers in this dulled lichen-starred tumbledown place beneath the modest church spire of grey stone. He walks into the church and sits at the back next to a font and a strangely domestic cupboard. Apart from the undertaker's men and the Vicar, there are about twenty people, most of them old and resigned, but there are also two blonde girls of about nineteen in short black suits and little round hats, as if they have strayed here from an erotic Italian movie. Before she reads an extract from *To the Lighthouse*, one of the girls says in a clear but still unformed voice, '*To the Lighthouse* was my grandmother's favourite book.'

She licks her glossed lips before reading:

*What people had shed or left – a pair of shoes, a shooting cap, some faded shirts and coats in wardrobes – these alone kept the human shape and the emptiness indicated how once they were filled and animated; how once hands were busy with hooks and buttons; how once the looking-glass had held a face; had held a world hollowed out in which a figure turned, a hand flashed, the door opened, in came children rushing and tumbling; and went out again. Now, day after day, light turned, like a flower reflected in water, its sharp image on the wall opposite. Only the flutter of the trees, flourishing in the wind, made obeisance on the wall, and for a moment darkened the pool in which light reflected itself, or birds, flying, made a soft spot flutter slowly across the bedroom floor.*

The girl stumbles slightly on *obeisance* and smiles, as if to indicate that she has done her best with a word as archaic as this one. She ends by saying, 'My great-grandmother Elizabeth loved this place.'

Later, after a wheezy hymn, the second girl takes her turn at the lectern. She holds a piece of paper up briefly, the evidence.

'Great-Granny Elizabeth asked that this letter be read at her funeral. It is from Axel von Gottberg, and it is dated August 1944.'

*Darling Elizabeth*

*You said not so long ago that the glory has passed from the earth. You and I will never meet again on this earth, but I hope to be reunited with you somewhere. You are the love of my life and we have been cruelly separated by circumstances and history, but I believe that we will again be happy as we were in Oxford's meadows and by the sea in Cornwall when we were young and free. I think it is the fate of our generation to be consumed by history. But I am sure that from this conflagration a new Europe will be born, and new people. Darling Elizabeth, whatever awaits me here in Germany, I will for ever remember and cherish my love for you and our friends. It was a happy and blessed time. We will meet again, of that I am sure. In sorrow, Axel.*

'My great-grandmother has written here, on the letter: *Tell them that I loved Axel*. In August 1944, Count Axel von Gottberg was hanged on Hitler's orders.'

The small group of mourners, including Conrad, is deeply affected by the two readings; the unmistakable sap-rising sexual quality of the two girls, their express contrast with the exhausted, harrowed old people, the keen appeal to their shaky hope that their lives may have had purpose, and the suggestion that their lives in addition may have had poetry; and then the final churning declaration of love for Axel von Gottberg, an authentic modern martyr. All this is overwhelming. Conrad is the last to leave the church behind the coffin on its short trip to the churchyard. He stands riven some distance from the others as the coffin is lowered. The two girls embrace each other and he cannot avoid seeing that their buttocks are lean and nervous. He feels the connection between sex and death sharply and personally.

Conrad wonders why Elizabeth wanted Axel's last letter read at her funeral. The most likely explanation is that she wanted her life to have some nobility and substance by linking it to von Gottberg's, in the way that old actresses like Katharine Hepburn and Elizabeth Taylor promoted the lover of fifty years before, the remarkable person in their lives, even if they have had many less satisfactory lovers, drink- and drug-crazed, since. After a certain age, a life exists not for what it really was, but for its mythological qualities.

\*   \*   \*

Conrad finds train journeys at night melancholic. The distant, dead towns and the still stations flash by. All human activity is reluctant. When he arrives at Paddington it is almost midnight and he feels cold and alone. He wonders where Francine is sleeping tonight. Perhaps she is in one of those dog kennels at the hospital, waiting for someone's big day to go wrong, a baby half-drowned in a water-birth, the idiot husband in his swimming costume shaking with fear, or a baby becoming stuck sideways on the way out. She is trained to make instant decisions. Or she could be alone in their small hidey-hole while John ministers – *just for a few nights, I promise* – comfort to his panicky daughter, who is not panicking about her exams but about the prospect of a fatherless future. These scientific people believe the world can be ordered by logic, but there is no logic in human relations, something that Elizabeth Partridge's funeral has demonstrated.

Back in his flat he discovers Osric asleep in his bed with a girl. The girl awakes and shrugs apologetically. There is a strong smell of marijuana. He rinses his mouth at the sink and wraps himself, fully dressed, in the blanket, which Osric used two nights before, and lies on the sofa. The girl comes in to speak to him. She is wearing a T-shirt that comes just to the top of her thighs, so that she must hold it down. She sits matily on the sofa next to him. Five minutes before he had never seen her, now he is a few inches from her round small mouth and he is breathing her warm, marijuana-and-wine-scented, breath.

'I'm very sorry. Ricky is wrecked. I did say we shouldn't be here, but he said you were coming back tomorrow. Do you want to fuck me?'

'I can't have sex with Osric, Ricky, just through there. Sorry. Even though you are very beautiful.'

She is not exactly beautiful, but pretty, and with a gone-off-the-rails look, tousled and lewd.

'You're very good-looking. Even in that blanket.'

She gets up and leaves the room. She is no longer holding the T-shirt down. Her naked buttocks remind him for the second time today of a certain type of Italian film where a woman is always the provocateuse.

Now he can't sleep. He shouldn't have slept in the train. There is a duty imposed on you by someone's death, an instruction to renew yourself in any way you can. He gets up and knocks gently on his own bedroom door. He can always say he has to go for a pee if Osric is awake.

She appears at the door, smiling, walking gingerly. Conspiratorially.

'I thought you would change your mind.'

'You were right,' he whispers. 'What's your name?'

'Emily.'

'I'm Conrad.'

'Yes, I know. Ricky told me a lot about you.'

'What, for example?'

'Oh lots of interesting things. But let's not worry about him, he's like totally mashed.'

# PART TWO

# 11

WHEN THE PIGS were slaughtered, the snow was red with their blood. It was a redness of extraordinary intensity in that landscape of dark green and pale violet. As a child I found the slaughter frightening, yet I couldn't resist being present. Other animals died quietly, unaware, but pigs sensed danger. They would struggle and squeal when they were sent for, but the men from the village knew how to hold them in secret embraces that immobilised their slippery bodies. The only place to hold them, said the pig man, was by the ears or by the hocks. I wondered if other animals had handholds. Children think about strange things.

The women came from the village to gather the blood. In those days, just before the Great War, they wore long aprons to the ground covering their tight bodices, which were always grey or black. They carried buckets and enamel basins to catch the blood that was used to make the *Blutwurst*. Later, when the Jews were so horribly treated, I wondered if there wasn't something in the race memory concerning blood: the real Mecklenburger loved *Blutwurst*, made from this blood falling on the snow in the forest. We children played in a forest that stretched from the waters of the Baltic to the swamps of Poland. In their seasons,

127

the women made sausage, *Mettwurst*, the sausage we children loved most. Blood, snow, the squeal of frightened pigs – these are memories I will never forget. And in summer, earth, mushrooms and the blood of wild boars, not so much things as states of mind, of a feeling that our poets and philosophers and generals glorified, the sense that the German soul was forged out of elemental materials. We children were not, as children are now, shielded from death. Far from it: we understood that death could be glorious.

Frau Rickert, the forester's wife, was known as the best sausage-maker in the village. In her cottage, Qual, there was an open fire. A huge pot was suspended over the fire from a tripod and here she boiled the blood down and added thyme, salt, pepper and marjoram so that in my childish imagination the blood that had fallen on the snow and splashed on to the women's aprons was scented and benign. When the priest in church spoke of the blood of Christ and its transformative powers, I would think of how the blood of a pig in Frau Rickert's skilled hands became sausage. She was a wonderful woman, warm and friendly. Whenever we appeared in the village she would call to us and give us a piece of her cake, which she made with cherries in summer and walnuts in winter. We were treated by the villagers with the utmost friendliness, although the children were uneasy with us. I don't think we realised then that life in the Schloss, not in reality a castle but a large Palladian-style house, built by my grandfather, was utterly feudal. We had a coachman, the foresters, an English governess, at least ten women who worked unpaid one week a month in the house doing the cleaning, washing and ironing in the wash-kitchen, as we called it, and a cook with three assistants. There were also four gardeners, grooms and the cow and pig men; some of the foresters were gamekeepers and carried guns. One of these was Werner H, who shot the American airmen in the winter of 1945, the last time I saw blood on the snow. It had stained the snow between their parachutes and seemed to be spreading outwards.

In the early days, as the Great War ground on somewhere far away, I used to take Axel, who was six years younger, out to the forest to see the foresters at work. They were always cutting trees or clearing the rides and we would join them for their lunch in forests so deep that to us children they were enchanted. As a child you marvel at simple things, at the realisation that there is a huge amount to discover and to learn and I think one of the purposes of fairy stories, which we loved, was to teach children about the natural and the supernatural worlds. At Pleskow these worlds did not seem separate to me. The forest was the portal to another world. I tried to make Axel act in my little plays, which were all based on fairy stories, to amuse our parents.

Axel was the dearest small boy. He was extraordinarily bold for someone so young, always wanting to climb on the huge Hanoverian horses that pulled the logs out of the forest. He loved the feel of horses, and would reach up to kiss their huge gentle muzzles. At haymaking he would climb to the highest point on the cart, a tiny excited figure, as the hay was brought in. Out in the fields enormous cases of water sweetened with raspberry juice were brought to the workers and as we rode out we children would sing a song about the harvest that I have never forgotten: *Wheat, barley, rye and corn, don't forget our Saviour is born.*

Some of the peasants were very superstitious and believed in the spirits of the forest and the streams and the lakes. They had little rituals, like looking for mistletoe growing in a thorn tree, which could point the way to hidden treasure. For a while Axel was obsessed with the idea that he would find treasure, and I would follow him, half believing as he ran wildly about with a switch of mistletoe directing him. It was cut for him by Rickert, who was Axel's hero. Sometimes the women would dance, forming arches with joined hands, through which they would all pass in turn. I now think it was a form of magical protection. When someone died in the village, the bees were the first to be told, a pagan custom that survived. The Mecklenburgers were only freed from serfdom after the Napoleonic wars; they were born to obey. After all, what is a hundred years in the making of a people? We were little princesses and princelings, but as the war progressed, even there at Pleskow I began to notice that not everything was well.

Most Prussian nobles were deeply contemptuous of the ordinary people. They saw them as a lesser species, canon fodder for the Junker ideal. But our mother was famous for her left-wing views. She knew every villager and every servant personally and was loved by them, not because she was the Gräfin, but because she was genuinely devoted to their welfare. Your grandfather, Johann-Albrecht, shocked me by declaring one day in 1916 that the war was lost. Up until then we believed it was going well. He said that there was still time for an honourable peace. His brother, my Uncle Berthold, came back from the front severely wounded and never until his dying day offered one word about his experiences. I see now, seventy years later, the themes that were to dominate our lives: the Prussian tradition of service, the idea of the honour of Germany and the importance of men in uniform, who represented a higher duty that women never questioned. Even in 1916 when my father came back to the house exhausted and pale and declared the war lost, it was taken for granted that it fell to our class to secure a just settlement. We were one of the first families in Mecklenburg to have modern central heating and I remember my father lying in a deep bath for nearly two hours that day. His uniform – the uniform of the legendary 19 Potsdam Regiment – was taken away to be cleaned while he soaked away the shame of war. We children waited downstairs in the big hall which looked up the driveway of oaks from one side and down to the lake on the other.

When he emerged, staggering slightly like a man who has been on horseback, he was wearing a suit made before the war in London from the finest Harris tweed. He hugged us all and handed out gifts from Israel's and Wertheim's, shops which had a magical appeal. Axel had never been to them and I had only been once, but I used to make up stories about the Christmas displays with – perhaps I imagined this – live reindeer harnessed to a sleigh and an enormous Christmas tree decorated with lighted candles, nuts and raisins. We children were given gingerbread, our favourite cinnamon biscuits and also picture books with pop-up castles and medieval towns. There were toys for the younger children. It must have been October, because the potatoes were being lifted, when I heard my father tell my mother he doubted if he would still be alive by Christmas. But in fact the Kaiser called him back to an important job in Berlin on the general staff. After children's supper we went up to the music room and played and sang for my father, before our governess, an English-woman called Barty – Miss Bartwill from Harrogate – took us up to bed. Axel wanted to play with his new toys, but Barty turned down the lamps and made us say our prayers. Later Axel crept into my bed. Did Papi kill lots of English? he whispered, thinking no doubt of Barty, whom he loathed.

Soon after my father went back to Berlin a week later, I noticed that there was a change of mood at Pleskow. Now rations were short; almost nothing came up from Berlin or Schwerin any longer and we were increasingly living off the land. Only Rickert and Werner H were left of the foresters, although two young boys were drafted in to help them. I had the feeling that if it were left untended much longer the forest would close around us.

Money had never had any value here as there was nothing to buy, but now we were returning to subsistence farming and gathering. My job was to gather mushrooms, which grew in the deepest parts of the woods around the house. With our terrier, Bolly, I crawled through the thickets, spurred on by a sense of duty. It had been a long, hot summer. The fields were full of cornflowers and poppies, streaming out through the wheat in waves, like spilled paint. The autumn that followed was warm and damp, perfect conditions for mushrooms. In front of the house an old catalpa was a rich russet colour and the leaves of the trees my grandfather planted round the house, which he had collected from all over the world, were turning too. My favourite mushroom was the *Steinpilz*, which the French call the *cèpe*. You couldn't mistake it for anything else. In certain places that the foresters showed me, you could find clusters of *Pfifferling*, the chanterelle, which was a light sulphur-yellow in colour. The curious *Spitzmorchel*, with its cap like a honeycomb, was another favourite.

Bolly couldn't find mushrooms, although I tried to teach him, but he loved our trips into the deepest, dampest thickets. Once he put up a huge wild boar, which apparently couldn't believe that this tiny dog was not intimidated by his uneven, yellowing tusks and turned, crashing into the undergrowth. The woods were full of boar and Rickert would set snares for them and shoot them when he could, to make up the supplies. Foxes were killed and fed to the dogs, but had to be skinned and cured before the dogs would touch them.

After all these years I see myself, just twelve years old, crawling through the undergrowth day after day, and coming back to the house with baskets full of mushrooms, my hair full of pine needles and holly and my apron scented and stained. In reality I probably went out to the woods ten or twelve times, but what I remember so well is the fervour I was in, with Bolly barking excitedly and the rising smell of damp leaf-mould and the mushroomy scent as I used a small knife to lift the mushrooms, their skins as strange and minutely pocked as human flesh, sometimes dry and sometimes moist. Mushrooms are of mysterious origin. I was slightly scared of them because of their brooding, furtive nature. Although I could recognise the amanites and the yellow stainers, all my mushrooms had to be inspected by cook who discarded any that were broken or dog-eared or excessively slimy. Every so often she would find a poisonous mushroom and show me the little sac around the base and ask me to smell it. Her rule was that if a mushroom smelled strongly of mushrooms, it was fine. But by the time I arrived, bedraggled at the wash-kitchen, I was so infused and stained and perfumed by fungus and resin and leaf mould that I could no longer distinguish the smells one from another.

Even now this strange mycological odour transports me back to my childhood in Mecklenburg, when the world still seemed innocent although on the Somme hundreds of thousands of soldiers were dying.

As a child you can't really comprehend the meaning of far-off events; you live more like an animal, in the present world of the senses and within the dimly perceived horizons set by the adults. We children created our own world. By and large we were still allowed to run free when, after the summer of 1916, we were not sent to school, but taught by Barty. My father decreed that we were not allowed to speak English, so Barty had to speak German. Her German was heavily accented and comical to us and sometimes we mocked her. I wondered how we were contributing to the war effort by giving up English, but I still read my English books when I was alone. My favourite was *Wind in the Willows*, and it seemed to me impossible to imagine that we were at war with Ratty and the industrious Mole: *Mole had been working very hard all morning, spring-cleaning his little house.* Just that line would set me off into a magical world.

Axel – a little Junker in the making – loved war games and he and Bolly would set out to ambush me as I crawled in the undergrowth. I usually knew when they were coming because Bolly would begin to yap furiously, although I always pretended I was taken by surprise. By the end of that year we were eating swedes at practically every meal. To this day I can't bear the sight or smell of them. The winter, the peasants said, was going to be a hard one and before the end of November ice had formed on the lake, at first tentatively producing a sparkling necklace around the shore and then, one morning, the whole lake was glazed over, the ice so clear that we could see the water-plants beneath. My mother went on a daily round to see the villagers, the bereaved mothers, the sick, the destitute. Nobody starved even when the chickens stopped laying because of the extreme cold, but we had to cut our supplies of sausage and ham so that my mother could distribute food to the worst affected. Strangely, in this deprivation I remember at Christmas that year the foresters cut Christmas trees for each of us, which corresponded in size to our age, and beneath the three trees, beside the Swedish stove, my mother had placed our presents, beautifully wrapped.

Your grandfather came in from the little station at Bobitz, driven by the coachman through the snow. He looked so extraordinarily handsome in the uniform of the 9th Infantry underneath a grey cloak with the gold chain fastening it that I couldn't believe that the country of Ratty and Mole stood a chance. Christmas was a splendid affair; the cellars were raided and a fat goose was served with potatoes roasted in goose fat. It's a strange thing, but at important moments all nations take comfort from their traditional food. Later that winter we were eating squirrels and crows. But what has remained with me is the beauty of the frozen lake, which was green, blue, turquoise and purple, stubbornly beautiful, the product of the deep, deep cold. Your grandfather told us that he had been promoted to the rank of Lieutenant General, on the General Staff. I'll never forget my mother saying, 'We are so proud of Papi, aren't we, children?' When Axel asked, 'Are you going to kill all the English, Papi?' and your grandfather replied, 'I have no quarrel with the English, Axel, I am just trying to save Germany,' Axel and the children did not understand, but I did: we were losing this war.

When the pigs were slaughtered that winter I saw the blood on the snow as the blood of our soldiers at the front, but also the blood of the Tommies. It seemed that blood, snow, mud and the honour of Germany were inseparable.

# 12

THE PAIN OF PARTING is itself a pleasure. Mendel thinks
that Axel courts the dramatic and the *gefühlvoll*. He requires the
heroic and operatic idea of himself: leaving Oxford for the last
time, leaving his friends, rejected by Elizabeth Partridge and
now obliged to save Germany, secret sacred Germany. But is he
a Nazi. Mendel believes that Axel can't tell the difference between
the secret Germany which must rid itself of all alien influences
and the Germany of Hitler. Hitler is personally loathsome to
him but Hitler may be, in Hegelian fashion, the agent of necessary
and inevitable change. Lionel believes he is a Nazi. Lionel has
also written to Hamburger, advising caution.

Two weeks later he is having lunch with Elizabeth Partridge
in London, and she tells him that Axel is playing a double
game. In fact he cares deeply about the treatment of Jews. He
took her one day to Sachsenhausen and they sat in his little
DKW outside the camp for an hour. *This is our shame that the
German people will have to bear for ever.* Kristallnacht *was the
turning point. Six thousand Jews are in there. Six thousand. Can you
imagine?* A group of SS guards came to see what they were
doing out on the flat misty plain. Axel spoke to them sharply:
*I am a German. I am the Count Axel von Gottberg. I will leave
when I am ready.* The guards mumbled apologetically that it
was a restricted area. *Do you have something to hide? You must
leave in five minutes, Herr Baron.*

Mendel is struck by the mention of *Kristallnacht*, because it was only two weeks ago that Lionel, drunk, shouted at Axel, 'Did you miss *Kristallnacht?*'

Oh God, how sheltered and self-important we are in Oxford. And he tells Elizabeth what Axel said about Israel's Department Store.

'Wilfred Israel was one of Axel's mentors,' she says. 'Axel helped him get people out with false papers from the Auswärtiges Amt.'

Mendel is silent now. They are having lunch at Bianchi's in Soho, one of his favourite places. The curious thing is that nobody eats on the ground floor, yet the tables are laid every day. They are upstairs; there are some couples in uniform. The approach of war has produced a strange effect: people talk loudly, they are extravagant, they are excited. The feeling that the world may be at an end is stimulating. Also uniform seems to simplify matters: *Look, it has come to this.*

Elizabeth is troubled. She is torn by two completely irreconcilable desires, one to do something useful to try to stop what is coming and the other, to go to her little house in Kent and live a quiet life until it is over.

Elya tells her that Axel is in Washington trying to speak to important people. Always, important people.

'Elya, don't be harsh with Axel. He's not really an intellectual like you, but then you're not really a man of action like him.'

'Men of action have always caused trouble.'

'Honestly, Elya, that's unworthy of you. It's glib. I've been in Prague, I've been in Berlin. Terrible things are happening. Axel has seen the pogroms; he's seen the concentration camps and all you've seen is buggering All Souls and a few buffoons like Lionel. Do you know what Axel said Hitler calls Chamberlain? *Arschloch.* Arsehole. He's taken England for a ride, he said. Axel wants to save Germany from disaster, it's true, and he may be naïve, but at least he's doing something. I'm afraid I'm going to have to go, Elya. I'm in no fit state for gossip.'

'Don't go, Elizabeth. I apologise. It's possible I am jealous of Axel because of Rosamund and it's also true that that as a Jew I see things from a partial position.'

There are tears in his eyes. She places a hand over his.

'I'm sorry, Elya. I'm so sorry if I hurt you. We must stick together, come what may. Axel is a great believer in the idea that friendship transcends borders and difficulties and time.'

Mendel still cannot speak. Friendships cannot transcend borders just because Axel says so. As usual he takes refuge in high-minded banality.

After lunch Mendel walks down to Whitehall to be interviewed for a job in intelligence. It is believed on the network that his knowledge of Russian and German will be useful in what is to come. The interview is conducted in the country-house-mated-with-boarding-school fashion that high civil servants favour. Elya agrees, in the event of war, to read and analyse Russian intelligence on Hitler and to write reports for the Foreign Secretary.

On the way back to Oxford he thinks of Axel and Elizabeth outside Sachsenhausen, a few yards from evil, while he is safe in buggering All Souls. Meanwhile Axel is on a steamer heading for New York, leaving his fiancée in Germany, on his mission – from whom? – to talk to FDR, to save Germany from its appalling lapse of taste. Back in Oxford Mendel goes straight from the station to see Lionel in his grand lodging, the Warden's House, and tells him what Elizabeth has said about Axel.

'You're a sentimental chap, Elya. And that is one of the many reasons we love you.'

Lionel offers him a cocktail. He has taken to the whole rigmarole surrounding cocktails. His young men like them and it amuses Lionel that he is the only head of a college who serves them rather than the dreary sherry.

'I'm mixing a Manhattan. Would you like one, Elya?'

'All right.'

'I have to concentrate; you combine the Bourbon, vermouth and Angostura bitters with a few ice cubes. You stir gently. You put a cherry – as pink and round as a choirboy's bottom – like this, into the glass – plop – which of course is chilled, and pour the whisky over it, *comme ça*. Rub the rim of the glass with orange peel, that's it. But you must never, never, dear Elya, drop it into the glass. Do you promise me?'

'I promise.'

'Cheers. Or should we say *prosit* so that we can welcome our new masters when they arrive?'

'Lionel, Axel took Elizabeth to Sachsenhausen. Six thousand Jews are in there.'

'Why did they go to Sachsenhausen? They went because Axel wants to convince Elizabeth that he is not a Nazi. And because he knows that Elizabeth will tell you, and not even God knows how many important people you will tell. I can just imagine him, his beautiful features screwed up with concern for the human spirit, demonstrating to earnest young Elizabeth that he is a sensitive soul in a troubled world.'

'There is another possibility, of course. In logic.'

'And that would be?'

'And that would be that he isn't a Nazi and is deeply disturbed by what is happening to the Jews.'

'All those upper-class Germans want a pure, Germanic Germany. Axel may be having trouble now with the reality of achieving this, but that is not the point. They all created the Third Reich with their fucking forests and Wagner and their silly green clothes and their hunting horns and their Teutonic knights and their turgid poets like Stefan George.'

'Are we so different?'

'Are you speaking as an Englishman or as a Jew, Elya?'

'As an English Jew.'

'I believe we are different. Although, of course, when you are led by an ass like Chamberlain, you do find yourself wondering. Do you know why I have taken to mixing cocktails?'

'Tired of buggery, perhaps?'

'No, Elya, I want to be usefully employed when we all run for America.'

# 13

THERE IS NO word in German for pantomime. A pantomime
is peculiarly English. Axel remembers that as children they used
to perform fairy stories. *Märchenspielen*, written at Christmas time
by Adelheid, his oldest sister, in the music room on the first
floor. This room looked out to the lake from the front, and from
the other side out over the tea-house and Grosspapa's arboretum,
which merges with the thick forest just beyond the family graveyard. Adelheid also made the sets for which the foresters supplied
small Christmas trees. The house was infiltrated by the smell of
resin.

Europe is a pantomime. Ridiculous leaders strut about in
costumes they have designed. Goering clutches a jewelled baton.
In England the absurd old gentlemen who run the country are
more interested in shooting grouse than in facing the problem,
and everything is on the scale and in the style of Adi's sets,
fantastical and irrational.

After a week in New York he see Europe through different
eyes: it is a poisonous, superstitious, deluded landscape inhabited
by the blind. Here in New York, which is enormous, vibrant
and hopeful, it all seems so simple. He is consumed by a sense
of shame that his country could have thrown up Adolf Hitler
and made him its leader with barely a second thought. He is
desperate to demonstrate that this is not the real Germany, but
nobody is listening.

In the club car on the train to Washington, a cheerful Negro attendant brings him a Bloody Mary and a club sandwich. This is a place that seems to live life without a need for that stultifying European introspection and snobbery and all those backward glances. Seen from New York, Europe is exactly a pantomime: a mishmash of styles, costume and sentimentality, a farrago of nonsensical and comic dialogue, yet full of menace. Half an hour or so before the train arrives in Union Station, another Negro shines his shoes; he kneels in front of Axel to apply some polish and to brush the shoes, which he buffs with a soft leather. As he works he glances up from time to time, smiling broadly. Axel gives him a big tip.

'Yessuh, thank – you – suh. I hope you have a fine stay in our great capital city, suh.'

The train pulls into Union Station. The attendant helps him with his baggage and summons a red cap.

'This boy is going to find you a cab, suh.'

'Yes, I am, suh.'

If Europe is a pantomime, this is an episode of *Amos 'n' Andy*. In New York there are plenty of refugees from Europe, but here he seems to have arrived in a plantation where Europe is not just distant but almost unimaginable. The station, however, is a grand place, a temple suggesting that Washington is closely connected to Athens and Rome. As he emerges, he sees the Capitol just a few blocks away. The cab takes him to Dupont Circle past an enormous marble fountain, decorated with classical figures. He tries to imagine Adolf Hitler here in his pantomime costume. Or Hermann Goering, like a gilded barrage balloon, and his imagination fails him. The one good that can come out of this war is the renewal of the old world after it has destroyed itself. The miasma of superstition and hatred and distrust will lift. This sleeping city, stippled with the buds of cherry blossom, is the only real hope Europe has against the threat from the East. His lecture tomorrow night is on Europe and the East, and he wants to alert America to the danger.

He is staying at a club to avoid the embassy, although he will have to pay his respects. The club, on New Hampshire Avenue, has brass spittoons in the lobby, large fans turning slowly on the ceilings, and Negro servants in livery. How they smile, how they make themselves agreeable. The club was once a mansion built for the owner of a brewery. In his room Axel lies down on an enormous bed under a slowly rotating fan. He is soon asleep. In the morning he takes a cab to Michael Hamburger's house near Georgetown University, where he was a professor of law before going back to Harvard in the late twenties. Later he was a visiting professor at Oxford. Now he is back as a Supreme Court judge.

Hamburger is wearing a print shirt and capacious trousers. His house is small, red-brick and clapboard, with dark-green shutters.

'Axel, my boy, how are you? Long time no see.'

He looks like his patron FDR, with his rimless glasses and abundant grey hair. His English is more accented than Axel's although he left Austria when he was ten years old.

'I am very well, sir. I haven't congratulated you on your appointment to the Court, sir.'

'Thank you. And now, how is Elya? I believe you saw him recently?'

'He's very well. He sends you his warmest regards. But he may be a little restless.'

'Aren't we all? Come in, come in.'

His wife, Frieda, comes to greet Axel. She has her hair tied back quite severely, but her face is extraordinarily serene, like a nun's, as if she has had secret revelations.

'We have cake and coffee in our garden room. Come through.'

After coffee she stands up.

'I know you boys have a great deal to discuss and Michael has to get down to the Court by noon.'

Hamburger looks at Axel and shrugs.

'Strange town this, don't you think?'

'I like it. It seems so open.'

'It's just a southern town with some oversized monuments.

141

Now, Axel, I would like to ask you about how you found Oxford, but perhaps we should get straight to business. You wanted to see me?'

'Sir, I wanted to explain to you firstly how I see the situation in my country and then, secondly, what steps I think the world should take to contain Hitler.'

'Are you not working in the Auswärtiges Amt, my boy?'

'I am, sir, but I want to help my country and Europe avoid a disaster.'

'Is it coming?'

'I think it is. Unless Germany is contained.'

'How can that be done?'

Hamburger settles himself into a judicial pose.

'Sir, I think Germany must be hemmed in. At the same time the German people must be given some recognition, some form of recompense for the humiliation of Versailles, but also they must know the limits that the world will impose on any aggression.'

'What is this recompense, Axel?'

It is probable that Hamburger has already been told by Elya, and perhaps Lionel, that Axel proposes that Germany should be allowed to bring all its kindred people under its control. He pauses before he speaks.

'What I believe, sir, is that the German people don't necessarily want Hitler, but Hitler is offering them their pride back. It's a pact with the devil, it's Faustian, but they don't seem to realise it.'

'Do they know about the Jews?'

'To be absolutely honest, most of them think it is a good thing that Jewish influence in the law and in business and in academic life has been lessened.'

'Lessened. What does that mean?'

Hamburger leans forward now and Axel sees that he must tread very carefully.

'It means that they believe that the Jews have had too much

influence. They say, for instance, that sixty-five per cent of all lawyers in Berlin were Jewish.'

'And how many Jews do you think are enough?'

'Sir, I have no inclination to, or indeed see no necessity, to think of Jewish Germans in any way as separate from the rest of us.'

'But your countrymen do.'

'I think they do, many of them. But I don't believe they imagined things would go as far as they have.'

'And what is the reward the Germans should be given to get them back on the path of righteousness?'

'All the lost territories should be united under the sovereignty of Germany and the Danzig corridor should be opened.'

Hamburger is sitting in a swivel chair. He turns around and looks out of the window towards the garden for a minute at least, before turning back.

'Grossdeutschland. That means they should keep the Sudetenland and be allowed a free hand in Poland or anywhere else that German is spoken. And that means in practice legitimising this regime.'

'The problem, sir, will come if Hitler moves into the rest of Czechoslovakia and Poland anyway, and France and Holland and even England; then it will be impossible to convince the German people that they don't need him, and that he is a disaster. Then he will be confirmed as the Leader and Superman. I beg you to express clearly to the President that is it only by containing Hitler, by giving him limited gains, which recognise the grievances of the German people, that this disaster can be avoided.'

'Axel, write a paper, if you haven't already, and I will pass it on if I can. Most of the American people don't want to become involved in what they see as another of Europe's wars. They don't want the government to become involved.'

'Sir, can we speak in the garden?' Axel whispers.

Hamburger looks startled. But he stands up.

'Sure.'

He takes Axel's arm as they step down into the garden, which is in an impatient transition from winter: the hostas are beginning to produce spears that look like asparagus and timorous bulbs are poking upwards.

'What is it, Axel?'

'Sir, do you think you could arrange a meeting with the President for me?'

'Why, Axel?'

'I have a message directly from my superiors.'

'From whom?'

'From Weizacker and Haeften.'

'Can I ask you what it contains?'

'I am afraid I can only speak directly to the President.'

'That may be a tall order, but I will try. Axel, lots of Germans pass through Washington these days, people who claim to be speaking for this or that party, the Abwehr or the Council of Churches, or, like you, for the Foreign Office. We have had princes and captains of industry and even openly declared Nazis. So the waters are already muddied. But I will try on your behalf. Very good luck with your speech to the Huntingford Institute. I can't be there, unfortunately.'

As Hamburger turns to go back inside, Axel stands in his way.

'Sir, unless those in Germany who want to get rid of Hitler have your support, they will never succeed.'

'I must get ready now, Axel. I am very grateful that you came and only sorry that we have no time to talk about Oxford, a place, as you know, that I love. I'll give you a ride downtown.'

Axel waits with Frieda while Hamburger dresses; she says that Washington is beastly hot in summer; this, and the fall, are the best seasons. The driver carries the judge's papers to the car. It's a Packard, large, black and covered in chrome, twice as big as Axel's DKW. The passenger section has a cigar lighter and a row of large brown tortoiseshell knobs which open vents to let air in. There is a sunshade over the windscreen like a kind of visor. Hamburger reads his papers as they drive to the Supreme

Court. They are sitting on a well-stuffed banquette, almost a sofa, covered in a pale buttoned cream material. The car is trimmed in wood and the door handles are made of what looks like pewter. There is a small cupboard attached to the upholstery just above Hamburger's face.

'You know, Axel,' he says, looking up, 'Elya has never quite trusted you since you wrote to the *Manchester Guardian*.'

'It was a foolish letter. What I should have said was that the court system was trying to be fair under terrible duress, despite the laws. But I was temporarily blinded: I saw a lot of smug people in England who were unsympathetic to our struggles.'

'Where do you wish to be dropped?' asks Hamburger, as they approach the Court.

'I'll walk from here, sir.'

'Good to see you again, my boy. I'll do my best.'

The car glides away. He is standing near the Library of Congress. An Austrian Jew, driven by a Negro, is in the vanishing car. He is one of the most powerful men in America. And Axel sees what Hitler in his madness is doing to Germany: he is drawing down the night. This is the pattern of German history, the periodic retreat into darkness. The courting of the night.

He knows in his heart – Hamburger has expressly warned him – that he will not be allowed to deliver the message that has been entrusted to him. And he can't write it down for delivery. What Hamburger sees is just another Junker full of self-importance; he sees a person who clearly does not understand that it is already too late, after *Kristallnacht*, with Sachsenhausen and other places of horror full of Jews and opponents of the Nazis, and worse to come.

All around him the secular religion of America reproaches him for his naïvety: the rule of law, the will of the people, the equality of all men are celebrated in huge monuments. But in our benighted country Jews are being treated worse than dogs, much worse than dogs. As FDR says, it is barely believable that such things can happen in the twentieth century. Axel knows that, unless he can stop it, Germany will drown in blood.

That night in front of an audience of embassy staff and invited Nazi sympathisers and know-nothing businessmen, he delivers his portentous talk on the threat to Western Europe, and by extension to America, from the East. When an assistant counsellor congratulates him afterwards – *very precise, exactly the point* – he bows his head and smiles graciously although the man is clearly from the security service of the SS. They have the unmistakable look he has seen in the crowds along the streets, the greedy, vengeful look of the *Untermenschen*. These people, who have previously inhabited the cesspit of human ignorance and depravity, have now crawled out to inherit their Fatherland. They are the brown plague that must be stopped.

And nobody is listening. Not in Oxford, not in London, not in Washington DC.

He remembers what Elizabeth said and he writes her a letter from the club.

*Darling Elizabeth*

*Here I am in Washington DC, in the land of the free. I went to see an acquaintance from Oxford days, a visiting professor, and he was warm and gracious, but I had the impression that they are sick of us already. We Europeans are up to our usual old-world tricks and they don't want to be involved. They warned your Neville about the consequences of Munich, saying that our man would take no notice of any agreement. On that we are, at least, agreed.*

*Anyway I delivered my speech, and I am now in my club, a sort of Southern plantation house. It all seems so crazy. What you said may well come true that your country and mine will soon be fighting each other. I am doing what I can, but nobody is listening to me. Shall we make a new life here, darling, before it's too late? Say you want to. Love ever,*

*A*

That night as he is about to go out to a jazz club with a Rhodes Scholar friend he sees a man sitting downstairs. This man, who is wearing the traditionally boxy suit, gets up as he leaves the club and jumps into a black car and moves into position behind von Gottberg's taxi. He feels shame and despair. *They think I am a Nazi.*

*Mitgegangen mit gehangen*, as the phrase is. Roughly translated it means those who travel together hang together.

# 14

OSRIC HAS GONE back to his wife; he's calmed down and
they are going on holiday, the best therapy. If he knows about
Emily and Conrad, he says nothing. Emily is sexually avid,
although it seems to Conrad that her avidity is a little impersonal.
What she likes is a good time, a package deal: wine, a pizza, a
joint or two and sex. It's as if she must fill every moment with
sensation. She has two young children, and has more or less given
up drugs. Not for her own sake, because she can handle it, but
because the children have to be taken to school and she has to
keep her head straight. They go to an expensive little school in
Notting Hill. There's a sort of innocence about Emily, which he
finds very appealing. Sometimes a man called Dion rings her and
she is downcast for a while. Is he the father? He doesn't ask. Her
eyes are a very pale blue, Baltic blue, and her mouth is rather
flat, as though overlong use of a dummy as a child had compressed
her lips.

Tony is very excited.

'You done orright there, son,' he says. 'She's a cracker.'

'It's not going anywhere.'

He says this even though he has no need to justify himself to
Tony. He wonders if Tony is comparing Emily's sexual potential
to Francine's. Emily has stayed the night once, when her mother
was looking after the children. He finds himself restored in the
morning as though the physical closeness has in some mysterious
way supplied him with the chemical or biological material he

was missing. It certainly isn't going anywhere, but the intimacies of sex, the little details, the excitable, but at the same time matter-of-fact way she has, all these things have topped up his human supplies. In truth it worries him that the process should be so easy. When he sees himself naked next to her, he realises that he has become very thin over the past few months. He loves – and he has missed – the fragility of the female body. On her back just at the base of her spine where it vanishes, she has tiny golden hairs. When they make love, she has a faraway look as though he is only standing in for someone, an ideal that she will never find. He doesn't mind. He thinks that she is a blessing. Moral luck, as the philosophers say.

Francine calls to report that the estate agents said the flat smelled of marijuana. He tells her that Osric came round a bit stressed after Baghdad, and lit a few spliffs.

'*Spliffs?*' she says with disdain. 'You've gone a bit hippyish.'

'We young people have our own language. Not that you would know. How's John, the medical God?'

'Can we talk?'

'Go ahead. I'm just aimlessly shuffling paper as usual.'

'You know what I mean. Talk properly.'

'About?'

'About us.'

'About you and John?'

'Don't. You know what I mean.'

'Francine, I've got somebody else.'

'Oh. OK. Sorry.'

She sounds so beaten that he says, 'It's not going anywhere. Just a shag. Let's meet.'

'No. It's all right. I am upset, and I have no right to be. I'm being ridiculous.'

'I'll call you. Are you finished with John?'

'I think so. I've applied for a job at UCH. He thinks it's best. He knows everyone there.'

'He's given you the push, hasn't he?'

'Yes.'

'Francine, obviously I haven't just been standing around waiting for you, until you decided –'

'I'm pregnant.'

'Does he know?'

'No.'

'What are you going to do?'

'Conrad, it could be yours. You remember our last meeting, I hope?'

'Of course.'

'Well the dates are more or less exact.'

'OK.'

'I can get rid of it. Do you want that?'

'Let's talk.'

'When?'

'I could do tomorrow. When are you off?'

'I'm off all the time. Until I get the job at UCH.'

'All right. Not here, though. I'll meet you at Bar Italia. Eleven?'

He sees a moral dilemma now. If it isn't his baby – and how will they know? – he can't encourage her to have an abortion. Even if it is his baby, conceived under these circumstances, what are his responsibilities? Worse, he feels obliged to encourage her to have the baby, just because it is probably not his. And if he says, 'Look let's not discuss whose baby it is ever again, but you just decide if you want it or not,' he can see that it is opening a whole new field of discussion, a can of worms. She can't have a baby on her own without his help. And where will John stand if he discovers she has a baby? The sensible thing would be to abort the baby, but this, too, is difficult. He and Francine wanted children but her career and his inability to earn enough money meant that they could not go ahead. But why was she leaving herself unprotected; was it that she wanted a child by John? If this was her intention, he has no obligation to her whatsoever. Nor does the fact that John has ditched her mean that Conrad is the natural successor.

Also he feels resentment: Just at the point when my life is becoming carefree, a heavy hand has been clapped on my shoulder. It's not fair.

They are going out together for the first time. Emily has booked the restaurant. She says she likes restaurants that are fun. Fun means loud and busy and in Chelsea. Everyone knows her at this restaurant and he feels a little foolish – the new boyfriend – yet sadly proud to be out with someone so lovely. She and her friends speak in a dialect known only in Chelsea. If they are not speaking to each other they are keeping their friends informed by mobile. This life demands a kind of upbeat casualness, as though thoughtfulness is only for brainboxes and losers. There can be no quiet moments: life is filled with parties and tequila slammers and dope and sex and dinners and spur-of-the-moment flights to see chums. These people are all wildly happy until they go off to rehab. Emily has a kind of sexual openness, which men recognise instantly. They go back to the flat in Camden much later. She thinks Camden is quaint and exotic, as one might a slum in Mombasa. As soon as they get through the door she starts to roll a joint; she has all the gear, a little box and papers. She finishes the joint neatly and seals it with a lick of saliva. Then she draws deeply and blows the smoke and her moist breath into his mouth and kisses him at the same time. He wonders what she thinks about when she's not busy in this way and he can't imagine. As he inhales he wonders if it is skunk, but he thinks it would be uncool to ask. At five in the morning, she leaves.

When he wakes, he finds a letter from the Bundesarchiv in Berlin. He opens it and reads:

Dear Mr Senior

Enclosed you will find a letter sent to the Archive in response to my enquiries which I posted on a film website for you in relation to the Wochenschau film you must try to locate. This gentleman, Mr Ernst Fritsch, has responded with enclosed letter, which I have sended to you. He is unknown to this department, but it can be a possibility for your research. With good wishes. (Miss) G. Eberhardt (Archiv: Film Assistant)

He reads the enclosed letter, which is typed on an old-fashioned typewriter. He translates as best he can, using his Cassell's dictionary:

> I am responding to the request for information required by an English television researcher, Mr Senior, concerning the Wochenschau films made on the orders of the Reichs Director of Film by the Firm Wochenschau in the year of 1944 at the People's Court and Berlin-Plötzensee Prison. I was an assistant cameraman at Wochenschau in those days, and it is possible I may be able to help with the research you have mentioned, concerning Count von Gottberg.
>     I am unfortunately unwell, so if Mr Senior wishes to speak with me I would advise some haste. Please ask this gentleman to write to this address explaining the nature of his interest in more detail and I will respond when I am able to do so. With all good wishes,
> Ernst Fritsch.

Conrad has almost forgotten his enquiry to the archive. Now, six or seven months later, this letter comes from a cameraman. He wants to write to Fritsch immediately but he has to leave for Soho to meet Francine. Events, inexplicably, are gathering force and congesting. (He remembers as a child his disbelief when he was told that thunder and lightning could curdle milk.) How quickly a world can change. He wonders what Ernst Fritsch wants. Probably money. His address is in Prenzlauer Berg, which used to be in the old East Berlin, the territory of the thriller.

Emily left at some time in the night without warning; there are mysterious demands on her time. But she left behind for a while the lingering scents of her presence; everyone has their own. When his mother died, he used to go to her wardrobe to smell her clothes. He was surprised to read years later that this is quite common amongst the bereaved.

When he arrives at Bar Italia, he remembers that it was in Frith Street, not twenty metres away, that Elizabeth Partridge and Elya Mendel met, and she told him about her visit to Sachsenhausen. They didn't know then that more than fifty thousand were to be hanged or gassed or that Nazi officials were invited to attend a demonstration of a more efficient killing facility, and watched ninety-six Jews being killed more efficiently to prove it; nor that the camp commander was ordered in 1945 to remove the remaining forty thousand prisoners in barges and sink them in the Baltic. In the event tens of thousands died on a forced march East.

Conrad sits on one of the high stools with a croissant and a cappuccino, the best in London, produced by an old Gaggia. Soon he sees Francine peering in. He stands up and goes to the door and kisses her briefly.

'What would you like?'

'What are you having?'

'A cappuccino and a croissant.'

'I'll have an espresso. Single.'

When he brings over the espresso they sit in silence for a few moments. He looks at her to see if there is any obvious change.

'What do you think?' she asks finally.

'Firstly, I am terribly sorry it didn't work out with John.'

'Not even a little bit pleased?'

'No.'

'That's sweet of you.'

'Do you still love him?'

'I never loved him. I just wanted a better life. Things were getting on top of me.'

'Including John.'

'Ho, ho. Same old Conrad. No, I felt desperate.'

154

He looks at her face; under the neon it is pale and wary. The familiar face that spent nearly ten years next to his and then positioned itself next to John's. The essence of a relationship is located here, in the face. That is why whores never kiss. It's odd that the sexual organs are the focus of attention in pornography, when kissing is a far more intimate activity. The Romans knew that. When Emily put her tongue in his mouth that first night, he was shocked and thrilled.

'It's not because of you. I was overwhelmed. But it is because of you that John and I have split up. He asked me if I still loved you, and I said yes. I couldn't lie. I realised it that day after all, but I was too stubborn to tell you.'

'Ah, that last, mythical day.'

'Don't mock.'

'Can I say one thing about this baby?'

'Please.'

She looks ready for a blow.

'Nothing should be decided on the basis of who the father is. Is that possible, anyway, to find out?'

'Not really. Not at this stage.'

'Presumably at this stage abortion, termination, is relatively simple?'

'Yes.'

She looks down at the counter.

'Fran, I mean it. Whatever you decide, it's not going to be because it is or isn't mine. One thing is sure, it's yours.'

'OK.'

'And?'

'I can't decide. I so want a baby. But as we know, it's not simple.'

'Because I am a wastrel and you have a career.'

'No, Conrad. I don't think that. Maybe I never did. I just thought you sort of disregarded me. Who is your new girlfriend?'

'She's just someone I met. She's called Emily. Trust me, it's not going to last. It was just a reaction. She thinks I am good-looking and I'm grateful.'

'You are good-looking.'

'And you are beautiful.'

'I am fading fast.'

'Just give me a couple of days to think it over and then we must decide what to do.'

'We?'

'We always wanted to have a child.'

'Oh Conrad.'

She is crying. He holds her hand. She looks so miserable, so crushed, that he feels his own eyes welling.

'What a pair we are,' he says.

There is kickboxing on the giant television screen at the end of the bar. He watches determinedly.

'I could do locum work until the baby is born.'

'Whoa. You're the one with the career path, remember.'

'Conrad, I have to tell you how dreadfully sorry I am for what's happened. All I can say is that it has been a terrible, terrible mistake. I don't expect anything from you. I don't deserve it, but I had to tell you face to face. I've got to go now.'

The colour is rising on her throat.

'Franny, always rushing.'

They walk up Frith Street hand in hand as they used to. But Conrad knows that nothing will ever be truly the same. He stops himself from pointing out the spot where Mendel and Elizabeth met to talk about Axel von Gottberg.

They turn into Greek Street. As she releases his hand, he feels this uncoupling deeply, the feeling you have when sex is finished, a symbolic separation which (the pain of the past minutes has made him extremely sensitive to these emotions) seems to speak of mortality, because each separation, each parting, depletes the material that binds you together. You know that you can never gather up the shards of innocence and blitheness to make something whole. And this, rather than the moment of death itself, is probably the meaning of mortality. He reaches over to kiss her, but she half ducks away from him and his lips just brush her cheek.

She turns suddenly under an arch, and she is gone. Is she going now to talk to John to tell him she is pregnant? It could be John's baby, after all. He can't bear the idea that she may have conceived with John's sperm. But nature is coldly undiscriminating; you can conceive a baby by a rapist or with a whore or in a one-night stand. What Mendel, who was eating lunch just there with Elizabeth sixty-five years ago, knew is that there is no generous intelligence at large in nature or anywhere else. At that time, just a few years before his death, Axel von Gottberg still kept faith with the idea of spirit making its way in the world of beings and things towards some conclusion. *The chaste, clear, barbarian eye*, as Stefan George the poet put it, could see these things.

As Axel sat with Elizabeth gazing at the electrified fence, the tower, the prison blocks of Sachsenhausen, had he realised at last what he was up against in this world?

Was it possible for them to imagine what was coming? Mendel discovered very early on that awful things were in process, while von Gottberg still chose to believe in the new order that was coming in Germany. But did he lose his faith outside Sachsenhausen? Did he forsake the *fable of blood and desire?* After Elizabeth rejected him, after his Oxford friends turned away, and after the FBI trailed him in Washington, Axel von Gottberg came back to Germany and later that year, four weeks after war was declared, married Dietlof Goetz's sister, Liselotte, in the Pleskow village church. All the foresters and cowmen still left on the estate, formally dressed, and the village women and children in their Sunday clothes, formed a guard of honour and threw flowers from their gardens in their way as Wicht the coachman drove them from the church to the house in the shooting brake, which was garlanded with flowers. Pulling the brake were the black and grey horses, Donner and Blitz.

In the pictures von Gottberg looks happy enough. Axel's best man is his brother, Berndt, who was to describe him as a traitorous dog less than four years later. Berndt has a duelling scar beside his mouth, which seems comical, even absurd to Conrad. Von Gottberg's father is not present, but in the formal wedding photograph his sisters and his mother sit on either side of the bride and groom, with scores of relatives all around. Upper-class people have extensive family ties, and their members are summoned for these occasions: like tastefully dressed migratory birds, they obey the summons. Within two months Liselotte is pregnant.

Everyone who has children says your life changes, nothing prepares you for the reality. But also having children can be self-centred. Some of Conrad's friends imagine that they have become creators, they have been trusted to keep the sacred flame alight: *zeugen*, to beget, which was a big idea with the German poets. They would beget a new society.


Later that afternoon before Emily has to go to pick up the children from school, which Conrad imagines is besieged every afternoon by huge four-wheel-drive vehicles until the tiny hostages are released, showered with lavish praise and equipped with their suspiciously accomplished works of art, she comes to the flat above the bakery. She is drunk.

'I had lunch with an old chum,' she explains cheerfully.

She has to take a phone call in the middle of their love-making. She is lying on her side and he is behind her. The shape of her back and thighs seems to be expressly formed for this. The conversation is short and tense. Quickly she gets up and dresses.

'Sorry, got to go. Love ya loads,' she says, fastening her skirt and then running her hands through her hair.

She bangs the door shut. Perhaps one of the children is ill or perhaps the mysterious Dion requires something of her. His penis has responded modestly, by retreating into itself. It's a defensive posture. Very strange how it seems not wholly dependent, like a small country whose foreign affairs are managed by a bigger, more sensible state. Like Andorra or Monaco or San Marino.

Conrad considers his life, so changed in a few days. He is sexually involved with a whacked Chelsea girl (girl-woman would be more accurate); his wife is pregnant and hoping for reconciliation; it is possible he is a father. Also a man called Ernst Fritsch claims to have knowledge of the film of Axel von Gottberg being hanged. There is no obvious link between any of these facts. The flat has been quiet for weeks, just the papers and letters moving and drifting, but now the place is the focus of energy, like those lay lines that new-age folk believe bisect the country at key places.

When he comes back with some milk and stamps, Tony steps out.

'Your bird was in a hurry.'

'She had to pick up her son from school.'

'She weren't properly dressed, you dog.'

'Jesus, Tony. Stick to baking.'

'Hehwah. I've got a nice focaccia for you. You got to keep your stremf up, mate.'

In Tony's eyes he's gone from recluse to dirty dog: Fuck a rat, it's the quiet ones you gotta watch out for.

The Bangladeshi who owns the corner shop is growing a beard. On the early evidence the plan seems to be to grow it straight down and untended in the religious fashion; back in the flat he wonders why it is that people are always looking for the incorrigible proposition. He remembers Mendel telling him that he took great comfort from the idea that life has no meaning. It frees you from irrational practices, like growing a beard as a billboard for your views.

Emily's Holly Golightly behaviour does not trouble him. For the moment the arrangement, unclear though it is, suits him fine. She calls, very cheerful, and suggests they carry on later where they left off.

'OK. I'm just going through the papers. I may have to go to Berlin soon.'

'Cool. They have some great clubs there. They really, really know how to party.'

In her world cities have no historical or artistic resonance; they are simply places to go and get mashed. Having a laugh is an imperative for these people: they fall off ski lifts; they run their jet-skis on to coral after too many rum punches. And they get off their faces in clubs in Berlin. So he imagines.

He starts writing a letter to Mr Fritsch, using his dictionary. He intends to say that he would be very much interested in meeting Mr Fritsch to discuss the filming both of the People's Court and the executions. Could Mr Fritsch suggest a suitable place to meet? He will discuss financial matters when he knows what Mr Fritsch is suggesting. He wants to check his German with a friend, but he decides he must keep his enquiries secret. He writes:

*Sehr Geehrter Herrn Fritsch, Ich bedanke ihnen für ihre Brief. Das ist für mir, wie historicher Forscher, sehr bedeutend. Darf ich bei ihnen in Berlin eine Besuch machen? Wenn sie für mich etwas zeigen kann, dan kann wir über Finanzen besprechung. Mit freundlichen Grüssen.*

Conrad thinks it is important to mention money right away: he imagines Ernst Fritsch in an East Berlin tenement desperate for some cash. As a Nazi he would not have received a pension and life in the new Germany is hard for the Ossis anyway. He seals the envelope and goes out again to post it, hoping it is not too full of errors.

He remembers Mendel writing that to be understood you have to share a common language and have the possibility of intimate communication. By the time war broke out, it seems that the plea von Gottberg had made for trust was misunderstood. But also it became starkly apparent that he and Mendel shared neither a common past nor common feelings.

# 15

WHEN BRITAIN AND France declared war on Germany on 3 September 1939, Oxford lost colour. It faded like an old carpet. For Elya Mendel the finer points of academic philosophy seemed not only trivial, but even ridiculous now. Other young dons were leaving town as officers, but he was not able to apply because of his foreign birth. He tried to take up the Foreign Office's offer of work, but they seemed to have forgotten him. He waited in Oxford, reporting to the Town Hall to roll bandages and check gas masks while the Foreign Office went through its checks. His birth in Riga was a handicap. He thought of moving to the United States; he was frightened of what might happen to him if the Nazi invasion took place. He wrote to Hamburger suggesting that some institution might be persuaded to employ him.

It was a miserable winter. His rooms were always cold and Oxford, despite Lionel's crazed bonhomie, appeared to be sinking into depression. Then he received a letter from the Foreign Office saying that it did not wish to employ him in any capacity. For a week he remained in bed. But – as Conrad sees so often in the correspondence – some important figure intervened on his behalf and he was asked to go to London after all to advise the Russian section. He wrote to Hamburger that he was scared of bombs, but went to work in London with joy. He had been shaken by his rejection, which was the confirmation of his foreignness even though he was a fellow of All Souls.

*My parents saw All Souls as their own acceptance in England. I haven't dared tell them that my first six years in Riga have returned me to the ranks of the alien. Nothing like a war for the noxious gases to seep out of the cracks.*

There is no mention of von Gottberg. The start of war was evidently the end of understanding. It may have been convenient, in the same way that families can forget after a bereavement, each member seeing for their own reasons an opportunity for an overdue dissolution of ties, something that happened at high speed when Conrad's mother died. He thinks that for Mendel the threat to the Jews was sufficient reason to forget his old pal. It was a threat that von Gottberg had fostered in a small way with his ill-advised letter. Von Gottberg was aware that he had lost Mendel's cherished esteem and he almost certainly knew that Mendel had briefed against him in Washington.

Conrad, living in the mouse-nibbled margins of London just a few minutes from great wealth and imposing solidity, sees the city not as home, but as a huge agglomeration of human frailty and greed, held in uneasy suspension. We live by assumptions which in reality we know nothing of, but our faith is as firm as that of religious fundamentalists. War demonstrates – perhaps it's designed to demonstrate – that we should not take any assumptions for granted. Elya Mendel was particularly sensitive to the terrible possibilities of history, while for von Gottberg six hundred uninterrupted years in Pleskow must have suggested something entirely different. For a Jew, six hundred settled years are an eternity.

Conrad has never felt settled in London. Wherever his home is, it is not here. London is too big, too burdened, to be held in the mind whole. He doesn't really know how planets work, but he sees London as a gaseous body bound together in some mysterious fashion like a planet.

The mystery of Emily's life is being revealed: Dion, who calls menacingly, is her drugs counsellor. He is himself a recovering addict. Crack was his downfall, apparently. Emily thinks of drug addictions as somehow honourable, a sign of higher striving. Dion has become a zealot for living clean, as he puts it. He has a hold over Emily, established when she was in rehab. She probably had sex with him; she seems to have had a lot of sex. In theory it doesn't worry him, but in practice he finds he wants to know not how many she has slept with, but on what basis she makes her choices. Their first encounter suggests that she doesn't need much evidence at all. What was it she saw, or glimpsed, in him? Whacked though she is, he has become very fond of her. Her calm, practical sexual expertise is at odds with her girlish, upbeat manner. It's as though all the categories in her world have blurred, so that life is now one long, looped film containing sex, drink, marijuana, ex-boyfriends, music, inchoate creative impulses – poetry, screenplays, painting are mentioned – all these melding into a whole that keeps revolving seamlessly.

And sometimes at night Conrad finds that his picture of the People's Court is like that too, played endlessly, as von Gottberg stands with his hands crossed speaking calmly and quietly, crossing his hands again, then speaking calmly again. These few minutes go round and round and they are unbearable because Conrad knows and von Gottberg knows that if the film stops he will be slowly hanged from a meat-hook, whatever he says, however considerate his demeanour. But something sustains von Gottberg and makes him calm. Even though he has small children and a young wife, and despite the fact that he has been tortured. And this is a mystery.

While von Gottberg was establishing himself in Berlin, his new wife stayed at Pleskow. She was welcomed by the family, especially warmly by von Gottberg's older sister, Adelheid, whose first marriage ended when her Jewish husband went insane in New York. He had been taken to Bellevue one night after he set their apartment on the Upper East Side alight. Adelheid told her new sister-in-law that the sight of her husband in handcuffs being pushed into a Black Maria had broken her heart. A financial blunder had unhinged him. At least he wasn't going to come back to Germany to face another kind of madness. Adi had visited him in Bellevue where he sat silent. Axel had visited him more recently in New York and reported that he did not recognise him. The doctors had given him a new treatment, electro-convulsive therapy.

Von Gottberg took a small flat near the zoo and sometimes, when he had to go to the main building in Wilhelmstrasse, walked the whole length of the Tiergarten, passing at last beneath the quadriga on the Brandenburg Gate. He went back to Pleskow when he could, taking the train to Schwerin to be met by the coachman; or sometimes he drove up in his car. His spirits always lifted as the house came into view, firstly across the lake, and then as they turned into the drive, by the oaks and the huge barns. The first thing he did when it was not too cold was to swim in the lake. The water had a unique taste and smelled of gently decomposing vegetable matter and aquatic plants, a scent that took him instantly to his childhood. Lake water, his own lake too. Next to the bathing hut was a wooden tea-house and there he and Liselotte, his mother and his sisters would meet over English tea. Liselotte said that there was always laughter and music although Axel was gloomy about the war. The panzer rush through Belgium and into France would make it more difficult to remove Hitler, he said.

Von Gottberg's life in Berlin was increasingly dangerous as he sought out others – there were many – who thought that Hitler was steering the beloved country to disaster. But he enjoyed the danger; he was a young man, plotting to save his country; he found the late-night discussions with like-minded colleagues in the Foreign Office and the Army and his meetings with Helmuth James von Moltke and his circle, his *Kreis*, exhilarating. He was forming the idea of an alternative Germany of spiritually conscious people, enlightened Germany, which would inherit when Hitler was gone. His friends in England did not understand; they wished to crush Nazi Germany into the dust. But they didn't realise that by saying this they were offering the German people no option but to stick with Hitler. He couldn't tell his family the details, but he was travelling to Sweden and Switzerland to pass on to the governments of Britain and America the information that there was an opposition that should be encouraged. He also passed on plans of annexations and invasions. Meanwhile, more and more reports of brutal killings by *Einsatzgruppen* were coming out and these too were passed on. In the spring von Gottberg went again to Sweden to met an English bishop, with details of the opposition in the Army and the Foreign Office, for onward transmission to Churchill. Soon after he met a young officer called Claus von Stauffenberg and reported to Liselotte that he had at last found a true friend.

The two cities, London and Berlin, where the old friends now found themselves, were sexually charged by war. With death in the air, sex scuttles in to fill the vacuum. Women stopped wearing hats all of a sudden, as if hats were keeping them down. Hair and sex became synonymous. Von Gottberg believed that casual sex with other men's wives or with girls he picked up in nightclubs or with waitresses in Kurfürstendamm did not count as adultery. And in London, Mendel found that he could translate his charm and urbanity into sexual activity. Women were liberated by the sense that the old world, for better or for worse, was finished. *Kaputt*.

Von Gottberg was working under enormous danger right from the beginning. He was never able to write a letter or use the phone or tell the names of his closest friends to other friends, for fear that when the reckoning came they would tell all. It was quite different in Whitehall, where Mendel treated his fortnightly digest of Russian intelligence as an essay. Very soon colleagues were talking of the brilliance and wit of his observations about Russian intentions; without demonstrating too much learning – never a good idea – he was able to suggest from his deep knowledge of Russian literature and history how the Russians would react.

In the Kreisau Circle there were endless arguments on matters of principle about whether Hitler could legitimately be killed, and about the attitude of the members to the threat from the East and the composition of the new government. Von Gottberg warned of the dangers of trying to restore a monarchy, or of allowing the proposed putsch to be the property of the *Alte Herren* of the Army and the aristocracy. England would not be keen on such a thing, he said. He was probably remembering Mendel's warning about the high-handed member of the Prussian aristocracy who had visited Oxford and caused outrage. Von Gottberg tended to see England and Oxford as the same thing.

Conrad sits above the bakery waiting for Fritsch. If Fritsch has anything for him he will go immediately to Berlin. What happens next depends on Fritsch. This old man – he pictures Fritsch as a sickly, shabby figure, trying to make a few euros out of his sordid past – may have the film or may know where it is. If he has been harbouring it for all these years it is probably only because of a sense of shame that he has not tried to sell it before. After all, he saw men being hanged. Or perhaps Fritsch is finding that his old mind is like a shallow boat, mostly gliding undisturbed, but occasionally touching on something submerged. Germany is full of people who would rather not remember. But then, Conrad's father was one of those too. Forgetting the unpleasant is a natural defence, probably Darwinian, and the belief of Freud's bastard children in recovering memory is utterly contrary to nature.

For more than a week he has rushed down for the post, but still there is no word from Fritsch. Meanwhile a child is growing within Francine, and it may be his child. Von Gottberg had three very young children when he was hanged. They were three, two and nine months old. It must have occurred to Mendel when he knew all the facts and when he met Liselotte for the first time in the seventies that nobody sacrifices himself recklessly if he has children. And now Conrad tries to imagine himself as a father.

He leaves the flat, hoping to avoid Tony, who has an unnatural interest in his new sex life. He can see him in his white coat, with his back turned, and tries stealthily opening the door to the street, which they share. The door has an electric buzzer attached, which makes secrecy impossible.

'You look a bit pale. Keeping your stremf up?'

'Tony, you have turned from the king of Camden's artisan bakers, maybe the only one, a legend in the field of farinaceous products, to a pervert. For Christ sakes keep out of it.'

'Orright, orright. Keep your 'air on, mate. I'm just joshing. You're a lucky bunny, that's all I'm saying, no more. That's it, *basta*. No offence?'

'I didn't take offence, it's just that I am beginning to feel persecuted. I can't go out of my own fucking front door without you or your little pal leering at me.'

'We're just jealous. Good luck to yer. And if you need some more fuel when you come home, there's loads of olive bread left over.'

'Oh Jesus. Bye-bye, Tony. Don't wait up.'

He is off to meet Emily. But passing the decrepit church on the corner just past the minicab office and the shop selling rubber-foam shapes – do-it-yourself furniture – he turns into the over-grown churchyard and towards the Victorian church. It has a tall steeple, not soaring but workmanlike, the sort of job you got for limited money in 1862. The porch smells of urine. Inside it is vast and unseasonably cold. He kneels on the floor and folds his hands across his face, in case anybody should be watching. There is some movement over to the right beyond a pillar and he sees between his fingers a man sitting on a pew eating something quickly and surreptitiously, like a dog picking up rubbish in the park. He hasn't been in a church on his own for years, although of course he's been to a few weddings and christenings. Guiltily he remembers his two god-children, who he has neglected criminally. He has never sent either of them a single present.

Mendel, who was an atheist, believed that religion should stick to its guns: the precepts of religion could not be altered at will.

And me? What do I believe?

He closes his eyes and tries to re-create the feeling of his few religious years at boarding school in Cape Town. The feeling was genuine, but was it, in any meaningful way, real? And, to his surprise, he finds he can re-create the feeling in part, through the physical: the pew against his buttocks (which Emily described, gratifyingly, as 'lovely tight buns') and the feel of stone under his knees and the sense that above his head there is a lot of unused, significant space. Religious space. The essence of religion is thought to live up there somewhere, although it can be lured into the heart by the bait of good behaviour.

And he thinks of fucking Emily. He can't bring himself in the privacy of his own head to use any other word. He counts the number of times they have fucked and at the same time he keeps his head buried in his hands in deference to the location. Fourteen. He is now very familiar with the topography of her body. In restaurants she encourages him to put his hand under her skirt; she parts her thighs briefly. She is always smoking or drinking or licking the paper on a joint. She doesn't eat much although she always orders a large plate of fries. She needs to fiddle, to handle, to taste, to suck. She is thin, but – he remembers a phrase in a Hemingway novel – made for sex. Tony and his lightly powdered chum recognise it. But now he must break it off. He's not sure she will mind; she'll move on fast and probably without regret; after all he remembers how they met. But he can't be having sex with her and deal fairly and squarely with Francine at the same time.

He says the words of the Lord's Prayer to his atheist self and remembers just how beautiful they are. Most of the hanged in Plötzensee were able to have last messages smuggled out. All these messages had a religious tone. Von Gottberg's, if he wrote one, was lost, to his wife's great distress. This need to believe, this need to profess some faith in something – God or decency or asceticism or conscience or homeopathy or country or the special qualities of animals or the Prophet's Night Ride or the imminence of a new order – is a curse. As he kneels there he sees that to confess to believing in nothing ultimately is to accept mortality unreservedly, which very few people are really prepared to do, although they know that the tide of death can only rise.

The man who was eating stops in front of the altar and crosses himself. Perhaps he was not eating but self-administering the host. He scowls competitively at Conrad as he passes. Conrad is now completely alone in this huge dark space. Water has seeped into the stone over the years, so that the pews and the hymnbooks feel musty. There is the whiff of mushrooms in the air. He stands up and walks towards the entrance. He sees a table with candles, none of them lit. *You may light a candle to bear witness if you make a voluntary donation.* He puts a pound in the box. It lands with a wooden noise that suggests that not many people have been bearing witness. Matches are provided, which could be seen as an invitation to an arsonist, although it would be hard to start a fire in this dampness. He lights a candle. The word witness, which the Church finds exciting, is puzzling. The way the Church intends it, it means to profess your faith openly. But it can mean to sacrifice yourself. His candle is in remembrance of his father. *Love cools, friendship falls off, brothers divide: in cities mutinies; in countries discord, in palaces treason; and the bond cracked 'twixt son and father . . .*

And he tells himself as he leaves the church that his cheap candle flickering in the dark is to restore the bond between son and father, even at this late hour.

When he meets Emily she is already drunk. She is with three friends, a young man and two girls, which makes him uneasy. She is sitting on a stool with a cigarette in one hand. Her denim skirt is halfway up her thighs. She introduces him to her friends and they pour him a glass of wine. The friends are like amiable

Labradors. They are simply waiting to see where the drink and the dope and the night will take them. They make noises that he can't fully understand. They whoop and laugh. He can in fact get the words, but he finds it hard to discern any sentences. They talk about friends who got mashed or arrested or crashed their cars – *whoop, whoop* – but it is never clear where or in what order these things have happened. They are unnaturally loud. The two girls have flat, bare stomachs and their breasts demand attention, not by being buxom or womanly, but by having a kind of life of their own, small lascivious creatures, barely under control.

'Emily?'

'Yuh?'

'Can I talk to you for a moment?'

'Go ahead.'

'Just you and me. Outside.'

'OK.'

She places a hand on his shoulder and slides off the bar stool, unsure of the whereabouts of the floor. He can see that she is wearing red knickers. When they are standing outside she kisses him.

'I can't stay, Em. I've got a problem. I'm going now.'

She isn't taking it in.

'Give me a bell when you're free. I don't know where we will be.'

'OK.'

'Love you a bunch.'

She stands on the pavement unsteadily. She's like a mountaineer at very high altitude: the air outside is too thin to sustain her. There is a tragic lapse before she gathers herself and goes happily back into the pub.

He walks down to the river and phones Francine. It is just dark enough for the lights on the embankment to show on the water, which is running full and dark. Francine doesn't answer, but he leaves a message.

'Fran, I would like you to come back, if that's what you want. And I think we should have the baby. I've told Emily I am not seeing her again, whatever.'

Although, of course, Emily has no idea.

# 16

FRANCINE, HE HAS realised, doesn't fully believe him. She thinks that this is just another of the delusions he has lived by for so long. She thinks, despite everything, despite the scale of her betrayal, that he is the unreliable one. Let's take it one step at a time, she says. She will do locum work and stay where she is until she is sure he is sure. She would also like to know if there is going to be an end to his work on Mendel's papers.

'Do you mean you would like to see me employed?'

'If we have the baby, I won't be able to work for six months and when I do go back to work, you won't want to be sitting at home all day looking after a baby and working on your papers at the same time. So yes, it would be better if you had a job and we could afford a nanny.'

Over this conversation hangs a conditional, which he can't contemplate: the existence or non-existence of a baby.

'Fran, we are going to have the baby. As for Mendel and his papers, I am going to follow this right through. I'm waiting now for a man called Fritsch to contact me. He may have some vital information. I know what you are thinking. But I can't tell you the nature of the information, it's not secret or anything, but I just feel I have to explore it myself. And then I'll know where this is leading.'

'Conrad, you must do whatever it is you think you have to. I've learned that lesson. All I am concerned with is the practical arrangements.'

It's not true of course. She's concerned with far more; even now, chastened, almost embarrassingly humbled, she is weighing up his reliability. She has had her hair cut, as if to suggest that she is shriven; although he said how much he liked it and how young it made her look, he was shocked. In fact she looks older and gaunt, even slightly potty. He remembers her walking hand in hand with John near the hospital, her hair incandescent – her hair was in love – and he sees this act of contrition as a realisation that she has to accept her lot: he is part of her climb-down. She must accept the unreliable, useless husband, indulging himself as usual. He sees the simulacrum of their relationship increasingly often amongst friends and acquaintances: the wife whose success and determination license the husband for a life of futility. It is a phenomenon of the new century. And often these house husbands drink or say they are writing a novel or profess to love children or they make furniture or sleep with the nanny. Has Mendel given me these papers to unman me? But then he thinks of Mendel in old age, with those small dark eyes, which appeared to consist only of irises, sitting in his collapsed chair, dressed in a three-piece suit, talking about Conrad's thesis and gently suggesting books he should read and opening his mind – how banal but how literal a phrase – to something extraordinary, a very personal but also wide-ranging understanding of human aspirations and longings. He remembers, as if it were spoken five minutes before, Mendel telling him that mankind's greatest delusion is the belief that one day the world will arrive at an ideal state of affairs, a heaven on earth where all values will be in harmony and all problems will be solved. Not only does he remember the words, he hears the way Mendel spoke them, with just a trace of his immigrant origins – a sort of East European warble in the vowels lingered in the oddly patrician English.

He had told Mendel that day that he had learned about his father taking money from the National Party to print stories about Mandela and the ANC that were untrue.

*Conrad, in times of great stress, of historic upheaval, people react in unpredictable ways. All I can say to you is that, in my experience, people under these circumstances are desperate to share the possibility of intimate communications. From what you have told me about your father, I would guess that he was expressing his understanding of the nature of truth. However personally disadvantageous, he seems to have decided that he could not subscribe to the idea that a heaven on earth was about to be ushered in.*

Conrad did not ask him to be more precise. He took this to mean that Mendel was suggesting that his father wanted to be true to something irreducible. He couldn't embrace another myth, another set of lies. And that was more or less exactly what his father, mad-eyed in the empty cottage, told Conrad a few years later. He sitting alone beneath his blue-and-red Balliol blade, *Bumped Ch Ch, Trinity, Pembroke, Wadham, 1959.* Conrad noted the names and weights of the crew, all recorded reverentially on the blade. His father asked Conrad not to contact him again under any circumstances. Conrad boarded the small train at Clovelly Station, the first step on his journey back to England, his heart broken.

No, Mendel wanted to draw him fully into the understanding of how things really work in history, among humans: what it means to be one of these creatures in a time of confusion and moral turmoil. And Mendel wanted him to try to understand what von Gottberg had done, which perhaps he hadn't fully understood himself. He wasn't expecting an answer, of course, only requiring that Conrad never cease from exploring this and other mysteries.

Shelley wrote in his *Defence of Poetry* that poets are hierophants – he had to look the word up – priests who carry the sacred knowledge from one generation to another. If he told Francine that he was carrying some sacred spark, she might have him sectioned. Doctors are entitled to do this.

He's waiting for Fritsch. In the meanwhile on a large chart

attached to a wall with Blu-tack, he is filling in von Gottberg's known movements. He sees patterns: he is in Berlin, meeting friends at the Romanisches Café, the Adlon and the Foreign Press Association, as he establishes himself in the Auswärtiges Amt at 137 Kurfürstendamm, which is the information and research department, as an expert on England. There he finds many like-minded people, who believe that Germany is being led to disaster. Increasingly often he has meetings with Helmuth James von Moltke; there are reports that they argue fiercely. He also finds that the generals, who have it in their power to end this madness, are unable to act decisively, although after the Russian campaign and more than a million German deaths they all see that the writing is on the wall. All except for the C-in-C, the Führer. He is living in a Wagnerian world.

Von Gottberg feels an overwhelming desire to tell the English the true story, that Germany is chaotic and that there is another Germany, which needs encouragement to forsake Hitler. Claus von Stauffenberg, who at the beginning came back from France exalted by military success, has returned from the East with 10 Panzer Division saying that the time has come for the secret Germany to assert itself. The generals have failed the people: the colonels must act. According to von Stauffenberg, the secret Germany is a nobler place with its roots deep in the past, deep in the forests. Its prophet is the poet Stefan George; von Stauffenberg and his brothers see themselves even now as carrying on George's task. He recites George's poem, 'The Antichrist', to von Gottberg in a flat liturgical way, the way the Master ordained:

*You will hang out your tongues, but the trough will be drained*
*You will stampede like cattle whose barn is on fire*
*And dreadful will be the blast of the last trumpet.*

The last trumpet had sounded at Stalingrad. Our armies, he said, were like a puff of wind on the steppes.

To his sister Adelheid, von Gottberg describes von Stauffenberg as a classical hero. He tells her that von Stauffenberg had once thought that, after winning the Russian campaign, the Army would be able to turn its attention to the SS. For the German nobility, Himmler is in many ways worse than Hitler. It is Himmler's *Einsatzgruppen* that have turned the people of Eastern Europe, potential allies in the war with Russia, against Germany.

As the war progressed von Gottberg travelled to Switzerland and to Sweden four or five times. But nobody listened. The Allies had already decided that anything less than unconditional surrender could not be contemplated. And, anyway, after his visit to Washington and his meeting with Hamburger, he was not taken seriously. Mendel had destroyed his credibility.

Mendel may occasionally have heard of von Gottberg's doomed efforts, or read his messages sent via the World Council of Churches and Swedish clerics and American journalists. Von Gottberg had a meeting with Allen Dulles in Berne, and a meeting with a British agent in Stockholm who advised him that the British Government would take the resistance more seriously if it produced results. Although von Gottberg wrote from Geneva and Stockholm to Elizabeth Partridge, there are no letters to Mendel.

By the end of 1943 von Gottberg has a son and a daughter and his wife is pregnant again, but he is unable to spend much time at Pleskow where his wife and children are kept company by his sister Adelheid and his mother. The effects of war have finally reached Pleskow, where the estate is neglected and the medieval reverie is over.

The conspirators are a loose band, diplomats, army officers, religious leaders. They meet and they drink and they argue, but their plans come to nothing, until, with the arrival of von Stauffenberg, there is a new determination. Von Stauffenberg is fearless and utterly convinced. Unlike the generals, he has no qualms about repudiating his oath to the Führer. In his mind, the Führer is the Antichrist. He is tireless in recruiting, and he relies heavily on von Gottberg and others for advice about how to order the new Germany that is to follow the removal of Hitler. By the beginning of 1944, soon after von Stauffenberg is appointed to the General Staff, a plan is drawn up to use the Reserve Army's emergency plan, Valkyrie, designed to mobilise Berlin in the event of an insurrection, as the starting point of a putsch.

In April 1944, Elizabeth receives a letter from von Gottberg, suggesting a meeting in Stockholm. Her husband has been killed in a plane crash in West Africa, but it is not certain if von Gottberg knows this; he makes no mention of it. The letter is postmarked Geneva:

> *Elizabeth darling*
> *Please let us meet. I will be in Sweden for a few days in May. Can you find a way of meeting me there? Leave a message addressed to the concierge of the Grand Hotel. Ask him to hold it for Mr Axel arriving May 4th. Our love will survive. But I fear unless you can come to Stockholm, we won't meet in this world.*
> *A*

Elizabeth has written *No!* on the letter and underlined it. As he waits for Fritsch and fills in his chart Conrad sees where this life is leading: to the gallows. Meanwhile Mendel is having a fine time – often in Washington, close to the seat of power, his reports read by Churchill, his advice valued and sought. He has even met the woman he is to marry some years later.

Conrad and Francine go to the cinema together as they used to, to see a French film. It is not a good choice under the circumstances, the enigmatic story of a woman in her thirties who has an affair with a total stranger; they never exchange their names and meet once a month in one of those small French hotels that appear to have been made entirely of gloomy lacquered wood with darkly atmospheric corridors on time switches. Once they make love at excruciating length, for a film, in one of the corridors when the lights go out. He glances at Francine to see if she is suffering any painful recall, but her face is set, resigned, although in the gloom it is hard to tell exactly what her expression indicates. Eventually the lover fails to turn up for a rendezvous and the woman wanders around Paris, chic even in her despondency. At the end of the film the woman is seen eating lunch on the Ile de Ré with her husband and two silent children. Seafood, in abundance. Nothing is resolved.

'Bit of a downer,' he says over dinner at a Vietnamese restaurant.

'Yes, not a good choice. Sorry.'

'No personal resonances, I hope?'

'Don't go there. You know I feel utterly ashamed and foolish.'

'Will you move back in?'

'I want to, but I don't think it's right or fair. Although I am longing to put everything back. It's not fair on you. We must be sure.'

'How long have we got?'

'Oh, some weeks.'

Conrad hears the sound of a clock ticking loudly. It's the Westclox in his grandmother's kitchen, on the window ledge beneath the flypaper. His grandmother looked after him and his sister when his mother died and his father was so busy with the newspaper. Often in that house the sound of the clock ticking and the flies battering themselves futilely on the windowpanes or struggling in the flypaper was amplified unbearably by the heavy afternoon stillness. The clock is now ticking for his – or John's – child. The ticking is entering the silences he and Francine cannot fill.

She won't come back to the flat. She takes a bus and he sets off walking to Camden. He wonders if they can be truly reconciled with this business of the child hanging over them. If they have the child, will he look out for physical resemblances or demand a test? It's easy for him to be magnanimous now, because he has found himself on the high ground. She is waiting for him to make some decisive movement, but it is not clear to him what more he can do than to ask her to come back without conditions.

She is the one who needs to convince herself, but characteristically she is transferring her doubts to him. He walks past King's Cross where there is always a thin stream of human activity of the marginal variety; here it is possible for illegal immigrants to pick up fares in their clapped-out cars, for touts from cheap hotels to look for custom, for prostitutes, whose shoes and clothes and hair reek of despair, to linger. In dog kennels selling fried chicken and cut-price burgers, pimps and drug dealers gather. In all cities railway stations have an allure for the desperate: with their massive anonymity and twenty-four-hour life they are power-stations providing the wattage these people need to survive.

It takes him twenty minutes to walk home. When he gets there he sees a brown Manila envelope propped up against his door. He opens it cautiously, to find some printed papers with a note from a friend, Karin. He has forgotten that he asked her to do a translation for him from German.

> Dearest Conrad, I am so sorry this has taken me so long. I have been travelling. Hope it's not too late. You owe me one – well, dinner, anyway. Love Karin.

He takes the manuscript up to the flat and places it on the bed. Then he showers in the unpredictable shower, which stands in the corner of the bathroom, a cheap little construction they had planned to get rid of. The doors of the shower don't close properly – they are of Perspex – and the water is barely warm. When he comes out of the shower he looks at himself closely in the mirror. Since Emily – crazed, sexy, Emily – told him he was good-looking, he has taken to inspecting himself. What he sees is that his hair is no longer vibrant. In fact it looks like von Gottberg's at his trial, resigned. As to whether he is good-looking, he reserves judgement. He imagines a stranger looking at him and Francine silently eating sizzling prawns and trying to decide who they are or what they stand for or what they do, he with his thinning hair and she with her Lenten haircut. What would the verdict be? Two people who have taken a few knocks, certainly, but beyond that probably nothing remarkable: he sees that they have joined the mass of Londoners, who have had the edges knocked off them and have adapted to the anonymity that the city prefers; it's a wary city, not cynical, but without expectations.

He starts to read. Karin, it is soon clear, has taken the job seriously.

# 17

For my children and their children,
A memoir. Liselotte, Gräfin von
Gottberg, June, 1982

I MAY BE imagining it, but the sun was always shining that
last spring and summer. In my memory every day was beautiful.
Sunlight fell silver on the lake soon after dawn and before you
woke I would stand by the window in the music room – the
best view – looking across the water. The light reminded me of
my parents' summer house on the island of Poel, a Baltic light,
still misty and indistinct in the early hours. It's the light of
northern Europe, magical and mysterious. I always loved this
view of the lake, looking over the boat-house, the bathing hut
and the tea-house, across to the village, the church and the windmill.

Your father was so busy that last year, those last terrible
months. One day in May he telephoned to say that he had a few
days' leave and that an important visitor would be staying for
the night. It was your second birthday, Angela, which he had
promised he would not miss. Knowing that he would enjoy
driving in the dark-green shooting brake, I asked Wicht – do
you remember him? – to take it to the station. He harnessed the
black and grey horses, Donner and Blitz, and put on his best
cap, the one he kept especially for your father and your grandfather
before him. He raised his whip in salute to me and to your Aunt

Adi and trotted off towards the station. I wanted to go with them but we were preparing a welcome for your father as well as his important guest. Also I knew that he would enjoy the ride back from the station and a chat with Wicht, the chance to breathe in his beloved landscape, and revel in the sense of arriving back home [Karin has put a note here: She uses the word *Heimat*, which is of course for more evocative than 'home'], catching sight of the house just before the road dips and you are lost in the trees for the final run to the park gates. There are certain places and certain sights in a life that raise one's spirits. For forty years I have thought about this place every day. And I know that never a day went by without your father dreaming about the lake and the house and the woods. He once said that as soon as he entered the avenue of oaks, planted by your great-grandfather, he felt true peace. In fact I think he felt that peace as soon as he plunged into the lake, which was the first thing he usually did, preferably naked.

It was nearly eleven when we heard the sound of the brake outside. Robert was in his sailor suit from Wertheim's and Angela, you were in your best frock. Puppi, you were still in Grandma's christening robe, I'm afraid. Aunt Adi was holding you. When they took the Jewish children away from the orphanage I burned the sailor suit. It was unbearable.

Suddenly there he was, so tall, so elegant in his grey suit, his hat pulled down and a brown travelling cape loosely over his shoulders, looking every inch [*Zoll für Zoll* – not an exact translation, K] the diplomat. He jumped from the brake and ran towards us. Robert began to cry: it was all too much for him. Dear Robert. Papi gathered us all in his arms.

'Swim, swim, let's swim,' he shouted. 'Wicht, bring the presents to the tea-room. Is tea laid?'

'Of course,' said Adi.

Your father and I pulled on our bathing suits. Babette held on to Robert and Angela, and your father carried Puppi into the water. How he loved you children. The air was soon ringing with laughter. We played hide and seek, with me carrying you, Puppi, and Robert and Angela stumbling around and trying to hide behind trees.

The tea was ready on the balcony in front of the tea-house. Although we had very little help now and supplies were short, we had made a special effort. Wrapped in a towel, his body white as a sheet, his face tired, so tired, still your father sang and told jokes and kissed you children. He was as gay and natural as ever, full of life and fun. I think it is true that this was the quality he possessed above all else that nobody could resist: the life-force ran so strongly in him. He shouted, 'What do we need for a harvest?' and you called out, *Rye, barley, wheat and oats, rye, barley and oats,* and then you sang one of your favourites, *I went through a grass green wood!* He had brought small gifts for all of us from Wertheim's and Israel's, beautifully wrapped as only they could in those days. Our friend, Wilfred Israel, had left the country before it was too late.

In the afternoon we had a small party for you, Angela, which you slept through. When you were all in bed your father said to me, 'Our guest tonight is Claus Schenk von Stauffenberg.' I had met Stauffenberg the year before in Berlin where he was regarded as a hero. At the time I thought he was a little naïve and vain in the old style, with his Iron Cross First Class and his cavalry uniform, but there was no denying his wonderful good looks.

'Don't be startled, he has lost an eye and a hand with Rommel in Tunisia since you last saw him. After we have given him something to eat, he and I must talk.'

And I knew then that it couldn't be long now.

When von Stauffenberg arrived at about ten, driven by his chauffeur (who had once been a professional magician), he came forward to greet me with so much charm and warmth that I was immediately won over. He had a black patch over his left eye, which increased his already considerable presence. We ate together and he talked of Shakespeare and Stefan George and Hölderlin. He seemed not to have a care on his mind. He had such enormous charm, such confidence that I really believed the great work could not fail. Your father and he had become very close friends. The right arm of his jacket was pinned to the pocket. The maids competed to cut up his food for him. In the kitchen the chauffeur was baffling Cook with card tricks. Von Stauffenberg called him in for our benefit. We, too, were baffled.

After dinner, although I longed to be alone with him, your father kissed me goodnight and said they would be talking very late. In fact they talked all night. They were planning the composition of the new government that was to take over when Hitler was killed, although I only discovered this much later. In the morning they swam and continued to talk in the tea-house and it was here that Werner H, the forester, who was later executed by the Allies, spied on them and reported to the *Gauleiter* in Schwerin. Werner's father and his father before him had worked on the estate, but loyalty counted for nothing in the madness of that time.

Von Stauffenberg did not come back into the house, but I saw him in the early dawn walking off to his car with your father round the side of the stables past the estate manager's house. This house was unoccupied then because so many of our people both from the estate and the village were at the front. I kept you children in the house until your father came in. We all had breakfast together and then, just before he set off again for the station, your father said something that put a chill on my heart: 'Whatever happens, you must always remember that you and the children have produced the greatest happiness I could imagine or hope for. What we are doing, we are doing for our beloved country and for them. You must never forget that. Particularly explain to Robert when he is able to understand. The time is coming.'

He looked so tired, so thin, that I wanted to beg him to stay and rest. He seemed too frail to be taking on the Third Reich. Part of me still believed that Hitler was invincible. It was only later that I fully understood that after Stalingrad all was delusion. And now the Allies were advancing across France.

I wanted to ask your father why he, especially, the father of three young children, had to do it, but I could not. Men, we all understood, had to do their duty, and women were not supposed to question them, quaint though that sounds to you now.

We spent the next few weeks keeping ourselves busy. Your Aunt Adi was so wonderful. She had a new plan for every day, from making toy theatres, collecting cornflowers to tie into circlets for your heads, or playing songs on her guitar to sing by the lake. Often we took one of the carts for picnics by the small secret lake in a remote part of the forest, and sometimes we would go over to our cousins at Schwerin and sail in their boats or take the ferry. And of course we swam. The water was, in my memory, always wonderfully warm. And somehow Cook always managed to find enough flour and butter to make a *Baumkuchen*.

On the 18th of July the stationmaster rang at about nine o'clock at night and he said that the Count had arrived on the Berlin train. He had set out on foot. The stationmaster said that your father had asked that the children be woken up as he could only stay until the early morning. I set off by car, while Babette got you out of bed. It was not completely dark, a warm, northern evening. About two kilometres from the station I found him, Axel, your beloved father, striding down the road in his suit without a tie. We embraced and he took the wheel. 'It's going to happen now,' he said. I knew what he meant, of course, but none of the details in case the plan failed. He had left Berlin to see us, although he was needed day and night. 'But I had to see you, just in case.' And what he meant was just in case the plan failed. There would be no mercy.

Back at the house a birthday table had been prepared and you were in your nightclothes in the hall by the big Swedish stove. There was no electricity but the table looked beautiful, with the red candles in the silver candlesticks, which I saved from Treskow. It was my birthday on the 20th and while I was on my way to find your father, Aunt Adi had prepared the table on which she laid little gifts: she added the gifts your father had brought with him, new editions of books I had wanted from Kiepert and some delicacies he had managed to get his hands on. I opened my presents: we sang, we perhaps shed a tear or two, but we were very jolly, and then you children were taken back to bed and he came in to kiss you before we were finally alone together, for the last time, in our room in the tower. He told me that he believed a new future for us and our country was coming.

In the morning you children were waiting at breakfast. Immediately after breakfast your father and I climbed into the brake and we waved goodbye to you, assembled with Aunt Adi and Babette on the front steps. We held hands all the way to the station: we were young then. As we approached the station, your father asked me if I loved him. 'Of course, my darling, I love you and I support you in everything you have to do.'

'It is only fifty-fifty, you know.'

He used the English phrase, 'fifty-fifty': at times he was happier speaking English than German. I think it reminded him of his Oxford days and his Oxford friends, who were very dear to him. He made no secret of the fact that he had been in love there and I felt no jealousy. He believed that if you had once loved someone, you should always maintain that love in some way.

He jumped out of the brake, seized me in his arms, thin and frail though he was, and swung me down. He said goodbye to Wicht, kissed one of the horses – 'I love their smell and the feel of their muzzles,' he said – and we ran hand in hand to the platform. We embraced and he jumped into the train. As it pulled away, a dark cloud fell on my soul that has never completely lifted.

The 20th of July was my thirty-second birthday. What a terrible, terrible irony. By nightfall we knew that the Führer had survived. In the morning we heard on the radio that a small clique of renegade officers, led by the traitor Claus Schenk von Stauffenberg, had been executed. But we did not know what had happened to your father. We could obviously not ask anyone.

Your aunt made a wonderful show of keeping things as normal as possible, but she and I went up to my bedroom to listen to the radio for news.

Conrad cannot sleep. He sees Axel von Gottberg desperate to hold his wife and his children for the last time. He sees the tall, romantic figure striding through the fading light for home; he sees the intensity of that evening, the startled children in their nightdresses, the poignant journey behind the horses back to the station and on to ruined Berlin, where the twilight of the gods has descended. He sees Axel von Gottberg exactly as he is in the trial footage, tall, hollow-eyed, agonisingly thin, but resolved.

And now, deeply moved by the memoir, Conrad wonders, as Liselotte did, how he could have done it. Was it courage or was it a kind of delusion, a *folie de grandeur*, that he, Axel, Graf von Gottberg, was destined to save Germany alongside his grand friend, Claus Schenk, Graf von Stauffenberg? But also Conrad sees the puzzled children, innocent, confused, their lives for ever blighted, the children of a traitor – or a hero. He has met one of the daughters; the son Robert died of diphtheria a few months after the Gestapo took them away to an orphanage in Bavaria in accordance with Hitler's policy of *Sippenhaft*, kindred seizure. The two girls stayed there, mute, until Christmas.

In those last days von Gottberg was gripped by a belief that, once von Stauffenberg had killed Hitler, he would be vital in establishing Germany back in the civilised world: he might even be able to secure a government for Germany by decent Germans, a government that would avoid humiliation and ruin and Soviet annexation.

There is only a paper-thin divide between idealism and delusion.

# 18

## 19 JULY 1944

VON GOTTBERG ARRIVES back in Berlin at Friedrich-strasse Station. He takes the U-Bahn to the office. The U-Bahn is still running although Berlin is being reduced to rubble by the bombing raids. If anyone doubts the madness of Hitler, they have only to look about. The great military genius is in his Wolf's Lair in East Prussia, his personal escape from the chaos he has caused to be rained down on the people of Berlin. Von Gottberg feels a kind of dull pain that constricts his chest. Perhaps he should see a doctor.

But as he emerges from the U-Bahn near the office, he is filled with the elation of knowing that the day is coming. He has work to do, preparing for the installation of the new government. The bad news is that Rommel has been injured when his car is strafed; he will not be at hand to lend his great authority to the putsch. But the Auswärtiges Amt is strongly anti-Nazi still, apart from von Gottberg's boss Dr Six, an SS appointee, and even he sees which way the wind is blowing.

He lunches with some friends including his brother-in-law, Dietlof Goetz; they don't talk about the putsch. But all afternoon he is busy co-ordinating the Foreign Office's reaction to the coup. Of course, they are in the hands of the military at the Bendlerblock, who will put the Valkyrie plan into operation as soon as news comes through of the assassination. It is the military's task to make sure that key locations in Berlin, Paris and Prague are secured. He also writes a letter to his wife, which she is to memorise and destroy: *In the next few weeks, you may not hear from me. Do not be afraid.*

That night he has a brief meeting with von Stauffenberg, who is calm, smoking one of his Brazilian cigars. On the way home von Stauffenberg stops at Martin Niemöller's church in Dahlem to bear witness. Nobody knows what von Stauffenberg and von Gottberg discussed, but it is probable that it was the nature of the announcement to be broadcast from the captured radio stations and transmitters. Late that evening von Stauffenberg returns to No 8 Tristanstrasse, and he and Berthold read their brother, Alexander's, latest poems.

# 19

KARL SCHWEIZER, THE former magician and von Stauffenberg's chauffeur, pulls up outside No 8 Tristanstrasse. The house stands on the Wannsee, one of the lakes that lie on the flat northern plain around Berlin. No 8 is built in the vernacular style popular in the prosperous and leafy suburbs: it has elements of the chalet, with a steeply pitched roof and a wooden balcony on the first floor. Part of the front of the house is faced in wood and most of the windows on three floors have shutters.

It has been a very hot summer and the garden, although untended, is flowering heavily, drooping lilacs scenting the air. Beyond the house is the lake, Wannsee, invisible from the street, but providing a wonderfully natural view from the back of the house through birch trees to the gently undulating water. Proximity to a lake is highly prized. In summer the beaches on the lakes are crowded with bathers, soldiers on leave with their girlfriends and wives, and children in family groups or with mothers only, all those in fact who want to get away from the ruin that is Berlin. The U-Bahn trains to Wannsee and Nikolassee from Alexanderplatz and Unter den Linden are packed at weekends. Unter den Linden no longer has any *Linden* – limes – because they have been replaced by triumphal Roman columns on the orders of Reichsmarschall Goering.

At exactly 7 a.m. von Stauffenberg appears at the door in the uniform of 10 Panzer Division with the light-grey summer jacket, the collar patches and shoulder flashes with two crowns that identify his rank and regiment. The piping around the sleeves of the jacket indicates that he is on the Army's general staff. He wears cavalry boots. With him is his brother Berthold, in his dark naval uniform. Berthold hands Schweizer his brother's briefcase, which contains two lumps of explosive, each weighing nine hundred and seventy-five grams, with two British primer charges and two thirty-minute fuses, also British. A shirt covers the explosive, a timing device and a pair of pliers which have been adapted for use with his brother's left hand. He wears a black patch over his left eye, also lost in North Africa. A colleague, Major-General Henning von Tresckow from Army Group Centre, has procured the explosives.

Claus von Stauffenberg and his brother settle in the back of the car for the drive to Rangsdorf Airfield. There is light fog, which looks as though it will soon clear. Von Stauffenberg clasps his brother's hand for a moment and then recites. His brother joins him in a whisper:

> *When this generation has cleansed its shame*
> *And thrown the serf's yoke from its neck*
> *And feels in its entrails the pure hunger for honour,*
> *Then, from battlefields covered with endless graves,*
> *A bloody signal will flash through the clouds,*
> *Then roaring armies will rush through the fields;*
> *And the horror of horrors will rage, the third storm,*
> *The return of the dead.*

Claus says quietly, 'For honour and secret Germany.'

Berthold repeats, 'For secret Germany.'

The car pulls in to the airfield, saluted by guards. The fog is thicker. Lieutenant Werner von Haeften, von Stauffenberg's adjutant, is waiting.

He speaks to the driver, Schweizer: 'Go to Spandau and get yourself a new suit.'

'Why do I need one, sir?'

'You will be needing many new things.'

Von Haeften and the brothers stand outside the low airport building until they hear the drone of the engines of the courier plane. It appears suddenly from the murk and lands with a bump, before taxiing to the buildings. It is 8 a.m. when von Stauffenberg and von Haeften climb up the short flight of steps and wave goodbye to Berthold before settling down for the flight to Rastenburg in East Prussia. Berthold is driven back to his office in the Naval High Command. The fog has cleared and below them Brandenburg and Mecklenburg, a patchwork of forests and lakes and fields, unrolls. Even from this height you can see fields of wheat and barley shot through with the red of poppies and the blue of cornflowers.

The plane lands at 10.15 a.m. A staff car is waiting. Von Haeften carries the briefcase containing the bomb and von Stauffenberg carries his briefing notes which concern the use of troops on leave in Berlin as an emergency defence force. The car pauses briefly at the gates that lead to the eastern command centre, Wolfschanze – Wolf's Lair – a compound ringed by two perimeter fences. Within the compound is the Führer compound, which contains Hitler's quarters, a casino, and houses and bunkers for leading ministers. Gorlitz station is beside this compound; the line separates the Führer compound from the rest of the Wolfschanze. To the north of the Führer compound are swamps, which provide a natural defence before the outer perimeter is reached.

Von Stauffenberg is invited to have breakfast with the Headquarters Commandant's staff. He is greatly admired; the Commandant himself has invited him to lunch after the briefing. The breakfast is lavish, with the best Westphalian ham and a variety of cheeses and freshly baked bread. A special delicacy is the local *Blutwurst*. After breakfast, at about 11 a.m., von Stauffenberg is driven to a meeting with the Chief of Army Staff, Lieutenant General Buhle. They discuss the divisions – the blocking divisions – that will be drawn up from somewhere to prevent a rout when the front-line troops in the East withdraw, which they must. Von Haeften rejoins von Stauffenberg outside Field Marshal Wilhelm Keitel's office for preparatory briefing before von Stauffenberg is summoned to the Führer's presence. Von Haeften is still holding the briefcase containing the explosives. He is not required in this briefing and stands in the corridor.

At noon Hitler's valet, Linge, phones Keitel to tell him that the morning briefing is delayed until 12.30, because Mussolini, who is due to arrive at Görlitz station in his special train, is late. At 12.25 Field Marshal Keitel is informed that his General Staff's chief of operations has arrived by train and the Führer briefing can begin. Von Stauffenberg wants to be sure that the Führer is going to be present. He is told that the Führer will indeed be there. He asks permission to change his shirt. Von Stauffenberg and von Haeften are shown to a sitting room, where, with von Haeften's help, von Stauffenberg changes his shirt. Keitel, Buhle and Keitel's adjutant stand outside the hut in the sunshine waiting for them. Von Stauffenberg puts his back against the door and starts to prime the bomb with the special pliers, using his three remaining fingers. Only he may do it: he is the assassin.

He has to remove the fuses from the primer charges and squeeze the copper casing with the pliers to break the glass phials inside. The acid must seep out on the cotton around the retaining wires. Too much pressure might break the wire; it has to corrode gently for the delay, a maximum of thirty minutes, to be effective. Then he has to look through an inspection hole to make sure that the firing pin is still compressed, remove a safety bolt, and finally put the fuses back into the primer charges. Eventually one bomb is primed. But as von Stauffenberg starts on the second, the door is pushed against his back by a staff sergeant who has been sent by Keitel. He calls through the door to say that there is a phone call for him and that the Field Marshal requests that he come immediately to the briefing. Then the Field Marshal's adjutant himself shouts down the corridor: *Stauffenberg, come along*. The

Field Marshal is agitated. Von Stauffenberg decides that there is no time to prime the second bomb. He gestures to von Haeften, who closes the briefcase and hands it to him and they hurry out past the staff sergeant. Keitel's adjutant reaches for the case, but von Stauffenberg pulls it away impatiently. His unwillingness to accept help, despite his injury, impresses itself on the adjutant.

Von Haeften stuffs the second lump of explosive in a brown-paper parcel and slips it into his own attaché case. His task now is to make sure that the car that is to take them back to the airfield is standing by. He slips out of Keitel's office complex and makes his way to the drivers' pool.

Von Stauffenberg is animated as he walks to the briefing complex where the Führer is already at work planning for the impossible, how to save the Fatherland. Outside the wooden building, von Stauffenberg hands his briefcase to the adjutant and asks for a place as close to the Führer as possible, as he has charts and maps to show him.

As von Stauffenberg enters the room, Hitler breaks off and looks at him. Keitel announces Colonel Claus Schenk, Graf von Stauffenberg, who will report on the new arrangements for the defence of Berlin. Von Stauffenberg, with his eye patch and uniform with one empty arm, looks directly back at Hitler. It is reported later that von Stauffenberg, six foot three inches and extraordinarily good-looking, is a proud figure, the image of a warrior of classical times and the picture of a general staff officer. Hitler allows von Stauffenberg to shake him by the hand, an honour. Keitel's adjutant asks one of the officers at the map table to move in order to allow von Stauffenberg to stand as close to the Führer as possible. Only Major-General Heusinger, who has been briefing the Führer on the situation in the East, now stands between him and von Stauffenberg. Von Stauffenberg pushes the briefcase as close to the Führer's legs as he can. It rests against the massive legs of the table support. After a few minutes, von Stauffenberg motions to the adjutant and asks him to get Lieutenant General Fellgiebel on the phone. The adjutant gives the order to the operator in a side office, hands the phone to von Stauffenberg, and returns to the briefing. As arranged, von Stauffenberg leaves the briefing room and walks to find von Haeften and Fellgiebel. They wait. At some time between 12.40 and 12.50, they hear an enormous explosion. Debris and a body fly out of the windows of the briefing room. They see another body being carried out, covered in the Führer's velvet cloak.

Von Stauffenberg and von Haeften walk calmly to their car and direct it to the airstrip where a plane is waiting for them. It is the Heinkel HE 111 of the Quarter Master General, Lieutenant General Wagner. At the first perimeter fence a guard stops the car. Von Stauffenberg, with icy calm, tells him that he is a member of the General Staff acting on urgent orders. They are waved through. At the second checkpoint, the outer perimeter, there is an absolute ban on anyone leaving the Wolfschanze. Von Stauffenberg has a lunch appointment with the Commandant, but nonetheless he tells the guard sergeant to call Captain von Mollendorf, the Commandant's adjutant, for permission to let him pass. He lights one of his black Brazilian cigars as he waits for the sergeant to make the call: the sergeant soon waves them through and salutes. As they pass through a stand of trees, von Haeften throws the second lump of explosive out of the car window. Fellgiebel, meanwhile, orders that all outgoing signal traffic must be stopped.

The Heinkel takes off for Berlin-Rangsdorf. An order is given that fighters should be scrambled and that the Heinkel should be shot down, but it is not passed to the Luftwaffe by the major on duty, who is the son-in-law of one of the conspirators, General Olbricht, who is himself waiting at the Bendlerblock, General Army Office, for von Stauffenberg's return to Berlin to take over the government of Germany and end the war. But already, by the time the Heinkel lands at 4 p.m., there is uncertainty and confusion. Karl Schweizer, the chauffeur, goes to the wrong airport. Von Stauffenberg and von Haeften have to borrow a car from a Luftwaffe officer. At 4.05 p.m. communication with the

Wolfschanze is restored. Reports are coming in that there has been an explosion at the Wolfschanze and that some officers have been wounded.

Before von Stauffenberg's car arrives at the Reserve Army Headquarters in Bendlerstrasse, there is already uncertainty. There has been a fatal delay in implementing the Valkyrie plans, drawn up to take over the key installations of Berlin in an emergency. The Guard Battalion, the armoured troops from the Officers' School at Krampnitz and the infantry regiments at Dobnitz and Potsdam, should, according to the plan, already have entered the administrative sector of Berlin and occupied all the main government buildings, SS and Party headquarters. The Berlin Radio Tower, all newspapers, and the radio transmitter at Tegel were to be seized, SS leaders to be arrested and the SS disarmed. But the order has not been given.

General Fromm, von Stauffenberg's superior, has been told that the Führer is not dead by Field Marshal Keitel himself. He is incensed when he is ordered by Olbricht to put Valkyrie into operation immediately. He and General Olbricht come to blows. Olbricht now puts out the orders under his own authority, with a proclamation declaring martial law and beginning: 'The Führer, Adolf Hitler, is dead.'

When von Stauffenberg finally enters Olbricht's office with von Haeften it is 4.30 p.m. He announces that Hitler is dead. 'I saw them carry him out,' he says.

Von Stauffenberg now goes to see Fromm and tells him that Hitler is dead. Fromm says that is impossible: Keitel himself has told him that Hitler is only lightly wounded. When Olbricht tells him that the orders for Valkyrie have been sent out, he slams the desk with his fist. He says it is high treason. They are all under arrest.

'On the contrary,' says von Stauffenberg, 'you are under arrest. I placed the bomb myself, right next to Hitler.'

Fromm replies, 'The assassination attempt has failed. You must shoot yourself.'

In the small panelled office, the atmosphere is almost farcical. Fromm is trying to save his neck. A pistol is pulled on him. Fromm is given five minutes to decide if he will join the uprising. After five minutes he declares that he considers himself relieved of his command. He is placed under guard in a side room.

At Wilhelmstrasse, the head office of the Auswärtiges Amt, von Gottberg has been waiting since soon after dawn, full of excitement. Hans-Bernd von Haeften, who is the older brother of von Stauffenberg's aide, Werner von Haeften, and other conspirators gather. They occupy themselves with office work and correspondence. They rejoice that it is the last time they will ever have to close letters *Heil Hitler!* At 2 p.m. they receive the agreed message, *Panta rei*, Greek for *All in motion*. Hitler is dead. The Valkyrie plans to seal off the government area of Berlin are to be put into operation right away from General Army Office. Von Gottberg looks out of the window for the movement of troops. People are walking unconcerned down Wilhelmstrasse and there are no soldiers in sight. Someone tells von Gottberg that there is a report that Hitler has survived an assassination attempt unscathed.

'It's a trick,' says von Gottberg. 'Stauffenberg himself confirms that Hitler is dead.'

But they can get no information from the Bendlerblock, Reserve Army Headquarters. Von Gottberg is desperate to speak to von Stauffenberg, and von Haeften tries many times to reach his brother. The lines are dead or overloaded. Two hours pass as they wait, helpless.

After placing Fromm under arrest, von Stauffenberg starts on a round of telephoning to assure the other conspirators that Hitler is dead. He tells them that it is impossible that Hitler has survived: he has seen the explosion and the body being carried out. He calls von General von Stülpnagel, the Military Governor of Paris, and other conspirators in Prague and Vienna. Some of the troops are ordered out, as the plan demands, and they set off from Potsdam to occupy the government quarter of Berlin. But a diligent Major Remer, a convinced Nazi in charge of the Guard Battalion, manages to speak to Hitler himself and orders some of the troops back to barracks. Tanks from the Officers' School in Krampnitz are moving fast, however. Von Stauffenberg's inner circle come and go, increasingly uncertain.

Wilhelmstrasse. At about 5.30 p.m. von Gottberg sees that the street below is cordoned off and steel-helmeted soldiers are taking up their positions on both sides of the road, right up to the Adlon Hotel. Von Gottberg and von Haeften are delighted; they embrace. They have a list of people who are to be arrested as soon as the military leaders are ready. Von Gottberg tries to call the Bendlerblock again, but still he cannot get through. They decide to delay any announcements and appointments within the office until they are certain.

At the Bendlerblock, an SS colonel arrives to ask von Stauffenberg to a meeting with the Chief of Secret Police. Von Stauffenberg has him arrested. The confusion deepens as reports come in that Hitler will himself soon make a statement. Support melts away. The conspirators are not, after all, in control of Berlin or of communications. Junior officers loyal to the Führer arm themselves and shooting breaks out. Von Stauffenberg is hit in the shoulder. Now he telephones Paris, his last hope, from Fromm's office, but he is told, 'The SS are advancing.'

He slumps in the seat.

'They have left me in the lurch,' he says to von Haeften, who is burning papers in a bin. At 6.15 p.m. the radio announces that an attempt has been made on the life of the Führer, but that he is unhurt.

At about 7 p.m. there is an awful moment: the troops below in Wilhelmstrasse are withdrawing and soon the traffic is flowing again. Von Gottberg, who has been deathly pale all day, has the feeling that the blood is draining from him with the soldiers as they file away. It is all over. He stays in the office until eleven, destroying papers, thinking of his alibi, hoping to speak to von Stauffenberg. Maybe General Stülpnagel is even now bargaining from Paris with the Allies about surrender.

At Army headquarters in Bendlerstrasse, Fromm is brought back to his office by the junior officers. He confronts von Stauffenberg and the other conspirators, saying that they are now under arrest and must hand over their weapons: they have committed an act of high treason. General Beck asks to keep his pistol in order to shoot himself. Fromm agrees. Others want to write statements. For half an hour von Stauffenberg stands in bitter silence as they write. Fromm declares that he has convened a court martial and that it has found the colonel, whose name he cannot speak, as well as Lieutenant von Haeften, Colonel Mertz von Quirnheim and General Olbricht, guilty. Von Stauffenberg now speaks: the others were under his command and he takes full responsibility.

The four men are led down some stairs and outside to where sandbags have been piled against a wall in the long, cobbled, rectangular courtyard. Drivers from the car pool have been ordered to light up the place of execution with the headlights from their vehicles. Ten non-commissioned officers stand ready with their rifles. The conspirators are shot one by one. It is reported that von Haeften tries to throw himself in front of von Stauffenberg, as a last act of devotion. Just before he is shot, von Stauffenberg shouts,

'Long live our sacred Germany.' *Es lebe unser heiliges Deutschland.*
One person reports that he shouts, 'Long live secret Germany,'
and that is possible, because the words *heiliges* and the unfamiliar
*geheimes* could easily have been confused.

Upstairs General Beck, who has shot himself in the head, is
still alive after two attempts. He lies groaning in a corner asking
if he is dying. Fromm orders an officer to finish him off. The
officer says he cannot shoot a German general lying wounded
and defenceless on the floor. He orders a soldier of the Guard
Battalion to do it. This man drags Beck into a corridor, leaving
a trail of blood from his head, and shoots him.

Von Gottberg and von Haeften stop off at the Adlon for a drink
with a colleague from their office.

'At least we tried,' von Haeften says.

'There is no more hope. Hitler has destroyed Germany,' says
von Gottberg.

At 1.30 a.m. they hear that Hitler has made a broadcast
denouncing a small clique of disappointed officers. The Führer
speaks to the German people from the Wolfschanze: a small, but
deluded, group of officers, including von Stauffenberg, has tried
to kill him, but he has been spared. He is very lightly injured.

That night he declares in front of Mussolini that he will practise
*Sippenhaft* without mercy. Mussolini is reported to be shocked.
The armoured divisions have withdrawn to barracks.

The bodies of the five dead men shot in the courtyard of the
Bendlerblock are loaded on to a lorry and driven to a graveyard
beside the Matthiaskirche in Schöneberg and hastily buried on
Fromm's orders in their uniforms and decorations. The next day
Heinrich Himmler has the bodies exhumed, cremated and their
ashes scattered in the open spaces of a park near by.

# 20

CONRAD'S BELL RINGS harshly. It takes him some time to understand what the noise is, as if he has never heard his bell before. In fact the sound is a kind of grating cry, the cry of a crow. He wakes where he has fallen asleep, on the sofa. He is losing a sense of the days. He has no idea of the time or the date. He goes downstairs and finds Tony, who hands him a registered letter.

'Morning, mate. This came for you. I signed for it. You weren't answering.'

'Thanks, Tony.'

'You orright?'

'Yes, I'm fine. I've been working hard.'

And Tony gives him some freshly baked bread, still warmly aromatic.

'Pugliese. Where me gran come from. You must eat, my son.'

'I'm eating, Tony. Trust me. But thanks very much.'

He goes upstairs with the bread and the letter. Fritsch has written to him at last. After how many weeks? He can't work it out. He opens the letter and reaches for his Cassell's dictionary.

*Sehr Geehrter Herr Senior,*

I have the only known copy of the film in which you have shown interest. This film has been in my possession since 1944. Many times I have wondered what I can be doing with it. I believe from the Bundesfilmarchiv that you are writing about some of the resisters. I was an assistant to Mr Steuben, of Wochenschau, deceased, and the footage filmed on B Camera, Arri 2C, by me was on August 15th, 1944, and never used. This is the footage of the execution of four of the plotters of July 20th, 1944, which event I believe is known to you. The four executed include Count Axel von Gottberg. I am not interested in selling this footage to you, but in making sure that it is given to a responsible person. It can never be shown in the public media. I have lived with this secret for sixty years. Also, I cannot allow this footage to be held in Germany. Many times I have decided to destroy it. If you can come to Berlin there is a possibility that I can give you this film and the negative. Please telephone this number to make an appointment.

Conrad immediately calls the number in Berlin. He is trembling as it rings. A woman answers and he asks for Herr Fritsch.
'*Papi. Telefon.*'
'*Guten Tag.* I am Conrad Senior. I received your letter.'
They stumble along in German. Conrad agrees to meet him in four days' time outside Schönhauser Allee 23, in Prenzlauer Berg. He imagines Fritsch in East Berlin – he has a strong urge, at times uncontrollable, to fill in the details of other lives – keeping this awful film for years, like some venomous creature, some poisoned substance, all through the communist days and then in the new united Berlin wondering what he could do with it, how he could atone, perhaps, for his part in this terrible act. And maybe all this time, sixty years now, Fritsch has never been able to talk about it or think of any way of disposing of it honourably until he sees Conrad's notice in the archive or hears about it at a showing or a reunion of other Wochenschau veterans.

Conrad feels faint. He hasn't been eating. He books himself a ticket to Berlin at a local cheap-flight shop. He has no money in the bank but his credit card is still acceptable, apparently. And then he goes to the café where workers and taxi drivers gather for breakfast. He tries to estimate how many days have gone by, conscious that during this time the baby has been growing. He leaves a message for Francine: *I must go to Berlin. I believe that this is coming to a conclusion now. Please call me to discuss our situation.*

He sits in this café. The taxi drivers are enthusiastic talkers. They meet here every day for a little *Midrash* of their own. He wonders how many taxi drivers are still Jewish. It was once the immigrants' route to accumulation. And the taxi drivers' test demanded prodigious feats of memory. Are Jews more intelligent than the rest of us? Is that what the Nazis really feared?

He remembers von Stauffenberg's guru, the poet Stefan George's, view of Jews: *One Jew is very useful but as soon as there are more than two of them, the tone becomes different and they tend to their own business. Jews do not experience life as deeply as we do. They are, in general, different people.*

It was the knowledge of the extermination of Jews and political commissars in the East that turned von Stauffenberg from conservative aristocrat to regicide. An army major reported to him seeing one thousand naked Jews shot by the SS in the Ukraine. Mendel wanted Conrad to determine in what state von Gottberg died. Did he die a German patriot or as someone who wanted to atone for the sins visited on the Jews, on Mendel's people? For Mendel that was the issue when all else was forgotten. And soon he may be able to provide the answer and then his task will be complete.


Francine has been doing nights as a locum, but she wants to see him before he goes to Berlin. They meet at the flower market in Columbia Road for breakfast on Sunday morning when she comes off shift. Night shifts affect her badly: he is distressed to see the imprint on her face, as deeply worn as the action of water on rocks, so deeply that she seems permanently to have aged. But worse for Conrad than this haggardness is the certainty that she is profoundly unhappy. She is possibly still in love with John.

They eat a bagel with smoked salmon and scrambled egg, and they drink dark Arabica. Outside the café, as though they are in a jungle clearing, is a dense wall of greenery and blossom. On a Sunday morning it is almost impossible to walk out on the pavement, such is the commingling of people and plants. Suddenly, to his utter dismay, he sees that Francine is sobbing. He stands up and puts his arm around her and leads her out into the flower market. They stand in a courtyard amongst coppery bougainvillea, tree ferns and large blue pots. He holds her until her sobbing eases.

'I've got rid of it.'

She stands, silent within his embrace.

'I love you,' he says. 'We'll be fine.'

But in his heart he feels a certain bitterness that she should have destroyed the child without consulting him.

'I've waited for days to speak to you. You never rang,' she says.

He feels her body quaking.

'I am so sorry. I was completely lost.'

# 21

IN THE MORNING von Gottberg and the others turn up for work as usual. They appear to be paralysed with disappointment. In the next few days they wait for the inevitable. Although he is offered several opportunities to escape to Switzerland, to France or to Sweden, von Gottberg is unable to leave his wife and children at the mercy of the Gestapo. In any event he feels a sacrifice is due to Germany. Different conspirators react in different ways. On the Eastern Front Major-General Henning von Tresckow, who supplied the explosive, writes a note: *Now everyone in the world will turn upon us and sully us with abuse. Hitler is not the arch-enemy of Germany, he is the arch-enemy of mankind. In a few hours' time I will stand before God to answer for my actions.*

He drives out into a wood with his adjutant, asks him to go back to the car for a map, and then blows his head from his body with a hand grenade. Other conspirators denounce their colleagues. A few escape across the borders by one means or another.

Five days later von Gottberg is arrested. Two Gestapo men are waiting for him in his office when he comes in. One sits, as is traditional, at his desk going through his papers. Von Gottberg is taken away to Gestapo headquarters, and then to Oranienburg. Dr Six sends an emissary to the prison: he is keen to keep von Gottberg and his foreign contacts as a bargaining chip when the final defeat comes. It is, for the moment, only Schweizer's logbook that ties von Gottberg to Schweizer's master, von Stauffenberg.

Later Six turns on von Gottberg saying, *Wir haben einen Schweinehund unter uns gehabt – We have had a schweinehund among us* – when a document proposing high office for von Gottberg in the new government is discovered. He is to be the ambassador to Great Britain. But Six may be playing a double game, speaking at the same time to his boss, Himmler; the prospect of a settlement with the Allies has been on Himmler's mind too. Who better to send as an emissary to Churchill than an Oxford man? Every day von Gottberg is brought from Oranienburg which is not far from where he and Elizabeth sat in the little DKW looking at Sachsenhausen six years before. Every day he is driven to Gestapo headquarters in Albrechtstrasse, where, the records show, he only incriminates people who are already dead or out of danger. Von Stauffenberg is one of these. Stauffenberg's remains are by now lost in Schöneberg, dispersed, ashes to ashes. The Gestapo are sure von Gottberg knows more and, at Himmler's behest, want to find out about all his contacts abroad.

Von Gottberg is beaten and he is made to stand for hours without sleep. Other conspirators are tortured on a rack, or half drowned in buckets of water. The guards are creatures of the movement; their continued existence is tied to the regime. They see these men, distinguished men, who are being dragged in in ever-increasing numbers, as the enemy within; it is always the case that the enemy within, the ones who refuse to accept the articles of faith of the masses, are hated most. The guards have dealt with Jews and Ukrainians and Poles and now they see that they have, in this patriotic work, been insulted by the privileged who own castles set in broad acres and from time immemorial have had everything – fine linen, wines, and leather-bound books – while they have had nothing. Worse, these are the very people who stabbed Germany in the back in 1918. It's an opportunity many of them cannot resist. Their vindictiveness and cruelty are beyond belief.

Von Gottberg's daily interrogations are interrupted. It is announced that he and the other traitors will be summoned before the People's Court presided over by Judge President Roland Freisler, to be condemned to death. The purpose of the court is to minimise the importance of the uprising; Freisler's job is to blacken the name of the conspirators for home consumption. They are a small group of deranged ingrates, who believe they know better than the Führer, which, of course, is logically impossible, because the Führer is the people. The Führer principle demands that the people hold no doubts or even opinions of their own. Throughout the trials Freisler is to enunciate these ideas clearly.

To Field Marshal von Witzleben he sneers, 'A Field Marshal and an Oberst General declare that they can do better than our Führer. You understand why we call this overweening ambition? You shrug your shoulders? Well, that is a kind of answer. We are of one opinion that the Führer is of the greatest help to us all alive and well.'

And to another defendant – although no defence is permitted – Major-General Stieff, Freisler says, 'What you reject is of as little interest to us, as the perverted desires of a homosexual are to the healthy German male; for if you do not see that that is rabid defeatism, then you are politically just as perverted. But here it is our healthy opinions which matter, not yours.'

To the former Mayor of Leipzig, Carl Gördeler, who says he wanted power restored to the General Staff, he replies, 'But we have that now! Yes, because we always have it in the person of the Führer. There is no more complete quintessence of all the powers emanating from the people.'

And then Axel von Gottberg's turn comes. The defendants have been given an assortment of clothes that look as though they may have been donated to help the homeless. He wears a loose jacket, a grey workman's shirt, and trousers without a belt or braces. His shackles are removed in an anteroom. Two guards lead him into the courtroom to a bench where the defendants wait. Behind Freisler, who is wearing juridical robes, is a huge Nazi flag. The light from the arc lamps is very strong, blinding to the defendants.

Just as von Gottberg, transparently pale, almost ethereal, is summoned from the box, there is a commotion outside the court on the landing. Two women are demanding to be let in. That they haven't fully understood what is going on is quickly apparent: 'We demand to be let in to attend this hearing.' They are led away and arrested. Von Gottberg recognises their voices, the voices of his wife Liselotte and his sister Adelheid. His head sinks into his hands, as though any support it had has gone. A few days later the children, Robert, three, Angela just two, and the baby, Caroline, are taken away to an orphanage where they are given the names Horst, Waltraud and Heidi.

Von Gottberg stands calmly, already imagining death, perhaps longing for death after what he has been through. He doesn't understand why there are film cameras in the court. The film is being made by Wochenschau on the orders of Reichsfilmintendant Hans Hinkel, to demonstrate to the public that the small claque of traitors is decadent scum, who never fully understood the legitimate and heroic struggle of ordinary German people under the Führer, a struggle against humiliation and unemployment and decline.

Freisler is particularly interested in Oxford and the Rhodes Scholarship.

'An English scholarship. Ideal preparation for a traitor. So your years at Oxford were not entirely wasted. You proposed negotiating with the armies in the West and capitulating?'

Von Gottberg replies *'Gewiss.'* Certainly.

He is going to his death with composure. When von Gottberg says, 'I believed it was best for the people of Germany to negotiate,' Freisler replies, 'We are not interested in what you thought. We are not interested in your view of foreign policy. We want to know if a German stands before us.'

Of course von Gottberg is not allowed to reply. But he stands there as if he has already passed from this hellish nightmare.

That night in the small block next to Plötzensee Prison six people are hanged; they are brought in – it is reported – half-naked and one by one they are slowly hanged. The cameras turn, as Hitler wants urgently to see the death throes of his enemies. But von Gottberg is not executed; he is held back for further questioning because the interrogators believe he has more information. He is held for eleven agonising days. Himmler wants his death sentence commuted so that he can use him and his contacts. When this suggestion is passed to Hitler he falls into one of his terrifying rages, which are becoming increasingly frequent, and he declares that the traitors at the Auswärtiges Amt are the worst of all.

'Hang them, hang them like cattle.'

Axel von Gottberg is hanged in a batch of four on August the 26th.

# 22

CONRAD HAS BOOKED himself into a cheap hotel in Prenzlauer Berg. The old tenements of East Berlin stretch away on either side of the road, some not yet renovated, others already gentrified. There is still plenty of scope for improvement, but there are cafés and bars everywhere and untended parks. In the streets and on the U-Bahn he sees young people with dyed Mohican haircuts, chains attached to their waists, body piercing and tattoos. Some have curiously resigned dogs. There are also what could be neo-Nazi youths with shaved heads and combat trousers. He has the impression that East Berlin is not completely won over by the new world on offer: in fact a huge banner, in English, hangs from one of the tenements: *Fuck the Free World*. Forty-five years of communism followed by the Stasi may well have produced a truculent, suspicious people.

The hotel is simple: the rooms are cell-like, functional, with one mean, flat warehouse window. It gives a glimpse of the tall, red-brick Zionskirche, where Protestant opposition groups gathered during the war. A square near by is named after Käthe Kollwitz who lived and painted here, recording the lives of the poor, and here he starts his researches into Berlin's cafés and bars and chic sights. His editor has made it clear that this is the last time she subsidises his travel. He sits in a café reading guidebooks. Very quickly he has a list of places he must, at the very least, look at.

And so, here he is in Berlin, a little drunk from the three

Bloody Marys he swallowed on the plane, strangely excited –
nervous – a man of thirty-five, largely unemployed, in an uncertain
state of marriage, but somehow – he feels – about to be instructed
in what it is to be human. This, of course, has been the aim of
philosophers and theologians, and even novelists, for many years,
but perhaps you can only have an insight into these matters, as
Mendel said to him about his father, when you see humanity
under the greatest duress.

He spends the rest of the day visiting the top bars and cafés
and sights of Berlin, culled from a book called *Berlin Top*. He
particularly likes a café near the opera house on Unter den Linden.
He sees some old men gathered in animated conversation and
writes in his notebook:

> *Historic Unter den Linden, after years of East German neglect, is
> once again the lively centre of this fascinating city. And here, not far
> from Berlin's renowned Humboldt University, where Albert Einstein,
> its most famous faculty member, is commemorated, is the Operncafé.
> This is the sort of place Berliners would rather keep to themselves,
> but get here early on a sunny day and you will find Alt Berlin
> pausing for a coffee and a* Himbeer *tart. It's as if they are paying
> their respects to the Berlin of Einstein and Brecht and Isherwood and
> Grosz. Here you can see their ghostly shapes passing. This place is
> No 1 in my top ten of insider's Berlin.*

What the readers of the travel pages don't need to know is that
George Grosz, the satirist and Dadaist of that extraordinary pre-
war period, wrote that it had come to him *that it was complete
nonsense to believe that spirit or anything spiritual ruled the world.* His
work, he said, *was a reaction to the cloud-wandering tendencies of the
so-called sacred art that found meaning in cubes and gothic while the
commanders in the field painted in blood.*

No, the readers don't want to know that Berlin – in this respect
just like Jerusalem – has been in the grip of the terrible, fatal,
belief in spirit, what Mendel called vaporous clouds of nonsense.

And it was Mendel's conviction that these vaporous clouds of nonsense – how similar, Conrad suddenly sees, to Grosz's cloud-wandering tendencies – led to Hitler and even to von Gottberg's sacrifice. And to the death of countless millions. The question of how many millions has not been fully agreed, as if a final determination could in some way fix the wretched twentieth century for ever in the past. Grosz was pointing to Mendel's deepest fears: when Hitler arrived it wasn't so much the commanders in the field who were painting in blood, but the brown plague of the SS, and also the Gestapo, directed by their beloved Führer, who had himself forsaken his own modest talents in watercolour for the new medium in which he was undoubtedly to become the modern master.

Conrad is in a hurry. He rushes around Berlin, walking the length of Unter den Linden, paying a quick visit to the Pergamon Museum – *top for antiquity, don't miss the Pergamon altar* – a lightning visit to Checkpoint Charlie – *unmissable reminder of Le Carré's Berlin* – Gendarmenmarkt – *wonderfully evocative square, ringed by fine restaurants* – Reichstag – *Norman Foster's sensitive and glorious restoration, wonderful views, long queues* – Holocaust Memorial – *reminiscent of the Jewish Cemetery on the Mount of Olives* – Brandenburg Gate – *utterly iconic*, and finally he walks all the way through the Tiergarten – *one of Europe's most inspiring parks, don't miss the English Garden* – to the zoo – *one of Europe's greatest and longest established* – and closed; but he gazes at the giant elephants that form the gates and then he tries to find von Gottberg's house behind the ruined Kaiser Wilhelm church – *soaring monument to Prussian dominance* – but it seems the Erotic Museum now stands on the site. It's late and he hurries to cover cocktails at the Adlon – *faithfully restored to former glory* – and Potsdamer Platz – *new hub of Berlin's sensation seekers* – a boutique hotel – *light, modern feel, low-carb food, which you might need after too much* Eisbein. He has never eaten an *Eisbein*, but he has seen it, reaching up from the plate like a cathedral spire in a bombed city, historic Teutonic cuisine.

When he finally gets back to his hotel he feels a certain resentment rising from the night porter who is watching television in a small office. He looks like a veteran rocker, with a ring in each ear, a ponytail tied back and a tattoo escaping underneath his collar, perhaps something he regrets now in the new, cool, low-carb Berlin. He hands Conrad his key brusquely.

The bed is narrow and prescriptive: *Don't try anything fancy here.* He lies down exhausted. His walk through the English Garden brought Oxford to mind. When Conrad arrived in Oxford to explore his destiny, he fell under the thrall of the place. The gardens, the glories of Christ Church Meadow, the endless surprises of the quads and fellows' gardens and the climbing roses on crumbling stone walls, even the tall cow parsley growing outside St Michael's Church in Carfax, all these whispered to him in a language he seemed already to have learned in another life. He saw that every cobblestone and every path and every carved ceiling and every inch of lawn in Oxford had been willed. Until that first year he had seen mountains and sea – landscape – as something created by accidents in geological time, but at Oxford he saw what hundreds of years of human tending can achieve, a harmony of place and ideas.

As Conrad wandered through the English Garden and darkness was closing, he saw that whoever laid out this place had captured an ideal perfectly, with small enclosed gardens of roses, arbours, gates, framed views to water through trees and a sense of a landscape that had been tended and controlled. For von Gottberg, as for Conrad's father, Oxford was seductive. In the English Garden, did he think of his excursions on Addison's Walk with Mendel or their brisk forays into The Parks and Christ Church Meadow? He has a profound fellow-feeling for von Gottberg, walking through the English Garden on his way to work, through the ruins of Berlin in those last days of his life. This garden must have whispered to him too, of his loss of the love of his life, and of Elya Mendel, his friend and mentor, and above all of his blithe youth. As he walked to work on that awful day, July the 20th, he must have known that he would almost certainly lose his life and family. But by then he had made up his mind. He was prepared, even eager, to sacrifice himself. Perhaps he decided the time had come to disperse the clouds of nonsense for ever.


Conrad is nervous. What does Fritsch have in store for him? His mind is teetering out of control. This condition is often described as racing, but it is not racing so much as an inability to settle. He feels clammy and cold by turns. The English Garden, the Sony Centre in Potsdamer Platz, the Holocaust Memorial, the martyrs' memorial outside Balliol, Francine's unborn baby, von Gottberg standing calmly in front of Freisler, Emily rolling a joint and blowing smoke into his mouth, they are all becoming scrambled as though they have lost any hierarchy of meaning. This is what it must have been like for his father. His father's doctor, who knew how distressed Conrad was to be sent away by his own angry father, wrote to him saying that he had early-onset dementia and had lost control of his emotions.

At last he sleeps and he dreams of Francine's baby, of a tiny foetus; and he dreams of minute, perfectly formed organs and then he dreams that the foetus is crying. He wakes up horrified, sweating. He calms himself by reading a guidebook. At random he reads that the zoo contains one thousand, four hundred species ranging from jellyfish to Indian elephants – *good-natured pachyderms*. The top attraction at the moment is a young gorilla called Sagha. He makes a mental note. He reads that the Huguenots brought culture to Berlin in 1688 after the Edict of Potsdam. There were one hundred and sixty thousand Jews in Berlin in 1933. He drinks some water.

By morning he has the impression that he has hardly slept, yet his wake-up call finds him profoundly asleep. He sets off to capture as many of the sights on his list as he can before his appointment. He loathes shopping, but he knows that shopping is important, so he visits, briefly, two centres – *lively Kaufhaus, the biggest in Europe, sensational selection of electronics;* pubs – *don't miss Berlin's famous bars; the Kneipen;* gay and lesbian scene – *lively, Christopher Street Day Parade in July is a fixture on the gay calendar;* the lakes – *Wannsee, infamous for the final solution. Visit Wannsee Haus, Nikolassee for bathing;* River Spree – *forty-six kilometres are within city limits: Athens on the Spree;* Nazi architecture – *Olympic Stadium, Air Ministry, creepy.*

He emerges from the U-Bahn at Senfelder Platz and walks up Schönhauser Allee, away from Kollwitz Platz – *lively, dotted with cafés,* he notes – and looks for number 23. Across the way is a park with a café promising barbecues and vegetarian food. Perhaps this is where Mr Fritsch wishes to meet. But the numbers on the right-hand side of the street are all odd numbers and sequential so he follows them until he comes to a cemetery, No 23–25. It is a Jewish cemetery. This is the appointed place. He waits at the gate. After about five minutes he sees, standing stooped, almost hunched, a man looking at him. He waves. The man walks over. He is elderly, dressed in a brown suit without a tie and he wears a small brown hat. He carries a Lufthansa bag of the sort that used to be given away to passengers many years ago.

'Herr Senior?'

*'Jawohl. Sind Sie Herr Fritsch?'*

They shake hands. Fritsch is about eighty-five, Conrad guesses. His eyes are yellowish, perhaps caused by liver problems. (Conrad thinks of himself as having medical knowledge by proxy.) His hand is very soft with the feel and instability of a gel; his face is minutely lined with surface-dwelling blood vessels. His back is curving forward, forcing his head lower than it wants to go. He leads Conrad into the cemetery and points to a box of kippas, exactly like the disposable kippas at the Western Wall in Jerusalem; Conrad places one on his head and Fritsch leads him away from the entrance into the overgrown cemetery itself where most of the tombstones lie on the ground or are tilted at an angle. It is a vast cemetery and Conrad for the first time has the feeling that Berlin's Jews were real rather than symbolic beings.

'Jewish cemetery,' says Frisch, although this is already rather old information. 'Here Max Liebermann is buried and many important Jewish families also.'

There are hundreds, perhaps thousands, of stones. A workman in a kippa passes with a barrow. Conrad catches sight of some of the names: Rosenblum, Goldfarb, Katz, Kaplan: he wants to know how Jewish names differed from German names. What was it that distinguished these names from those of their Aryan neighbours?

Fritsch has thought this meeting through. He leads Conrad deeper into the cemetery and points to a stone bench that looks directly at a fallen mausoleum of the Nathansohn family. Conrad feels as they sit that they are in the middle of Jewish Berlin. He has the strange sensation that he has been here before. This is the true Berlin, crowded with the dead. Fritsch takes from his flight bag a small, lined exercise book. It becomes clear that he has prepared some questions and answers and has written some English words down. There is nothing in the bag that could be the film whose existence hangs over Conrad now.

'You are a historical researcher?'

Conrad recognises his own word, *Forscher*.

'Yes. I am interested in the life of Axel von Gottberg. I have the letters Count von Gottberg wrote to my teacher, Professor Elya Mendel, at Oxford University. I was told that a film was produced by the Deutsche Wochenschau of the execution of members of the resistance, and I wished to see it. That is the reason I asked the Bundesarchiv, film section, to make enquiries.'

Conrad believes that the introduction of the word Oxford into the conversation early on is a good tactic.

'Who is Mr Elya Mendel from Oxford?'

'He was — he died seven years ago — a friend of Count von Gottberg at Oxford and they were separated by the war.'

'Mr Mendel was a Jew?'

Conrad thinks, Oh shit, this is the end of our conversation.

'Yes, he was a Jew.'

'I am a Jew. My mother was a Jewess.'

The words *Jude* and *Jüdin* spoken here by this elderly man carry a powerful charge. He has never before heard these words spoken although he has read them many times. His Cassell's dictionary does not contain the words *Jude* or *Jew*.

'Why do you wish to see the film?'

Conrad thinks that he should explain to Fritsch, who is sitting with his notebook ready, his relationship to Mendel, but he cannot. He could probably not do it in English.

'I believe,' he says, 'that as an historical researcher I must know everything I can about von Gottberg. That includes' (the word *einschliesst* comes unbidden to mind as though he has suddenly become German-speaking) 'his terrible death.'

This cannot be strictly true.

'Why are you interested in von Gottberg?'

'His friend Mendel gave me all his papers. He wanted me to write the story of their friendship after he died.'

And it seems to Conrad as he struggles with the words that this is the heart of it.

'Was Mr Mendel well known?'

'He was one of the most famous men in Oxford.'

They sit silent for a moment in the flickering, underwater light of the sun through the tall, unruly trees. Only the workman's wheelbarrow makes a noise. This wheelbarrow is a leftover of East German times, a long, unwieldy cart with an iron wheel.

Then Fritsch asks him a strange question.

'Did you love Mr Mendel?'

'Yes. Yes, I loved him like a father, perhaps a grandfather.'

'In this time I was a young man working for the Wochenschau. I am eighty-nine years old. My family home is not far from here. My mother died when I was young. I was not known to be a Jew, although I was informed on – *informiert worden war* (Conrad remembers the phrase from his reading) – and my boss at Wochenschau protected me. When I was ordered to go to Plötzensee

Prison for this work, I wanted to kill myself. But I could not refuse my boss.'

The conversation is halting and they have to stop many times for clarification, but in retrospect Conrad remembers it running unhesitatingly and directly, because neither of them is able to elaborate or explain. Instead they have the simple narrative:

> *I am a Jew; I had to film the hanging of the resisters.*
> *I loved Mendel; he asked me to write about his friendship.*

And so the narrative proceeds: Fritsch filmed three of the nights of hanging. His boss, Mr Steuben, was preoccupied with the technicalities; he brought in many lights so that the place looked like a film set. The night that von Gottberg was hanged it was said that the Führer wanted the film sent to the Wolfschanze in East Prussia so that he could see it before he went to bed at 3 a.m. A plane was standing by at Tempelhof. The rolls of film Fritsch shot on B Camera were processed but never given to the editor; Fritsch's boss, the chief cameraman, said that it would not be necessary; all the executions had been covered in a technically satisfactory way on his camera, A Camera.

'So, I have kept this film for sixty years.'

'Why, Mr Fritsch?'

'I believed it was necessary to remember.'

'But you never told anybody?'

'No, I could not. The problem was very simple: I was a Jew and I had taken part in this terrible (*schreckliche*) crime. With the Stasi it was dangerous for me and my family. But I could not destroy the film or tell anyone about it. Only my daughter knows about it. After the end of the GDR I wanted to do something, but my wife was dying and my daughter came to live with me and we never discussed the matter until I saw the notice in the Filmarchiv.'

Fritsch suddenly reaches for his hand.

'If I give you this film, you shall promise me that you will never tell anybody where it is from.'

The soft, gel fingers hold the back of his hand insistently: Conrad thinks of a chameleon's grip. As a boy he used to catch chameleons and take them into the house to help his grandmother's war on flies. Proximity to a fly, even if the chameleon was perched warily on Conrad's finger, always caused its long tongue to shoot out.

'No, I will never tell anybody where I got this film, I promise. I make an oath to you now.'

'I have never looked at the film again. I cannot look at this material.'

He releases Conrad's hand. His frail shoulders are hunched: his back is toppling and as he leans forward silently for a full minute Conrad sees a disturbing round lesion on his throat.

'Here my mother is buried,' he says. 'She died in 1934. After that no more Jewish burials were allowed here. I was no more a Jew until 1989. Now I go on Shabbat to the synagogue to remember my mother and her family. All gone. You shall take this film and you must do what you want with it, but please do not tell anybody where it comes from.'

'I promise.'

The light in the cemetery is flickering steady so that there is an aquarium background to their conversation.

'Do you have children?'

Conrad finds it difficult to answer, such is the awful intensity of his feelings.

'No. Not yet.'

'You must have children.'

'OK.'

'I believe you are an honest person, Mr Senior.'

'I hope I am.'

'I have one more thing to say.'

'Yes.'

'These Junkers who died were very brave. Von Gottberg was brave. That was one man (*Es war ein Mann*) but please do never forget that six million Jews died also. Sometimes I see that nobody in Berlin wants to remember that. They want to make themselves feel good with the expensive memorials from famous architects, but the reality is now forgotten. And I think that only those people who experienced those times can truly understand. We are fewer every year. My life has been very difficult. Can you understand?'

'I can.'

Now, as Fritsch speeds up, Conrad is able only to follow his story in segments. But the gist of it seems to Conrad overwhelmingly clear: an ordinary man, a film technician, has had his life utterly destroyed by people who believed that spirit operated in the world.

Eventually Fritsch stops, as if he has run dry.

'Tomorrow I will meet you here at 10 a.m. and give you the film.'

From his airline bag he produces a brown padded envelope.

'In here is a letter to E.A. Mendel of Oxford. It was given to me by Pastor Schönborn at Plötzensee. He asked me to send it after the war. But it was not possible and then it was too late. The Russians came and . . . you know what happened.'

'Now I understand why you asked me about Mr Mendel.'

Fritsch smiles briefly, a smile from the forgotten depths. The small red veins move about and then settle back.

'Yes. I must be sure you are, as you say, honest.'

He says 'honest' in English. He has it written in his notebook.

'Honest. Yes, you will keep it. I have not read the letter.'

They leave the cemetery, replacing the kippa in the box at the gate. Conrad makes a small donation for the restoration fund. Seventy years after the place was destroyed by Brownshirts in one night it is still a long way from being restored. And the whole monstrous Third Reich, which destroyed this old man's life, lasted only twelve years.

They part at the gate. Fritsch walks with difficulty: over the years, his back must have moved upwards and it is threatening to crush him. It is looming. More and more you hear people discussing their backs, blaming them for their problems, as if backs have a malign intention for the rest of their bodies. They seek help from people who manipulate and placate or propitiate their recalcitrant backs. But Fritsch's problems seem to belong to another order, something with mythical significance. From *Grimm's Illustrated Fairy Tales*, Conrad remembers an illustration of two trolls knocking their heads on a spike in order to make a rich soup from the chunks of dislodged flesh that fell into a large pot. He watches Fritsch as he walks stiffly across the road and past the park.

He feels light-headed, as though he has emerged from under water. He and Francine once went scuba diving; emerging from the cemetery is a strangely similar feeling. All the while he was in there with Fritsch he was submerged in another country and now it is a surprise to find Berlin outside the gates of the cemetery, just as it was.


Back in his room, he opens Fritsch's package. A makeshift envelope, of folded paper stuck down, is addressed to:

> E.A. Mendel Esq.,
> All Souls College,
> Oxford,
> England.

He stares at the envelope. God knows what state von Gottberg was in when he wrote this letter. The pastor must have provided him with a pen and paper. Conrad cannot open the letter. For five or ten minutes he stares at it or out of the window to the church spire. Von Gottberg's familiar, impeccable handwriting is intact, despite everything that has happened to him. It is as though handwriting is immortal. A man's last letter should only be read by the intended recipient, but then Mendel has passed all his papers to him to make what he can of them. He opens it finally. Outside, the spire of Zionskirche is, apparently for his benefit, lit by the dying sun. Conrad's hands are shaky. Until he engaged on Mendel's task, he was unaware that his hands could shake uncontrollably or that he could sit bolt upright at night from the depths of sleep. The paper is brittle.

*26 August 1944*
*My dearest Elya,*

*I am soon to be hanged. One of the things that I have missed most since we were together in Oxford is our talks. Walking in the English Garden here I have often thought of Addison's Walk and I thought how we must have looked to any passing stranger, arguing and laughing as we strode along. They would have heard you say, 'Whenever you are in a corner, you turn to Hegel.'*

*My dear Elya, I loved you and it is one of the great regrets of my life that I shall never see you again. Please, if you can, make contact with my family when this is over, which it must be soon, and try to talk to the children and help them to understand. I shall also miss our friends; as you know I loved Elizabeth. Earlier this year when we met, just a few months ago, although it seems like years, we talked of you.*

*Now Elya, I must pass to something painful. It was clear to me in Washington in 1940 that you and Lionel had told Michael Hamburger that I was a Nazi, or at least a conservative nationalist. Elya, whatever I did was for Germany, certainly, but also for us, for our deep friendship and for a belief that a new world must be born and that people like us should be the midwives. I could have escaped Germany many times, right up to the last, Elya, but I believe that the true nature of a man is revealed when he is prepared to lay down his life for his beliefs. I tried to prevent what was coming, but I have failed. We have all failed. But I go to my death with this consolation: at least I tried to show that there was another Germany. It was always in my mind that I must demonstrate to you, Elya, that my principles are not, as you put it as we walked in Oxford, vaporous nonsense.*

*Goodbye, my dear, dear friend. Think well of me. I will for ever think well of you, day and night, if such a thing exists where I am going. Don't grieve for me; I am calm.*

*A*


Conrad reads again: *My dear Elya, I loved you and it is one of the great regrets of my life that I shall never see you again.*

The letter, possibly the last words he ever wrote, is unbearable to Conrad. He has read what Mendel never could, that von Gottberg knew his friend had betrayed him, but still declared his love and forgiveness. And Conrad remembers painfully that earlier today he was wondering if von Gottberg was reminded of Oxford as he walked in the English Garden. And Fritsch said to him that only those who were there could truly understand, but Conrad believes that he has heard the dead speak, if only in whispers.

To calm himself, he decides to go walking. The night porter hands him his key without speaking to him. Conrad walks the city, preparing himself for what is to come. The city is curiously expectant; despite all the building works and projects, he sees that it is waiting for the dead to rise from the cemeteries.

He remembers walking in Jerusalem and seeing in an upstairs room the wild flailing shadows of Jews, who were waiting for the same thing.

# 23

CONRAD WAITS OUTSIDE the cemetery. Fritsch has decided he is a just man. In these surroundings he feels like a character in a thriller waiting for a drop; it is surprisingly difficult to be nonchalant and inconspicuous. Perhaps the passers-by are inspecting him to see if he is Jewish. Fritsch appears unexpectedly behind him, from within the cemetery, carrying his antique Lufthansa bag. He has been to his mother's grave, he says. Perhaps he has been praying for guidance. He reaches within the bag and produces a neatly wrapped parcel, which he says contains three rolls, the negative, the positive and the sound. The running time is twenty-four minutes. Even now Conrad sees traces of the meticulous technician in the toppling, frail figure of Fritsch. They have little to say this morning. They shake hands and Fritsch bows his head briefly. They both act as though they are in some way guilty.

'The smell was awful,' says Fritsch. 'I cannot forget it.'


Now Conrad is waiting once more, outside the Imperial War Museum. He has asked to see the show trials again. In his bag he has the rolls of film given to him by Fritsch. It is a damp morning. Summer is ending in a few soft, apologetic wet days and the leaves, for no obvious reason, get the message and start to fall. Nothing dramatic, just a sort of surrender. They are already lying, diseased, on the forecourt of the museum.

Yesterday he called Francine and told her he was home. She sounded more cheerful. Even as she says hello he is always able to tell from the timbre of her voice how she is. Sometimes he asks her, 'What sort of day have you had?' and she reads a little list of things that have gone well, or badly. It's as if every day must be assessed and marked. It's a habit of mind, he thinks, inculcated by the life of science or the belief in progress and order.

'Hello, darling,' she answered.

'Good day?'

'Yes, I got the job.'

'Brilliant. Wonderful. When do you start?'

'In two weeks. How did you get on in Berlin?'

'I have found some unseen film footage.'

'Of what?'

'Of von Gottberg in Berlin.'

'Anything more specific?'

'No, I haven't viewed it yet.'

'I'm glad the trip was worthwhile.'

He detects a note of scepticism, but he decides to ignore it.

'It was. How are you about, you know?'

'I don't want to talk about that at the moment. But obviously I feel a lot more cheerful since I got the letter.'

She can't talk about the lost baby and he can't talk about the poisoned film.

He stands on the steps watching the leaves make their slow, despondent descent on to the wet pavement. He seems to be standing there for ever. He has a churning, sick feeling in his stomach. He thinks there is a connection between the termination – the death – of his baby (he's sure it is his) and the death of Axel von Gottberg. Of course the only connection runs through him, but it is the inexplicable nature of consciousness to make personal meaning and significance out of the random. Walking around Berlin in the night he looked for the site of the Roman-

230

isches Café which Freisler so detested, the place where the aristocratic traitor had met with his effete friends to plot the subjugation of ordinary, honest Germans. He couldn't find any trace of it. It's lost under the post-war reconstruction. But he has seen pictures of it, ornate, elegant, opening on to Tauentzienstrasse, the waiters in long aprons moving attentively between the seated dilettanti. And it was while he was walking that he realised that he had neglected, in the terror of reading von Gottberg's letter, that he had mentioned meeting Elizabeth. That could only have been in Stockholm, he sees. And now he understands her final, defiant statement from the grave: *I loved Axel von Gottberg*. Perhaps in Stockholm they discussed flight. As he wrote to Mendel, he had many opportunities to get away, but his duty was to die.

The doors of the War Museum annexe open and he goes in. Upstairs he is shown to the same small viewing room and the rolls of film he has requested are brought out and laced up on the Steenbeck. He watches carefully how it's done. As soon as he is alone, he removes the film, takes Fritsch's film from his bag and laces it up, lining it up in the same way, film on one set of ratchets, sound on another. It's dark. He starts the film, afraid that after all these years it will disintegrate, but more afraid of what he is to see.

# 24

AXEL VON GOTTBERG and three other prisoners are taken from Haus III to the condemned cells on the ground floor, which is known as *das Totenhaus*, the House of Death. They are in shackles and wearing only their trousers.

Since the Nazis came to power thousands have been executed here, half of them Germans. The House of Death is next to the execution block, which is an outbuilding, almost a shed, with large opaque windows at one end. From the roof of this building an iron girder was suspended in 1942. There are six meat-hooks attached to the girder. A guillotine also stood in this space, above a drain set in the floor, until it was destroyed in an air raid on the night of 3 September 1943. Three hundred prisoners were in Haus III that night. All these prisoners were hanged in the next four nights, although some had clemency proceedings outstanding and some were awaiting trial. The order for execution was given by telephone, without waiting for the paperwork.

Axel von Gottberg has been kept by the Gestapo for eleven more days, tortured and abused.

In the execution shed, Wernher Steuben, the cameraman, and his assistant, Ernst Fritsch, set up their Arri cameras. Steuben is close to a breakdown. This work is appallingly stressful: on the one hand the film is to be shown to the Führer and must be technically perfect, and on the other the people he has to deal with at the prison are barbarians. They don't understand the demands of film – lighting focus, reel changes, sound. The hangmen themselves are usually drunk. A bottle of brandy stands on a small table to the side for their benefit. But worse for Steuben is the fact that none of the camera team at Wochenschau want to do this work, and who can blame them? He has been forced to do it because the Reichs Director of Film has told his boss that the Führer himself is insisting that these executions be filmed. And Steuben, without being specific as to the consequences, has told Fritsch that it would not be in his interest to refuse, although of course he has only to say that he has looked after him in the past, but he may not be able to do it for ever; things are very different now.

Five or six times Steuben and Fritsch go through the plan. It's simple enough, but has one unpredictable element: the condemned take different lengths of time to die, depending on their weight and the hangmen's whims. Fritsch has to start running his camera, B Camera, three minutes after Steuben's camera, so that there is time to change reels as A Camera runs out, or between executions, whichever comes first. He could run longer magazines of film, but they are inclined to pick up dirt and hairs which blemish the film.

Axel von Gottberg is cold. It has been a very warm summer, but in the House of Death it is always winter. He sits on a form, his hands and feet shackled. He tries to imagine that he is with his family at his beloved Pleskow, and he tries to believe that it has been worth it to sacrifice everything. Death, he hopes, will be like an endless swim in the warm, vegetable water of the lake, of his own lake.

And now he is awaiting death shivering with the cold, as though he is perhaps anticipating the natural condition of the dead. The pastor comes to visit him. Von Gottberg asks to write another note and the pastor opens his bible in which he has concealed some paper and a pen. He returns half an hour later and takes the letter addressed to E.A. Mendel of All Souls College

Oxford, England. Because the guards have taken to searching him as he leaves the prison, he passes it to one of the camera crew, who are decent enough people, when they meet at the urinals, and he asks him to mail it when he can: 'God will thank you for this Christian act of witness.'

Usually executions take place at night, but the Führer is at Wolfschanze, and the film must reach him tonight. Steuben has been told a plane is waiting.

Von Gottberg hears the guards taking the man from the next cell. He is a trade-union leader called Franz Liebherr, who was supposed to call workers out on strike after Hitler's assassination. The guards shout at him, 'It's a short walk. You don't want to be late for your next appointment.'

Near by someone is praying. After ten or fifteen minutes another man is led away. He calls out, 'Goodbye, friends,' but the guards shout at him to be silent. His shackles scrape and clatter on the floor as he leaves the building.

Von Gottberg longs to die. Another minute of this hell is unbearable. The evidence of the degradation of his people, of the descent into inhumanity, has already killed him. The prison grapevine has informed him that his wife has been arrested and his beloved children taken away. And they have been taken away because of what Elya called his taste for intrigue, a remark which Elizabeth reported to him in Stockholm. Surely this is the refutation, this Plötzensee, this House of Death, the hanging that waits. It is common knowledge in Plötzensee that it takes some time to die by strangulation.

At last they come for him. He stands up, as straight as he can, well over six foot, despite the bruises and burns.

'Gottberg, your time has come.'

He nods. The two guards lead him, shuffling out of the building and across the courtyard, half-naked on these bare stones. He is led through a door. Inside the execution room there is a blinding light, puzzling after the days and nights that have collapsed into each other so that he has lived in degrees of darkness and shadow.

There is a smell in here of excrement. He has no idea what the lights mean or what the black, drawn curtains to his left are hiding. His death sentence, very formally couched, is read to him: *Im Namen des Deutschen Volkes.*

Now the hangman takes over. He holds von Gottberg by the arm. 'This way, my lanky friend. You should eat more, you know.' His assistants laugh. The assistants now lift him up and place the noose, which is attached to the meat-hooks, around his neck.

'For our sacred Germany,' says von Gottberg calmly.

The hangmen remove his trousers, to speed the clean-up, and then they release him.

# 25

CONRAD LURCHES FROM the building. He is sick in the street, until bile appears in small, bubbled strings. When he has voided himself, he sets off at a fast, snivelling jog, like a five-year-old.

Fuck that smiling bastard Mendel. Fuck you, you great toad, you amateur gentile, with your three-piece suits and your sly charm and your hairy ears and you five languages and your house in Headington with tasteful English garden, loud with roses, and your wonderfully urbane theories about how the world works and your barrowloads of honours and honorary degrees and membership of every fucking rinky-dink order of letters and science in the whole fucking world and your illuminated addresses and your knighthood – Sir Elya Mendel KBE and *macher* – and your love of Schubert and Beethoven and opera and the hampers spread on the grass at Garsington in the company of intelligent women, who all fuck like rabbits after you have given them the warm-up of Herzen and Turgenev – in fact anybody they have never read in English, let alone in Russian, Estonian or Aramaic. And your wonderful war in the Reform Club on Welsh rarebit and devilled kidney and claret – *Just a little of the '36 left, Mr Mendel* – and your high-minded intrigue in the Foreign Office and the British Embassy in Washington, your elegant dispatches and your cosy notes to Michael Hamburger: *A second-class intellect, I'm afraid, Michael, gets the wrong end of the stick; deep dark Teutonic forests, goose-girls, duelling scars. By the way, can you come to All Souls*

*for a Mallard Supper? We sing a ridiculous song about the mallard –
I will give you the words – and then we eat one. More conventional
food is also provided. Absurd really, but I think symbolic of this place,
teetering on the edge of farce, but always self-aware.*

Lovely war. Lovely old stones. Lovely gossip.

While your friend hanged slowly, his eyes bulging, his bowels
opening.

Conrad reaches Westminster Bridge, his lungs gasping hopelessly for air. He leans over and looks down at the water. It's
high, although still running in from the sea. Why did you ask
me to do this? Why? Why? His stomach produces a wretched
spasm, a violent heave. Nothing but a clear, thin dessert spoon
of liquid escapes him. His eyes are, by contrast, full of liquid.
He reaches into the bag and takes the film can and drops it over
the side. For a brief moment it floats, turning once, and then
vanishes.

Hanged men are frequently priapic, Elya.

These also are human qualities.

# 26

'YOU LOOK A LITTLE peaky, if you don't mind me saying so.'

Tony is concerned. Conrad hasn't left the flat for days.

'I'm fine, Tony.'

'I'll get some food in, if you like.'

'No, it's OK. Emily's coming round later.'

'Blimey, that would cheer anybody up.'

'Tony, I'm going to be leaving soon.'

'I thought you and the missus was getting togever again.'

'We were. But it hasn't worked out.'

'Sorry to hear that, I really am. Come in for some bread. I'll do you a panino. I'm just about to do one for meself. Mozzarella, tomatoes? 'Ow's that sound?'

'Great. You're a pal, Tony.'

He is touched by Tony's solicitude.

In the back of the bakery is a yard. Tony has a little table there, and a vine growing out of a tub. He sits Conrad down.

'This is nice, Tony.'

There are tubs of white and red geraniums, rosemary bushes and a bay tree. It's a secret garden, Tony's own *Hortus inclusus*, his own fellows' garden. The desire for an enclosed personal space, a small piece of your own paradise, is a powerful one. He remembers the Maasai villages out on the plains beneath the Maasai Mountain of God, in all that vastness, round enclosures of branches and thorn trees into which the Maasai retreated at sunset from

239

the threat of lions, leopards and hyenas. In there they and their cattle were safe, bathed in firelight, the night locked outside.

Tony comes back with two cappuccinos and two panini stuffed with mozzarella and plum tomatoes as he promised. Conrad takes a bite.

'Any good?'

'Lovely. Fantastic.'

'It should be, it's Naples buffalo mozzarella. *Mozzarella di bufala*. If you was fed this when you was a nipper, like I were, it is in your blood.'

Conrad begins to weep.

'You orright, my friend?'

But Conrad cannot reply. He nods.

'I'm sorry, mate,' says Tony. 'Don't worry, whatever it is, take your time. Just a sec.'

He comes back with some paper napkins.

'It's Francine, is that it?'

Eventually Conrad is able to speak.

'Sorry, Tony.'

'No problem, mate.'

'Tony, it's not Francine. I have seen something no human being should see. I can't tell you about it, but trust me, Tony, you're the only one I've even mentioned it to, it's something beyond imagination.'

That was my mistake, he thinks, insufficient imagination.

'Don't say no more, Conrad. Just eat if you can. I'm going to make you another. Mortadella? Prosciutto?'

'Whatever. Thanks.'

In all Conrad eats four panini. He discovers that he has been starving.

Francine was extremely honest: John had reflected during their separation and then he had left his wife, without first discussing his decision with Francine. It was the only decent way, he said, leaving her free to decide.

'So you both cleared the decks. How fucking noble.'

'You're a shit, Conrad.'

'Good luck with the rest of your life.'

But she was not done: three estate agents will value the flat; he can choose any agent he likes. And she will buy him out of his half at the median estimation. It is this detail, this coolness – *the median estimation* – which finally allows him to squeeze Francine from his being. And just a day later Emily rang, as if aware of a vacuum. She has a sad story: she crashed the car on the way to Notting Hill to pick up the children. She was drunk – totally mashed – at two o'clock in the afternoon. She's been fined and has lost her licence. It was just the wake-up call she needed. It's only been a few weeks but she's clean now and she wants to see him. He has been unable to sleep for more than twenty minutes at a time and now he hopes that her frail but sexually knowing body will soothe him. It's the sort of arrangement she understands. He has offered to drive the car when she picks up the children, if her mother can't do it. They will help each other at a time of need in this utilitarian fashion.

In the past two weeks he has asked himself if he has any grounds for complaint against Mendel. He has come to think it was wrong to hope that Mendel had any aim in mind for him, other than to have him complete, perhaps write, the story of his friendship with von Gottberg. And, he has also come to see, he led himself into this: he has a regard for his own ideas and sins and afflictions: they are, after all, just about all he has that he can call his own. And he has always had a certain arrogance, readily picked up by Francine, about the importance of his inner life, his human qualities. Now that confidence has taken a blow, perhaps a mortal blow.

He goes back to Elizabeth Partridge's papers, and finds a thirty-year-old obituary for her husband, Lord Dungannon. He is survived by his widow Elizabeth, Lady Dungannon, and is succeeded by his only son, Erroll O'Brien, as the seventh Earl of Dungannon. There is nothing, apart from the one letter with *No!* written on it, about Stockholm. He finds the phone number on a sheet of paper. The paper is quite thick and the address and phone number, Dungannon 23, are embossed in cerulean blue, lying on the paper in serpentine filaments. It takes him no time at all to establish the dialling code. He speaks to the estate manager, who tells him the Earl is presently in Dublin, but that he rings in every evening to see how the harvest is going – they are harvesting at the moment – and he will pass on the message to call Mr Senior. Conrad has the feeling that he is phoning not another country so much as another time in history.

But the death of von Gottberg has left its appointed time, and projected itself into his consciousness. It is inhabiting not just his mind, but his skin and his clothes. He remembers a film in a Polanski retrospective at the National Film Theatre, where he often used to go with Francine. In this film Françoise Dorleac, or her sister Catherine Deneuve, finds the material world disturbingly motile, refusing to obey the laws of physics. At the time he thought that it was an interestingly surreal conceit. He knows better now. In this way, von Gottberg's death has defied all physical laws and become present in his own time. It's come to inhabit and possess what should by rights be his to control. He understands now Fritsch's anguish: nobody can understand. He has been given, maybe he sought, just an inkling of what true horror means, what human beings are. That's it. That is what has happened to him: he has been given a lesson in reality. Never mind what philosophers say about the reality of things.

He longs for Emily to still his mind with – how to put this honestly? – her body. When Emily finally arrives, he sees that the two of them are ghosts.

Dungannon does not call him immediately. Perhaps he has aristocratic insouciance: vulgar to thrust, old chap. But Conrad feels, as he had hoped, more calm. Emily's children are still with her mother and she stayed the night. Their love-making was subdued but intense as if both of them required something beyond physical pleasure. They both need in their own way to re-enter the world of the familiar. Her breath had a slightly chemical scent, not unpleasant, but artificial, perhaps from the pills she is taking. He too is taking pills, tranquillisers. Her body had somehow changed from the sexually active to the defenceless. They are like two survivors of a plane crash finding each other in the jungle and thanking God they are not alone.

She asked him no questions about his absence. She said she called because she felt he was the only person she wanted to see.

'I rang you because, like, I knew you would not judge or criticise me, but that you would accept me. You were always on my mind when I was in the bin. I heard your voice in my dreams.'

He feels a little irritation at her self-centredness, but then he has no wish to talk about von Gottberg to her, so he is happy for her to ramble on, and describe her own feelings in detail for him. Without drink or drugs – he realises he has never seen her completely sober before – she seems very vulnerable, even puzzled, as though the business of life is a mystery. They have arrived at the same point by different routes.

She tells him she has a cottage in the country and she is going to live there with the children and be a proper mother. The notion of being a proper mother seems to be the only aim she can conceive of in this new, blank, featureless world, other than an inchoate appreciation of his human qualities. His cursèd human qualities.

Conrad could warn her now that there is no symmetry in this world, although we are always looking for it, but he has come to understand that the looking for it is also a part of being human, and unavoidable.

# 27

CONRAD HAS NO money. He has borrowed the fare to Dublin from Emily against his payout on the flat. She seems to have plenty anyway. Dungannon rang and said he would meet him at the Shelbourne, which is his base when he is Dublin to escape the demands of an estate at harvest time. He listened closely to Dungannon's voice on the phone: he spoke in that way that only the high-altitude upper classes maintain without embarrassment, yet it was unmistakably Irish with a sort of Celtic richness as though Gaelic had left a lyrical residue. He proposed dinner and gave a very specific time: seven twenty-five in the Horseshoe Bar. Conrad has booked himself into a rat-trap at the airport, a special deal offered with the cheap flight. He takes a bus into town in plenty of time. He is aware that he has neglected his clothes; his wardrobe has had no additions for three years, but he has a tweed jacket he bought in an Oxfam shop when he first arrived in Oxford under a colonial misapprehension, and he thinks this will be appropriate for Dublin, which he envisages as tweedy and literary in an old-fashioned sort of way: Guinness, poetry, the *craic* and pub crawls.

He announces himself to the concierge who takes him through to the bar. A balding man of about sixty is reading the *Racing Times*.

'My lord, your guest has arrived.'

He takes off his glasses and stands. He is very tall in an elegant light-grey suit with slanted pockets. For some reason the aristocracy favour pockets on the diagonal.

'How do you do?' he says. 'I am Erroll Dungannon. Welcome to Dublin. Would you like a drink?'

Conrad is bemused.

'You look just like him,' he says, although he hasn't meant to bring the matter up too suddenly.

'So my mother used to say. I wouldn't know,' he replies cheerfully. 'Two special whiskies, Sean.'

'Right away, milord.'

'Now,' says Dungannon, 'I saw you briefly at the funeral, but you didn't stay.'

'No, I didn't want to intrude.'

'Not at all, jolly good of you to have come.'

'The two girls who read must be your daughters.'

'By my second wife. Lovely girls. They live with their mother.'

His face is long, like von Gottberg's – like his father's – with deep, dark eyes and a strong nose. The little hair that he has is silvery and brushed backwards so that there is a large open brow. He seems to be running on a lower voltage than his father, however.

'Why was the funeral in Cornwall?'

'My mother insisted on it. She said that she had been happy there. She loved this hotel, by the way. She and her cousin, the novelist, were often here.'

His manner is light and amiable, as though the fact that he is von Gottberg's son is merely incidental and that talking to Conrad is a minor, but unavoidable, chore, whereas for Conrad it is extraordinary to see him here, looking – he finds it unsettling – like a sixty-year-old version of his thirty-five-year-old father.

'My mother, of course, came to believe that she had always loved Axel von Gottberg, but the truth is that for fifty years and more I heard nothing about him. She and my father – I mean Dungannon – had a friendly but passionless relationship. He was, as people say now, gay, although he never wanted to live that life. She married him soon after her first husband died in an air crash. I was thirty-one when my father – Dungannon – died and she told me about my real father. To be honest, it was too late. Too much to take in. In fact I was rather angry, thinking that as she became older she was glorifying a one-night stand. Also, of course, I understood that I had half-sisters in Germany, and it was far, far too late to disrupt their lives. Anyway my mother said before she died that you were asked by Elya Mendel to write something about Axel von Gottberg?'

'Did you know Elya Mendel?'

The whisky arrives at this moment. The barman pours two large glasses.

'Irish whisky. Forty years old. Older than you, I would imagine. They keep a little reserve for me here.'

They drink and Dungannon says, 'Rather good, don't you think?'

'I do.'

Conrad suspects that he is a drunk.

'You asked me about Elya Mendel. He was my godfather. He and my mother were very close. They wrote letters and telephoned often right up to his death. Of course he must have known I was Axel von Gottberg's son, but it was never mentioned. I had the conventional sort of upbringing, Eton, Oxford in the early sixties, and came back here after a spell in the Guards. Didn't suit me, I am afraid. At Oxford Elya Mendel was always kind and helpful. I probably wouldn't have got in without him anyway. I think I disappointed him a little. In the beginning we used to go for walks at Magdalen, but I wasn't up to the mark. I used to go for lunch on Sundays in Headington quite often in the beginning. I loved Oxford but I was not really an Oxford man. I spent a lot of time out with hounds, the Bullingdon and so on, and left after a year and a term. Balliol. Of course I didn't know then that it was my real father's college. Anyway, after the Guards I came back here, and here I have remained on the estate with some business interests in Dublin and London. I used to hunt, but my back is crumbling and my doctor has warned me off. Probably sounds a dull life to you, but I have been happy. Any more questions?'

He laughs loudly and unexpectedly, and Conrad remembers that friends spoke of von Gottberg's sudden laughter, rising from geological depths. The laugh has a curious and charming retrospective effect, inviting a certain irony about what has gone before. Conrad realises, as they go into dinner, that Dungannon has decided to give him just enough information to get rid of him.

Dungannon doesn't eat much: he has chosen grouse which he inspects and prods and then slices a few bits off. But he drinks freely and Conrad keeps up. After dinner they move to another bar for port.

'To be honest with you, Conrad, I am not very keen to be dragged into this whole business. I would appreciate it if you kept me out of the story or whatever you are proposing. Of course I am aware, very well aware, that my mother and Elya Mendel had, as they say nowadays, an agenda. And of course you will want to be true to Elya's wishes, but can I ask you to leave me out of it? There is no definite proof that I am Axel's son and in a way it was just an accident, a sideshow. I have no claim to any involvement. Do you follow me? No interest in digging up the past?'

'I haven't decided finally what to do with what I have, but yes, I promise to leave you out.'

'You're a good chap. How old are you? Thirty-five. You could be my son, just about.'

He laughs again, that astonishing laugh.

'Why do you think your mother never told me about you?'

'She probably thought you would work it out. I don't know. I have the memoir left for you. It's in my room. Remind me to get it before you leave. When are you off, by the way?'

Back in his hotel, Conrad lies drunkenly on his bed. He has come to see von Gottberg's son, and perhaps to tell him something of his father, but, for Dungannon, the world he knows is enough. He can't even contemplate the prospect of discussing his father.

Conrad understands that his mother, who loved von Gottberg, wanted Conrad to know, after all those years of secrecy, that she was still true to his memory and had produced his son. Mendel wanted him to know that, even if it was at a distance, he had done something for his old friend, and helped Dungannon into his father's college, where he and von Gottberg had first met all those years ago. The most poignant detail for Conrad is that Elya Mendel took this gangling doppelgänger on a few laps of Addison's Walk, perhaps hoping they could take up where he and the father had left off.

Conrad sees them. He wonders if anyone notices the resemblance, the tall youth with the startling laugh, the deep eyes, the long Mecklenburg nose, walking briskly with the small, chubby figure of Elya Mendel, who barely draws breath as he explains how the world is organised.

# 28

MY LAST MEETING WITH AXEL VON
GOTTBERG, A MEMOIR. ELIZABETH PARTRIDGE,
DUNGANNON HOUSE, 2001

ELYA MENDEL HELPED arrange my flight to Stockholm.
He always knew who to talk to. I was flown out with some
Foreign Office people, who did not speak to me. I was supposed
to report back on my meetings, although only Elya knew who I
was meeting. By this stage of the war, the Luftwaffe was beaten,
but it was still a nervous flight, arcing far out over the North
Sea and then curving back over Norway. The windows of the
plane were blacked out and it was very cold and bumpy inside
the plane, but we landed safely somewhere outside Stockholm.
The Foreign Office people were met, but I was left to find a taxi
to take me into town to the Grand Hotel, where I was to make
myself known as the guest of Mr Axel.

Axel had left a note for me that read: *Welcome. I will be back
as soon as I can. Love A.* He had booked a room for me that over-
looked the water across to the Old Town and the vast Royal
Palace. There were flowers in the room, ordered, I was sure, by
Axel. Down below the ferries were setting out from the quays
to the islands as if everything in the world was as it should be,
ordered, unruffled and calm. The madness and destruction of the
war seemed to me to belong to another world, a world that, now,
I could barely imagine. It was suddenly quite literally unreal, as

though I had dreamed it and woken up, to discover my confusion. But of course, it was real. All too real. I sat on the terrace of the hotel in the warm sunshine, my heart full of bitterness and shame. How had we allowed our world to be destroyed? How had we got to this? Why had our wonderful, enchanted lives been ruined, our friends killed? All it needed was to get rid of Hitler. That, above all else, was what we should have been striving to achieve to avoid this Armageddon. Here in orderly, sensible, calm Sweden, the folly of war was so overwhelmingly obvious.

I walked up to a small park near by and ordered a coffee and a lingonberry tart and watched with deep envy ordinary people doing the everyday things, looking after their children, walking in the sunshine, reading the newspapers, chatting, without the sirens warning of V-1 rockets, without the rationing and deprivation and without the destruction of my beloved London, which now lay ruined. Utter, utter waste, the product of hundreds of years of human striving, lying in ruins. And Axel's Berlin, I knew, was far worse with more to come and the Russians closing relentlessly from the East. A young woman in the national dress of tight bodice and wide skirt brought me the tart, such a simple, homely pleasure, and this sight made me feel so deeply for Axel, who had spent the last five years trying to get rid of Hitler, travelling God knows at what risk to himself, to ask that the German resistance be given some encouragement. But the blood rage of war demanded unconditional surrender, which meant unlimited destruction.

When Axel arrived at the hotel in the early afternoon, he noticed immediately my shock although I tried quickly to hide it. He was gaunt and his eyes had retreated deeper into his head; his elegant grey suit hung from him. His hair was thin, too.

'Is it that bad? I have grown old, but you look just the same, my darling.'

'Axel, no, you just look very, very tired and thin. But wonderful as always.'

We embraced and only later did it occur to me how it must

have appeared, a German diplomat and an Englishwoman in each other's arms, the Englishwoman in floods of tears.

'Let's have a drink. We both need it.'

He was so worn and tired, but as always full of life. We sat on the terrace.

'Did you have a terrible flight? I worried that our Luftwaffe would shoot you down. And to be honest I wasn't sure you would come. I am overwhelmed that you are here.'

'I wasn't sure you were going to be here at all. Axel, why did you ask me to come?'

'You don't need to ask. You know the answer to that question. I love you. And I heard, of course, that Roddy had died. Do you miss him?'

'I do miss him. I feel guilty, too, that I never loved him. How are your children?'

'They are divine. That is the worst thing about this whole business, the thing that worries me most; our chances of success are not high and the price we will pay, and our children will pay, will be terrible.'

'Axel, for God's sake, you must get away. I have been asked to suggest it to you. Can't you take the family to Switzerland or come here and hide until it's over?'

Of course I knew that he could never leave Germany. Germany needed him; his fate was bound up with his country's. Whatever happened in Germany, and we could all see that the end was near, he was a part of it. Over the next few days I realised that he had become obsessed with the idea of restoring Germany's honour by killing Hitler. He talked quite freely, although Stockholm was full of Nazis and agents from every power.

'We have to get rid of him and then it will be my job to ask the Allies to deal with us, who got rid of him.'

'Is it soon, Axel?'

'Very soon. I have a surprise for you. Tomorrow we are going to go out into the archipelago, to the island of Grinda to stay in an inn.'

253

We walked around the town, past the Royal Dramatic Theatre where Greta Garbo started her professional life and down to the Old Town, which in those days still had fishermen and their families living above the nets and herring barrels. We walked hand in hand and perhaps were followed. The worst moment for me was when I saw one of the Foreign Office people in the street looking at a Dala horse. I broke away from Axel and pretended to be deeply interested in the contents of a herring barrel. Axel thought it was funny. He didn't speak about Liselotte, although I felt deeply uneasy about being here in Stockholm with her husband. I think all women believe adultery is a betrayal of themselves as women, while many men, in my experience, think of it as an endorsement of their true natures. But Axel asked me about Rosamund, and I told him that she was happily married with a baby girl and that she was quite well known now after her third book *The Wings of the Dawn*.

'Does she speak about me?'

'No. I think she has tried to put you out of her mind.'

'And Elya, does he ever mention me?'

'We always talk about you whenever we meet.'

'How does he feel about me?'

'You know we have all been swept up in this awful determination to crush the Nazis and of course Germany, for ever. I think he still believes that you should leave the country.'

'I can't. I know that you actually understand. I can't because we have to demonstrate that Germany is not the same thing as Hitler. Elya knows that.'

I saw then that Elya was always on his mind. What would Elya think? What would Elya say? Now I believe, after all these years, that Axel sacrificed himself for Elya. It seems ridiculous to say it, but he was trying to atone for that letter to the *Manchester Guardian*, which lost him the friendship and trust he most treasured in the world. In the night we became lovers over again but now with a fearful intensity of feeling because we knew that everything was lost. I found him at four in the morning staring out over the harbour.

'I haven't slept for four years,' he said apologetically when he saw that I was awake. I could see the ribs on his back.

After breakfast we took a ferry out to the islands. They were so beautiful, the light soft and hazy, each small rocky island with its own jetty and red, deep-red painted cottage, with a boat moored near by; it was a vision of what life could be, what life was supposed to be. So different from the gloom and fear and despair and deprivation of London and the utter desolation of Berlin.

'Can't we stay here, Axel, until it's over?'

'I can't.'

'But please, get your family out at least, Axel.'

'I have to go through to the end. I have friends and colleagues who are risking their lives every day. We have to do it or die trying.'

We were standing at the prow of the ferry as it eased its sensible, pragmatic way past countless small islands and skerries. Here we were free as we hadn't been for years, not since we were young and blithe. Now, of course, I am immensely old, but then Axel and I already had the feeling that we had lost our youth. The war had taken it. He was obsessed with saving Germany, but I saw that it was almost suicidal. He looked so terribly worn. But for those two days, we were carefree again. It was as if we had been given a blessing from heaven. The strange thing was that I could easily imagine that this landscape, these astonishing islands set in the magical archipelago, were the real world and what we had left behind in Berlin and London was completely unreal, the stuff of nightmares. I had the feeling that we could just step out of our lives. And also, I knew after that first night that I was pregnant. I can't explain how I knew, but now I believe that it was fated.

The ferry came into the jetty at Grinda, I think after about an hour, and a pushcart from the inn met us to take our bags, which were very few. We walked up a track through woods and meadows that were deep in wild flowers. The Grinda Wärdshus turned out to be exactly what we craved, a haven of utter tranquillity, with not a sign of a German or a British agent. In fact there was only one other guest, and he was a botanist, I think, from Uppsala. Probably nowhere in the world did the awful, cruel, relentless war seem further away.

Axel and I swam at a lovely sandy beach. I hadn't realised until then that the Baltic is more or less a freshwater lake, although I had seen eider ducks paddling by in flotillas. The water itself had only a slightly brackish taste. Our room looked out over a meadow to woods with the gleam of water beyond. We didn't talk that night or the next morning about the war. We seemed to understand that these were our last blessed moments together. Nor did I mention escape again. To tell the truth, I saw a certain stark beauty in Axel's attitude to the war: for him it had become a simple matter of principles and courage. Only by believing in these things could he justify himself and his existence. He did ask me to tell Elya that what his country had done to the Jews could never be forgiven. I didn't tell Elya.

We walked across the island through the meadows of flowers. Memory, famously, plays tricks, but there in that season I remember the fields full of marguerites, orchids, primroses and wild gentian. At the edge of the meadows, on fences or scrambling up trees, were pink and white wild roses, what we would call dog roses. We spent all that day walking, swimming and picnicking, happy, but also, as the day wore on, oppressed by the knowledge that this was just a reprieve, release on parole, as Axel put it. Still Axel's talent for wild enjoyment had not diminished, even under immense duress. I loved him so deeply that even as I write these words I feel this love surging through me.

Late that evening as the sky dimmed in summer twilight, we took the ferry back to Stockholm. We clung together watching this world separate from us. We could have stayed. In Stockholm at midnight the sky was an inky blue; I mean the colour of my Parker's Quink at school, a deep royal blue. We glided in past the Royal Dramatic Theatre and round to our berth outside the Grand Hotel.

In the morning, Axel had to leave early, before breakfast.

He woke me and said, 'Goodbye, my only love.'

I never saw him again and I have missed him every day, although as our son grew I saw his likeness and it has been some consolation to me.

Although Elya remained a true friend, in my heart I believed that he was in some degree responsible for the fact that Axel courted death. As Axel said to me in Stockholm, even if we fail to kill Hitler, we will be doing Germany a service by demonstrating to our friends that there is a more noble Germany. He died a hero.

# 29

CONRAD IS WRITING every day. By assembling this story on paper – he writes in wire-bound notebooks in the Bodleian Library – he finds a strange calmness. He has heard it said by a writer that he doesn't know what he thinks until he has written it down, and this seems to be true also for him. He was gratified to find that his name was still on the library's roll as a member of the university, and his reader's ticket, which bears a picture of him looking like a Moonie, allows him access to Duke Humfrey's Library, where he sits late into the winter gloom. Sometimes he brings a pile of papers with him; sometimes he delves into the library's collections. At the end of the day he cycles seven miles back to Emily's cottage. After six months or so, she more or less gave up her plan to be a good rural mother, but she and the children come from London most weekends and she is happy for him to look after the place in return for his room.

He likes the children, a boy of six called Jamie, and a little girl of four whose name is Lamoxie, a name that apparently came in a vision, but which Emily now believes may have to be changed to something more sensible as she is already being teased. They have taken to kissing him when they arrive on a Saturday morning. He wonders if this kissing is a form of anxiety caused by the fact that they are not sure who their fathers are, or whether kissing is so commonplace in expensive little private schools that they kiss anything animate.

When he leaves the library, the gas lights are lit and they are suffused gently by the damp air, so that if you didn't know better you might think this light contained particles of minute, Cheddar-cheese-coloured matter hovering around the lamps. Cyclists go by, past the Radcliffe Camera, up the Broad or down Holywell. They call happily to each other above the sound of the bikes on the road; his youth is going by. Sometimes he cycles home via Holywell, in the hope of hearing music escaping from the Music Rooms, and then he goes on past New College, with its glimpses of silhouetted figures in the quads beyond, and then he swings up Longwall Street and Magdalen in honour of Elya Mendel and Axel von Gottberg, whose lives, as he labours in the library, he is trying to shape. He struggles sometimes with the fear that in the process of writing about them he is trivialising their story or introducing new falsehoods into it. As he progresses he has to decide what material to ignore and what to include. But he sees that there is no objective truth possible. To the one over-whelming fact, as far as he knows, he and Ernst Fritsch are the only living witnesses.

When he finally reaches the house down a long, bumpy farm road, he lights a fire and heats some soup and reads or watches television. One night he sees with a shock that his friend Osric has been kidnapped in Baghdad. Two nights later he is out, after a miracle escape through a tiny window. He is selling his story. A happy, contemporary, ending. Conrad wonders if he was encour-aged to escape because the Iraqis couldn't stand another night at close quarters with him.

As for himself, he is happy spending most nights alone out here. But he doesn't lead a hermit's life. He finds that he has friends who have stayed on or come back to Oxford; and he has been invited to eat at high table in various colleges, a sort of sacrament. He sees himself being absorbed into the fabric of the old place, so that he is just one more hopeful and slightly seedy seeker after truth, bicycling in the gloom, walking by the river, breathing the damp air, longing in a subdued way for the peace of the mind.

It's spring now, and sometimes he takes a break from the library, and walks down the High to Magdalen, where the fritillaries are out in the meadow beside Addison's Walk. They are curious flowers, speckled and venomous. He sees, more faintly with every passing day, Axel von Gottberg and Elya Mendel striding along and now he hears only snatches of their conversation and their ill-matched laughter.

# POSTSCRIPT

IT IS A HOT summer. The barley and wheat fields of Mecklenburg are strewn with poppies and cornflowers, though it is common knowledge that there were far more flowers along the roads and in the fields in the old days before fertilisers. Yet Mecklenburg has remained strangely untouched. It is not true calm, of course, but the narcolepsy of communism that has kept it this way. The only discordant notes are the brutal public buildings, barracks, schools and oddly non-specific factories – all moribund – set down according to some five-year or ten-year plan in the middle of a village or in a field. A woman is selling strawberries outside her small bungalow. Conrad pulls in. He asks for a large punnet. The strawberries are sandy and she offers to wash them. He accompanies her to the back of the house and he watches her as she rinses the pale sand – the sand of the Mecklenburg plain – from them. She is wearing a pinafore, with tabs at the side, in a blue-flowered pattern. She seems to be taking a long time deliberately, perhaps because she has nothing better to do. She tells him that there is no work in the area and that they are obliged to grow strawberries. She stands rather wistfully by the gate as he draws away, reaching occasionally across for a strawberry. They are the most richly flavoured strawberries he has ever eaten, also containing in some unexplained fashion the essence of the countryside. *Erdbeeren*, earthberries, after all.

He drives on through sleeping villages. He loves this unhurried process through an unknown country. He stops for a drink at a café by a green river, which runs steadily – he imagines – towards the Baltic, through reeds and stands of birch. He is served by a woman who appears surprised to see a customer at all, let alone a foreigner. It is chicory coffee, *Ersatzkaffee*, which East Germans have learned to prefer to the real thing.

After an hour he is coming closer to Pleskow and he imagines he knows the landscape. It becomes more wooded and in the woods lakes gleam dully, pewter-hued. The road dips sharply to von Gottberg's ancestral villages, which cling to the estate. Here a village woman collected pig's blood for sausage and as a boy von Gottberg discovered that Frau Rickert always kept a piece of her famous cake for him. And it was from here that Liselotte and Aunt Adelheid and the fatherless children escaped the Russians, driven away long before dawn in a cart by the loyal Wicht, behind Donner and Blitz, to the safety of their second, smaller house across the Elbe in the British-occupied zone. It was an appalling journey of three days and nights. In the middle of the village, with its small baroque church and cottages and windmill, a concrete block of no obvious function stands without windows or doors.

The road now rises and at the top of the hill he catches sight of Pleskow, an Italianate palace standing on a lake, and he remembers Rosamund describing to her cousin Elizabeth how proud Axel had been to stop the car here to demonstrate mutely to her why his lands and forests and house were a part of his soul and spirit. Conrad, too, stops the car and stands by the road for a few minutes. The water of the lake below is briefly ruffled as a gust breathes on it. Out of the car it is very hot. He longs to dive into the cool, vegetable depths of the lake.

Now he turns through a housing estate, and sees the driveway down to the house, and the holm oaks that von Gottberg's great-grandfather planted and the huge medieval barns that line the driveway. One half of the house is covered in scaffolding. There are a few cars parked under the trees and a band is unpacking its instruments from a van. The members of the band wear a green uniform with peaked caps. At the house itself he is greeted by Angela and Caroline, who take him to speak to Liselotte in the vast entrance hall, which looks out on to the lake. She is ninety-four years old now and her daughters have warned him that her blindness has become almost total since he first met her.

She shakes his hand and says in near-perfect English, 'I am so glad you could come for this great day.'

Off the main hall, with the Swedish stove, is the drawing room, which is decorated with a classical frieze, not yet fully restored, and there they offer him tea or coffee or a beer. The house, Pleskow, is in the hands of a trust after years of wrangling. Today the tea-house, where Axel von Gottberg and Claus von Stauffenberg met, is to be opened by the Mayor as a monument to the resistance. It is also the house where Axel and Elizabeth spent almost the whole night talking. The resistance has entered the historical record, even here. It is hoped that tourists will, in time, come to visit. Conrad walks down to the lake; the band is now setting up alongside the tea-house which is, he sees now, a small pavilion. The grass and the reeds have been roughly scythed down to the lake, giving a fair impression of the rolling lawn that was once there. He walks up to the family cemetery, on a hillock beneath some enormous Douglas firs. Like the Jewish cemetery in Prenzlauer Berg, it lies in ruins, as if standing stones are a reproach. He remembers a verse: *The marks of pain trace countless lines through history.* He can't remember where he read it. A tomb, half underground, has been prised open by the action of roots over the years, and this reminds him of how long ago everything happened here, everything that has so gripped and convulsed him.

From the tea-house he hears the band now starting to play what his parents would have called oompah-music. A few people are milling around. A microphone is being set up on the balcony of the tea-house. The lake below the house is, as Adelheid wrote, violet and shimmering like the wings of a dragonfly.

The ceremony to open the tea-house is under way. The Mayor

talks of the heroism of the resisters. He praises particularly the self-sacrifice of Axel, Count von Gottberg, a noble son of Meck-lenburg and a true patriot. When he has finished, the microphone is passed to Liselotte, who says how delighted she is that her husband should be honoured in this way; then she declares the tea-house open. A plaque is unveiled, which reads:

*In this small house, Axel, Count von Gottberg of Pleskow met with others in an attempt to save Germany from the Nazi tyranny. In August 1944 he was executed with friends in Berlin-Plötzensee. It is our sacred duty to heed their example.*

There is ragged applause. Now Conrad is summoned so speak. In carefully prepared German he reads:

*When I was a student at Oxford University, at the same college as Axel von Gottberg, although nearly sixty years later, my teacher was Professor E.A. Mendel, who had been a close friend of Axel von Gottberg before the war.*

*Professor Mendel gave me all the papers in his possession relating to that period, and particularly to Count Axel von Gottberg. I have been working on a book, soon to be published in Germany, called* A Tragic Friendship. *The tragedy lay in the fact that the war caused a great rift between them. Professor Mendel believed that the events of the past century, which hang over us still and cast a deeper shadow in Germany than anywhere else, arose from the mistaken idea common to both fascism and communism that it is possible to build a terrestrial paradise, where all conflicts will be resolved and all values will be harmonised. I think we know now, after the heavy price paid in my country and yours, that this will never happen, but that we must instead accept things as they are and refuse to be deceived.*

He has gone too far. He has lost them, or annoyed them. He sees the Mayor's wife fanning herself with the programme. They want to hear – and why not? – something uplifting.

*Professor Mendel was very fond of a quote from Alexander Herzen, who asked,* Where is the song before it is sung? *To which Mendel replied,* Where indeed? Nowhere is the answer. One creates a song by singing it, by composing it. So, too, life is created by those who live it step by step.'

*I believe it is true to say that Axel von Gottberg lived his life according to his principles and beliefs, step by step. As Major-General Henning von Tresckow, one of the brave resisters, said,* Not one of us can complain about his death. The real worth of a human being begins only when he is ready to lay down his own life for his convictions. *I am honoured to have been invited to say a few words on this great day, in the presence of Axel von Gottberg's wife, two daughters and family. Thank you.*

The audience claps warmly.

Now they file into the tea-house for cakes and beer and tea. Conrad stands next to Liselotte with the two sisters and a great-granddaughter, to greet the guests as if he is part of the family. He is introduced to local dignitaries and outlying members of the family.

Later, when they have all gone, he asks Liselotte if she minds if he goes for a swim in the lake.

'No, of course not,' she says. 'I wish I could see you swimming. Axel and I loved to swim.'

'I know.'

He undresses in the bathing hut, which appears to have been used for many years to store odd bits of machinery and implements, so that in the gloom he sees a toothless rake of an old-fashioned design, a few shovels with broken handles and some pieces of what may have been an outboard motor, including a propellor, oil filters and fly-wheels. Over the lake there is now a dove-grey haze, which hangs more thickly in the small bays. The sky above is gauzy and pale, the blue of the egg of a wild bird, not true but lightly stippled.

The remains of a jetty stretch out from the bathing hut, but the few whole planks are broken or rotted. He lowers himself into the water. It is warm. He wades out a few yards, clear of the reeds and the weed, and then ducks his head under; the water has a distinct taste, of grass and freshwater fish and gentle decomposition. He is swimming in Axel von Gottberg's lake. He sets off strongly in the direction of the church in the village, whose baroque tower is poking above the haze on the far side of the lake.

This was von Gottberg's terrestrial paradise, his own lake, his own landscape, his own history. Conrad had not mentioned, of course, that it was Mendel's chief complaint against his old friend that he believed all values would inevitably be harmonised in some mystical synthesis. And as he swims steadily onwards, he thinks that – intended or not – this is Mendel's legacy to him, that he should understand – actually there is no other choice – that a life is made, day by day, as best you can.


After that awful day when he looked at the film, it took him six months to recover. He suffered from terrible headaches, so bad that he thought he was about to have a stroke as his father had. At times he thought he was going mad. He could not complete simple tasks. He would start on something, perhaps turning on the kettle, and forget what he was doing. Compulsively he would shift Mendel's papers, all seventeen boxes of them, emptying each one on the floor, but before he could begin to sort them he would lose heart, change his clothes or shower or toast a piece of bread. His meals bore no relation to the time of day and he slept or woke without pattern, so that sometimes if he found the television on he would watch a programme about alligators in the Everglades or fusion cookery for five minutes and then he would go to his computer to try to write. But every time he wrote a word, he thought of von Gottberg's death and he was paralysed. It was as though there was a direct connection between his writing, the act of writing, and the event he had witnessed, although he couldn't see why that should be.

One day as he tried fitfully to read a book by W.G. Sebald, he came across a striking passage:

> *It does not seem to me that we understand the laws governing the return of the past, but I feel more and more as if time did not exist at all, only various spaces between which the living can move back and forth as they like, and the longer I think about it the more it seems to me that we who are still alive are unreal in the eyes of the dead, and that only occasionally, in certain lights and atmospheric conditions, do we appear in their field of vision.*

He was not sure of Sebald's exact meaning, but he realised that he had been expecting something from the indifferent dead that they were unwilling to offer him. He was expecting some answers. Gradually, over months, order was restored to his thoughts and he began to write his account of the friendship of Axel von Gottberg and Elya Mendel, organising the hundreds of letters, the recorded conversations and the memories of friends, as well as archive material. He did not mention the curséd film that he dropped into the river. Gradually his account took shape and at the same time he saw himself slipping back into his own life, as if he had been away, inhabiting the life of another.

He swims on. Here in von Gottberg's lake he feels closer to him now than he has ever been. It seems a minor thing, a trivial thing, but this warm, vegetable-scented water affects him deeply, in just the way that scents linger in a room after someone has left it or as a forgotten childhood can be summoned by the smell of food or plants. He is finally freed of the horror of von Gottberg's last moments, which once he foolishly and recklessly imagined would increase his understanding.

From across the still lake-water he hears the band playing on. The sound reaches him in snatches each time he surfaces.

No, the dead do not speak in clear sentences, nor do they give advice.

# AFTERWORD

THIS STORY IS based in part on the friendship between
Adam von Trott and Isaiah Berlin.

For some time I had known that von Trott, a Rhodes Scholar,
had been hanged for his part in the bomb plot of July, 1944. I
was in the early stages of researching a book on Oxford, when I
was looking at some footage of von Trott's show trial and I was
struck by his apparent calm, almost serenity, facing the prosecutor,
Roland Freisler, although the outcome had already been
announced and the defendants had been tortured. It seemed to
me that von Trott was aware that he was sacrificing himself for
some greater good.

Seeing that astonishing film in the Imperial War Museum in
London, and knowing that von Trott had been repudiated by his
Oxford friend, Isaiah Berlin, I was gripped by the desire to write
the story of their friendship as a novel, particularly as Isaiah
Berlin has long been a hero of mine.

A novelist's job is to imagine conversations, motives and states
of mind which is, of course, what I have tried to do. But I have
also been very conscious of the obligation to the known facts of
these terrible events – and an obligation to those who have helped
me – to be true at the very least to the spirit of what I have
discovered in London, Oxford and Berlin. The events of that day,
20 July 1944, and Colonel Claus Schenk von Stauffenberg's heroic
attempt to rid the world of Hitler, I have reproduced as faithfully
as I was able. But for me the most interesting part of the whole

enterprise has been to try to understand how it happened, firstly that the German people and their traditional leaders were unable to rid themselves of Hitler even as he was leading them to their ruin, and secondly how Nazism could have taken hold and then subverted so quickly all Germany's institutions in the process, in what is routinely described as one of the most civilised countries in the world.

I imagined that there was something in the estrangement of Isaiah Berlin and von Trott that would give some clues, but of course a novel is an act of the imagination and I am not claiming – if there is such a thing – any incorrigible historical truth.

# ACKNOWLEDGEMENTS

I HAVE RECEIVED generous help with this book from people whose families are intimately acquainted with the facts. First among these have been various members of the von der Schulenburg family, both in London and Berlin. I have had from them extraordinary insights into the events of those days and their consequences. I have also visited their estates in Mecklenburg, lost as the Russians advanced, and I have been pointed by them to some of the key sites of the resistance. I have discovered that there is a great loyalty among the families of the German resistance, and so I wish to make it clear here that nothing I have written about my fictional characters is in any way the responsibility of any of those who have helped me.

In Berlin, Bengt von zür Muehlen has given me films, booklets and advice: nobody knows more than he does about the films of the Third Reich. He has filmed and documented the families of the resisters, and I have found these films both moving and enormously instructive.

In Oxford, Henry Hardy of Wolfson College, Isaiah Berlin's editor, has pointed me in the right direction and often corrected my mistakes. The Bodleian Library has been more than helpful.

My agent, James Gill, has gone far beyond the call of duty, and has helped me enormously, both with his warm and sensitive suggestions and much more.

At Bloomsbury I must thank Michael Fishwick, my editor, who was extraordinarily perceptive, Mary Tomlinson, copy editor, who spotted many mistakes and tactfully corrected them, and all those, including Rosemary Davidson, Tram-Anh Doan, Arzu Tahsin, Colin Midson, Katie Bond, Liz Calder, Nigel Newton, Minna Fry, Will Webb and David Ward, to whom I am indebted in many ways.

A NOTE ON THE AUTHOR

Justin Cartwright's novels include the Booker-shortlisted *In Every Face I Meet*, the Whitbread Novel Award-winner *Leading the Cheers* and the acclaimed *White Lightning*, shortlisted for the 2002 Whitbread Novel Award. His previous novel, *The Promise of Happiness*, won the 2005 Hawthornden Prize.

Justin Cartwright was born in South Africa and lives in London.

A NOTE ON THE TYPE

Linotype Garamond Three – based on seventeenth century copies of Claude Garamond's types, cut by Jean Jannon. This version was designed for American Type Founders in 1917, by Morris Fuller Benton and Thomas Maitland Cleland and adapted for mechanical composition by Linotype in 1936.